THE SUGAR SKULL

MANUEL RUIZ

CONTENTS

Get my Starter Library FOR FREE

Sign up for the no-spam newsletter and get a NOVEL, TWO NOVELLAS, and a BOOK OF SHORT STORIES, plus more exclusive content, all for free.

Additional details can be found at the end of this book.

Get your free Starter Library here:
manuelruiz3.com

ISBN: 978-0-9984486-3-3

DEDICATION

Dedicated to the four people who were with me one late night when a young girl appeared and left a haunting memory that inspired this story.

My Grandmother
Eulalia "Lala" Ruiz

My Brother
Marc Eric Ruiz

My First Cousin
Rick Ruiz

My Youngest Aunt
Melba Ruiz

CHAPTER ONE

"HERE, KITTY, KITTY."

The sound of a young girl's voice walking by the open window stopped the two best friends from talking. The hair on the back of their necks rose. A shadow eclipsed the light from the streetlamp that played over part of their bodies as they lay on the bed.

The voice grew louder.

"Kitty? Here, Kitty, Kitty."

The boys froze. Ricky heard Freddy gasp, but he couldn't make a sound. Ricky's little sister Myra whimpered from the opposite side of the room.

Ricky opened his mouth and tried to yell, but nothing came out. His neck tightened and his face felt like someone had splashed cold water over it. The sides of his eyes hurt from not wanting to turn his head.

"Grandma Bea!" Myra finally yelled.

That yell is all it took to trigger Ricky's flight instinct. He bolted from the bed, not caring that he smashed Freddy in the stomach as he flew over him.

Freddy didn't notice and jumped out right behind him.

They darted from the room as the hall lit up when Grandma Bea turned on the lights.

"What?" she said.

Myra had rushed out before them and had her arms wrapped around her grandmother.

"Grandma! Little girl! Outside! Kitty!" Myra screamed.

There were tears in her eyes.

Grandma Bea looked right at Ricky and knew something was wrong. Ricky just nodded.

Grandma rushed to the living room with the boys and Myra right behind her. They were much braver with an adult between them and the entryway.

Grandma opened the door and looked outside. She turned back. "I don't see anything."

The moment she finished her sentence, the voice returned.

"Here, Kitty!"

The three jumped back and Grandma stuck her head out the doorway.

"Hello," Bea said. "What are you doing out here so late? It's after midnight."

A little girl's voice answered. "I was just looking for my Kitty. She ran away from me."

Ricky moved forward and craned his head over his grandmother's shoulder, her body still protecting him.

The girl was tiny and wearing a green, one-piece bathing suit. She was barefoot and had a small towel over her shoulder.

"Where are your parents?" Bea asked.

"Oh, they're not home."

"Are you by yourself?"

The little girl didn't answer right away. She looked at Ricky, then peered in the doorway around Bea's other side. She stared at Myra and Freddy.

"Who's that?" she asked.

Ricky turned around. His mother, Lori, was standing there in a tee shirt and black underwear.

"What's going on?" she mumbled.

"Don't worry about it," Grandma Bea said. "Go back to sleep."

The little girl looked back at the grandmother.

"She's pretty."

"Where do you live?"

She pointed to her right. "Back there a few streets down. On the corner."

"Is anybody at your house? And were you swimming?"

The little girl just smiled. "I have to go find Kitty."

"Wait!" Grandma Bea said.

The little girl turned around and walked down the driveway by Grandma Bea's parked truck.

"Ricky, go make sure she's okay. Hurry!"

The conversation had calmed Ricky down and he ran out in his socks to the end of the driveway. The little girl turned left as soon as she got past the vehicle, just before he reached her. When he looked in her direction, she was gone.

He looked around the truck in case she had ducked on the other side, but nothing.

He shook his head and turned back to his grandmother.

"She's gone!" he yelled.

Grandma Bea forgot about her bare feet and went running towards him.

She looked down the block.

"That's not possible," she said. "The next seven houses have connected fences. She'd have to go halfway down the block before she could turn back towards her street. She couldn't have run that fast."

They all slept on Grandma Bea's floor that night.

CHAPTER TWO

The next day was a school holiday, but Grandma Bea woke Ricky up early. They were still shaken after the visit from the little girl and the boys hadn't fallen asleep until almost 3 am, so she had to shake him by his shoulders to stir him.

"Grandma," Ricky said. "What's wrong?"

"I have to leave and should be gone a few hours. Your mom's still asleep and I'm sure she will be for most of the day, but just look out for your sister, okay? There's plenty of food in the fridge."

"Okay, Grandma," Ricky mumbled.

He fell back to sleep by the time she walked out of the room.

Ricky and Freddy woke up around noon. They were sore from sleeping on the floor in Grandma Bea's room but got up and ate, then played video games while Myra watched television in the living room. They didn't mention the little girl at all.

Grandma Bea finally returned later that afternoon. She

had been gone for hours and walked through the door with a concerned look on her face.

"Grandma, what's wrong?" Myra asked.

Ricky heard the door open and his sister's question from his room. He paused the video game, and he and Freddy walked out to see what was going on.

Bea looked at Ricky and he knew something was up.

"Myra, go to your room," she said.

Myra looked at her grandmother, disappointed. "It's about that little girl last night, right?"

"You're too perceptive for your own good, little one. I hope that helps you when you're older. Still, go to your room. If you behave, I'll get you some extra junk at the Fiesta tomorrow."

Myra did as she was told. She had been excited about the Fiesta all week.

Once they heard the door to her room close, Ricky moved toward his grandmother.

"What is it, Grandma Bea?"

"I went to see a few friends from the neighborhood. I covered almost ten houses across three different streets over seven blocks. Three different people saw or talked to that little girl last night. And those were just the ones that wanted to admit it."

"They saw her, too?"

"Yes, some did. Mrs. Blackmon down the street said that she also heard the little girl chasing after her cat, but it was Janie that had the best information."

"The nosy one that's always asking about Mom?"

"Yes, that one. Well, her nosiness helped for once. She asked the little girl where she lived like I did, but after she pointed and told her, Janie kept pressing her. She asked her where exactly. She told her on Creek Street on the corner."

"That's like three streets down, right?"

"Yes. So this morning, Janie went down to that street because it sounded familiar to her. She went to the house and saw what was left of it. In all the years we've lived in this neighborhood, that place where her house sits has always been empty and just seems like it's an extended side yard. Janie said there's a foundation slab, but it's covered in grass."

"So there's nothing but a slab?" Ricky asked. "Was there ever a house there?"

"This is where her nosiness goes to another level. She went to the Stone Creek County Clerk's office to get the property history and found out the last residents there were a family named Seger. They were a married couple that lived there over thirty years ago with four kids, and one night the house caught fire. They all got out, but one of their daughters ran back in looking for her cat. Her parents rushed in after her and the house collapsed. The three of them were killed, leaving three orphans behind. The house was never rebuilt since no one wanted to build there after finding out such a horrible tragedy had occurred, so the city decided to maintain ownership and leave the lot empty."

"Are you sure it was that little girl?"

"Janie got a record of the incident and showed me a copy. The little girl loved to play in her small plastic pool and wore her bathing suit to bed sometimes. She was wearing it that night and when they found her body, she was holding her cat. Its name was Kitty."

"Are you saying," Freddy said, his voice rising, "that we talked to a ghost?"

"It seems it's at least possible that happened," Bea answered without hesitation.

"I think I'm going to be sick," Freddy said.

Ricky was struck silent for a few seconds before his face lit up.

"Are you kidding? That's one of the coolest things that's

ever happened. We saw a ghost! If she would have tried to kill us or looked like Freddy Krueger, then okay, that's not cool and I'd be terrified, but come on! How many people can say they saw and talked to a ghost?"

Freddy half smiled. "I guess you're right, but I still feel like I might pass out."

A look of concern came over Ricky's face. "Grandma, so has she been haunting this place all this time? I mean, has anyone else seen her before last night?"

"That's what's strange," Grandma said. "No. I've lived here so long and know most of the neighbors on the next few streets, but I've never heard about her before. If a spirit had been haunting this area, you'd think someone would have said something or seen something long ago."

"So, why now?"

Grandma Bea shook her head. "I don't know, but that same question has me worried."

"Worried about what?" Ricky asked.

"If that girl appeared to so many people last night, she had to have a reason. It's not a good sign. A spirit usually wanders because it died suddenly or has unfinished business. She did die in a tragedy, but as far as we know, she's never been seen before and that makes me think she was here for a completely different reason. From what the neighbors said, it sounds like she was looking for something more than her Kitty."

CHAPTER THREE

Ricky's alarm went off early the next morning. His first thoughts were about the little girl, but Myra came running into the room for a welcomed interruption.

"Hurry, Ricky. Today's Fiesta!"

"You're supposed to knock, Myra."

"I'm sorry, but come on. I want to get there early in case they run out of funnel cakes!"

Grandma had promised to take them to Fiesta this year. She had taken Ricky when he was twelve, but they hadn't returned since. Fiesta, an annual festival held every April in San Antonio, is a huge event that shuts down part of the city for ten days. Various locations host vendors and music in a massive celebration that involves the local communities, businesses, and universities.

Freddy was going with them but had stayed at home the night before to clean his room or his mother wouldn't let him go. Ricky realized this would be the first time in almost a year that the entire family would be going somewhere together. Things had been bad with their mother Lori for a few years, but the last year had been the worst. Some days she was completely incoherent and wouldn't get out of bed. Ricky was hoping it would be a good day for them all, especially Myra, but was trying hard to not show his excitement.

Ricky got up with Myra tugging at his shirt. He was riding on only a few hours of sleep. He texted Freddy to make sure he was up and getting ready.

Ricky had showered the night before and was ready within twenty minutes. He peeked in on his sister and he could tell she was as excited as he was without making any effort to hide it. She was wearing a green Mexican dress with bright yellow and red flowers around the top and hem.

Ricky walked to the living room and heard his grandmother in the kitchen.

"What time are we leaving, Grandma?" Ricky asked.

"Maybe another 15-20 minutes," she said.

She didn't make eye contact with him and Ricky's heart sank. He knew his grandmother better than she realized.

"She's not coming, is she?"

Grandma raised her eyes and they were moist.

"No. She can't get out of bed."

Ricky didn't want to ask, but he couldn't help himself.

"Why?"

"You know why."

"No, but why specifically this time. Did something happen?"

She looked at him a second.

"Grandma, I'm almost eighteen. I'm about to start my senior year. Just tell me."

Bea let out a deep sigh. She knew he was right.

"She left the house sometime last night. I heard her come in about an hour ago. She could barely walk and I only understood a few words."

It was something Ricky had seen more times than he wanted to admit.

"I'm not going to let Myra down. She's been looking forward to this all week. I want her to have a good time."

"I want you to have a good time, too, Grandson."

Ricky walked up to her and hugged her. "Thank you, Grandma. I will. Freddy will be there, too, so that will help. We'll have fun."

Grandma smiled. "Good. Then go make sure Myra's ready. Go ahead and break it to her. It's easier coming from you."

Ricky walked into her room and Myra was still looking at herself in the mirror and swinging her dress from side to side.

"You ready, Myra?"

"Yes, is it time to go?"

"Almost. I have a little bit of bad news."

"Mom's not going, right?"

Ricky nodded.

"It's okay. I know she gets sick a lot. I heard her and Grandma talking."

She tried to look happy, but Ricky saw her face drop.

"You're pretty smart for a ten-year-old, Myra. We'll have fun. I'll buy you an extra funnel cake if it makes you feel better."

Her smile brightened again.

"And a churro, too?"

"Don't push your luck," Ricky said as he smiled.

"That's a yes. Okay, I'm ready."

Myra had her big brother wrapped around her little finger as long as she stayed out of his room, and she knew it.

They left twenty minutes later. They were in Grandma's 4-Runner and had plenty of room during the trip.

"How long will it take to get there?" Myra asked.

She was bouncing in her seat. She had been to Fiesta when she was smaller but didn't remember much more than the food.

"Once we get out of Stone Creek, maybe 45 minutes to an

hour, depending on traffic," Grandma said. "I haven't driven into downtown San Antonio in a few months, but traffic never changes and Fiesta will make it worse."

"I can't wait!" she screamed.

Ricky and Freddy were on their phones, playing a game against each other. Ricky was only half paying attention. He usually destroyed Freddy on this particular game but was thinking about what kind of junk food he would get instead.

They were on their 10th match when the truck slowed down.

Traffic was backed up.

"We're close!" Bea said.

Ricky looked up and saw the exit signs for downtown San Antonio.

"Is this the only place we're going?" Myra asked.

"We'll see. This will be the busiest location. I wanted to see the Fiesta King crowned, but we're already too late. Let's see if we can find parking."

The traffic exiting from the interstate was slow but moving. They found paid parking about two blocks from an entrance.

The boys and Myra walked fast, making sure to ease up enough for their grandmother to catch up.

They hit the first fenced entrance and walked in. The music was already blaring. They passed the stage and Myra slowed down to watch the band that was performing. Grandma rushed back to pull her along. There was already a slowdown of people. The stage connected to an enclosed indoor area. They passed the stage and walked in to the mass of vendors surrounding every side and corner of space. The indoor vendors sold a profusion of interesting, artsy knick-knacks and clothes. It was still early, so they walked outside to the food vendors. There was already a pack of people but they wanted to be sure they got something good before anything ran out.

"What does everybody want? Nothing sweet yet!"

Grandma stared at Myra as she said this, although it was Ricky who stopped himself halfway to saying, "Funnel cake!"

Grandma and Myra got some breakfast tacos.

"I want a turkey leg," Ricky said.

"At ten in the morning?" Grandma asked.

"Of course. It's Fiesta!"

She handed Ricky some money and he and Freddy walked down towards a turkey leg booth. The line was already eleven people deep.

They got their turkey legs and met Bea and Myra in a central area filled with tables. There were no available seats, so they stood up in a circle.

"I want to hear some music," Bea said.

They returned to the stage where they had entered and listened to a Tejano band for about 30 minutes before Myra got antsy.

"Grandma, can we go? I don't even know what they're saying."

"Okay, after this song. Your Grandfather and I used to dance to this. It was one of his favorites."

"You miss him?" Myra asked.

Bea nodded and smiled as she finished listening to the song. Myra gave her a hug.

Once the song was over, they returned to the indoor shopping area. This time, however, they walked through it, perusing the various merchandise. Bea checked on some purses and blankets, buying a small red coin purse for herself. The boys followed, but other than checking out a few guitars, they stayed with Bea and Myra. Once they finished shopping, they walked to the opposite end of the building and went outside again to the larger open area. They were thrust into a mass of wall-to-wall people and drifted as the crowd formed dual lines against each other, like cars trying to stay in their lanes on a small road. Myra held on to her grandmother and Ricky stood behind her, making sure she didn't take off. Myra turned her head trying to see what she could, but her view was mostly blocked.

"This is so cool!" she said.

She pulled on her grandma. "Can I get one of those?"

Grandma Bea stopped. She cut left through the oncoming line of traffic and made it to where Myra had pointed. It was a vendor tent filled with handmade jewelry.

"I want a necklace, Grandma!"

They started browsing.

Ricky looked over and saw a booth with glass frames with various pictures in them.

"Grandma, we're going to go to that booth with the pictures, okay?"

She looked over to make sure she knew which booth it was.

"Fine, but either stay there so we can meet you or come right back here."

Ricky nodded.

He elbowed Freddy. "Let's go!"

This routine continued for the next few hours. They checked out the vendors, bought junk and stopped at different stages to hear a few bands. Grandma danced to a few songs she recognized, and Myra got up to dance with her when she wasn't stuffing her face. Ricky bought her the extra funnel cake and churro he promised her.

Myra ran up to her grandmother with white funnel cake powder still all over her mouth. Ricky smiled as he saw them laughing and dancing together, lacking the embarrassment most teenagers might have had seeing a parent or grandparent dancing in public. Ricky was just happy to be away from home and doing something they could all enjoy as a family. Even if Lori wasn't there.

He knew his grandmother was the reason.

As the day progressed, they made it to one of the last streets in the downtown area filled with more vendors. Myra had worn herself out and was in a sugar coma, tired and dragging. As they moved, Ricky looked down the line of stores behind the line of outdoor booths. Something caught his eye.

"Check that out!" Ricky said, pointing to a store window.

"Cool!" Freddy said.

Ricky looked at his grandmother. She nodded and moved to an empty bench.

"We'll be right there," Ricky said as he pointed to the store with a multitude of items in the window.

The boys rushed into the store. Various objects filled the walls and displays, but it was the sugar skulls that had caught his eye. The shelves held various sizes of ceramic skulls with multiple designs and patterns adorning them. Some were about the size of his hand, others were the size of a regular human skull, but most were several sizes between.

"These are awesome," Freddy said. "Are you going to get one?"

"I don't know. Just want to make sure I get something I want. Something cool to remember today by. Are you getting one?"

"Dude, I came here to eat. I'm buying at least one more sugar filled fruit cup and another funnel cake. If I don't puke tonight, this trip wasn't worth it."

Ricky glanced through the different skulls that were spread out in different sections and then reached the end of the aisle he was on. These sugar skulls were arranged from smaller to larger sizes. The smaller ones were nice but Ricky wanted something he could display.

"Some of these look great," Freddy said. "You find one you like?"

"I'm not sure. I want something from this section. Some great stuff. I like the mariachi skull with the electric guitars painted on it."

Ricky scanned the area, and then something stood out. The skulls, although different sizes, all had similar coloring. There were some with red flowers, blue streaks and black eyes, others with black or blue eye sockets and yellow or pink coloring. The one that stood out was a mid-size skull, sitting in the middle of the section alone, almost hidden in the back.

Ricky picked it up.

"This one is different," he said.

The skull was white, with blue flowers and designs all over with dark red trim around the eyes and a red rose on either side of the upper skull. He stared into the empty sockets. Something about it kept his attention. He stared at it and moved it around, checking for cracks.

"You going to make out with it?" Freddy said.

"Nah, I'll let you. Closest thing you'll get to a girl this year."

Freddy tried to punch him in the arm but he darted away.

"Hey!" the worker at the cash register yelled. "You break you buy!"

They looked around. Almost everything in the store was fragile.

Ricky stopped.

"Get it over with," he said and closed his eyes.

Freddy gave him a solid punch on the shoulder. Ricky winced, but let it go.

"Totally worth it, but I'm taking your girlfriend home."

Ricky pulled out his wallet. He had money saved up from mowing a few lawns and a little that he hadn't spent yet that Grandma Bea had given him.

He went up to the register. He didn't see a price tag on it.

"How much is this?" he asked.

"The medium-sized ones are twenty-five dollars."

That seemed pricey, but it was Fiesta. Prices would be higher. He thought for a moment. He held the skull up and stared into his eyes. He would always associate this with Fiesta and this day. He thought of Myra and her dancing with Grandma Bea and enjoying hanging out with his best friend. He also thought about the new game he'd been saving up for. He looked at the skull a few seconds longer and opened his wallet. He could mow a few more lawns and get the game later.

"I'll take it."

He paid and the clerk bagged the skull with a few layers of paper before sticking it in a plastic bag.

The boys left and met Bea and Myra on the bench. Myra was laying her head on Grandma's shoulder.

"What did you buy?" Bea asked.

"One of the sugar skulls," he replied.

"A *calavera*? Let me see it."

"They wrapped it so it won't break. I can show you when we get home."

"Okay. Are you boys ready to go? Myra has had enough."

They had been there almost nine hours, but Ricky and Freddy looked at each other and smiled. Grandma shook her head.

"ANOTHER funnel cake?"

It had been a good day.

CHAPTER FOUR

THE FIESTA TRIP HAD WORN RICKY OUT, SO HE SLEPT IN. FREDDY had gone home. Ricky woke up close to eleven to the sound of Myra playing in the living room. He looked up at his desk and his sugar skull was right where he had placed it the night before next to his computer. He smiled as he remembered Myra's happy, content face on the way home before she had fallen asleep. It had been a good time.

Once Ricky realized he wasn't going to go back to sleep, he washed up and walked into the living room where Myra was still going full speed.

"It was fun yesterday, right Ricky?"

Ricky grunted and gave a small nod.

"Where's Grandma?"

"She went shopping. She just left a little while ago."

"Ricky!"

It was his mother Lori's voice. She came running into the living room wearing a snug tee shirt and tights, and her hair looked like it hadn't seen a brush in days.

"Ricky! Myra! Let's watch something!"

Lori's words were falling over each other and she barely

breathed between each staccato syllable. She jumped on the couch next to Myra and hugged her tight.

"My baby girl! I love you sooo much! What do you want to watch, honey?"

Myra looked up. "Something Disney? *Lion King*?"

"Yes! *Lion King* sounds great! Ricky, are you in?"

Ricky had stuff to do. He wanted to play games online with Freddy and some other school friends on his PlayStation or PC, but this was a rare opportunity. The last time it was just him, Myra and Mom doing something family-like was over six months ago. Even though he figured she was trying to make up for missing Fiesta, the excitement on Myra's face already told him what he would do.

"Sure, Mom."

He sat down as Lori leaned over Myra and hugged him around the neck. She kissed his cheek.

"I love you, baby boy! You're the best son ever!"

Myra squealed, "My nose!"

Lori had scraped her shirt sleeve on Myra's face when she planted the kiss on Ricky.

"Grab the movie, honey!" Mom yelled. "Oh, wait, we need snacks! I'll make something. Get the movie ready!"

Myra was excited and rushed to the console. She looked around frantically.

"Ricky, where's the remote?"

"You used the TV last. Where were you sitting?"

"There, next to where you are. Check the insides of the couch."

Ricky stuck his hand between the cushions on one side, but found nothing. He reached between the side of the couch and the cushion he was sitting on and felt something sticky and mushy between his fingers.

He already knew what it was.

"You were eating marshmallows on the couch again?"

Ricky asked as he stared at the white stuff now embedded between his fingers and in his nails.

"Yes, sorry. We're out now. Grandma's gonna buy me more."

"You need to clean this up, Myra. This is gross."

"Oh, never mind. Found the remote!"

She ignored her big brother as she pulled the remote from under some letters on the coffee table.

Ricky grabbed a few paper towels, cleaned up the rest of the marshmallow mess and walked off to the bathroom to wash his hands. He returned and saw his mother in the kitchen. Lori opened the refrigerator, then closed it as she rushed to the pantry. Ricky eased back to his seat but couldn't stop looking at his mother as she followed a manic pattern of opening the refrigerator, pulling an item out, then returning to the pantry and coming back, then opening the fridge again and putting back items and pulling out new ones. This process went on for over seven cycles before she started looking in the drawers for utensils and the lower cabinets for cookware. She pulled out three different size pans before settling on a medium-sized one.

Lori placed the pan on the stove and opened some items from the fridge.

She pulled out a tomato and started slicing it, and when she got to the last piece to slice, she raised the knife and brought it down like she was a human guillotine. The tomato splashed and she laughed, sporting the biggest smile she had shown her children in a long time.

She was having fun.

"What are you making, Mom?" Ricky asked, still unable to figure it out.

"It's a mutt!" she yelled through smiling teeth. "A little mix of this, a little mix of that."

She continued making whatever she was making,

throwing weenies in the pan, some onions and green pepper slices, then added a second pan and threw in some kind of meat. This continued for about ten more minutes when she returned to the pantry one more time.

The smell of something burning overcame the room while she was in the pantry.

"Mom," Ricky said louder than normal, trying his best not to yell.

"Yes, honey?" came her voice from the pantry.

"I think the food's burning."

She rushed out with a bag of popcorn in her hand.

She picked up the first pan and slid the food off onto an empty plate.

"It's okay. It's Cajun style. Extra spicy!" she emphasized the last word with a hiss and a smile.

She was enjoying every second.

Lori put the bag of popcorn in the microwave and set the timer before returning to the second pan.

"Is the movie ready, Myra?" Lori asked.

Myra nodded. "Yes, Mom. Just waiting for you."

Mom smiled. "You are so beautiful, sweetheart. Did I ever tell you when you were born that you ripped my insides out so bad I couldn't sit for two weeks?"

Myra made a horrible grimace. "No, but it's okay if you never tell me that ever again."

Lori started laughing. "You put a whole new row of stretch marks on me! But they were worth every one to bring you into this world."

She reached her fingers up and blew her a kiss. "I love, love, love you!"

Myra's eyebrows ruffled. "I love you, too, Mom."

Lori returned to her pan and used a spatula to move around whatever she was making. She returned to the pantry one more time and came out with hamburger buns.

Ricky thought burgers were a good choice.

Lori pulled out more plates and started putting stuff together right as the microwave started beeping. Fortunately, she hadn't overset the clock and the popcorn smelled great. She poured it into a bowl and went back to preparing the plates of food.

"Come help me, Son. This is going to be soooo incredible! Movie time with my babies! Couldn't ask for a better day."

Ricky walked over and grabbed some plates. He wasn't sure what they were, though. The buns had something in them, but he didn't want to risk making a face and making his mom feel bad.

Instead, he moved back to the coffee table in the living room and set a plate in front of Myra and the place his mom would sit. He went back for the last one.

"Grab some drinks!" Lori said, almost singing. "Get whatever you want!"

Ricky went to the refrigerator and grabbed a juice for Myra and a soda for himself. There were a few cans of beer, but he decided to grab a soda for his mom, too.

He returned as Lori was placing the bowl of popcorn on the table. She sat down, looking at the menu screen for the movie.

"Go ahead and start it, honey."

Myra had her plate in her hands and looked at the burger. Ricky sat down and watched her pull the top bun off. The weenies were cut into pieces and were black all the way through. Cheese and potato chips were also mixed in with tomatoes, pickles and what looked like jelly. There were also pieces of ham slices that were scorched. Myra was about to say something. Ricky saw her lips moving and interrupted.

"How's the popcorn?" he asked.

Myra looked at him. He gave her a look and after her forehead scrunched up, she got it.

"All good," Myra said. "Let's start the movie."

Ricky picked up his smorgas-burger. He looked over and Lori had her arm wrapped around Myra and was smiling as she ate some popcorn. Ricky closed his eyes, pulled the burger up and coughed as the burned meat wouldn't go past his throat.

Lori turned to look right at him. She still had that crazy happy smile.

Ricky gulped, smiled back and forced a swallow. It wasn't bad, in fact, it was terrible. He feared that somehow it would burn a hole in his stomach and he'd be in the emergency room in about twenty minutes, but Lori was still looking at him so he took another bite.

"Honey, why don't you try your burger?"

Myra's eyes widened. She glanced at her brother, who was trying to use his eyes to point towards the bowl on the coffee table.

"I'm okay, Mommy. I'm not that hungry, so I'll just have some popcorn."

Lori smiled as Myra reached into the bowl.

Ricky put his burger back on the table and pushed it as far back as he could so he wouldn't have to smell it.

The family was calm as the opening scene started.

Lori reached over and grabbed her burger. While still staring at the screen, she took a huge bite. Her eyes closed with each chew.

"That is so good! I surprised myself!"

Her excitement sounded genuine and Ricky wasn't going to do anything to spoil the moment.

"Thanks, Mom," Ricky said. "It's really good."

"Oh," she yelled just as Simba was being presented to the animals on Pride Rock. "I just remembered I have a blank canvas. Let's paint!"

Myra looked at her. "The movie just started, Mom."

"It's okay. We can do both."

Lori leaped from the couch and ran towards the back of the house. She returned a few minutes later with a box, a canvas and an easel. She pulled the coffee table aside and set up the canvas.

"Come on!" she said, pulling Myra off the couch.

Lori pulled out some tubes of paint and laid some papers on the floor. She picked up the tubes and squeezed the paints on the paper.

"Ready?" she said, looking at Ricky and Myra.

"Ready for what?" Myra asked. "Where are the brushes?"

"No brushes!" she squealed as she dipped her hands into the blue paint and started forming small shapes with the fingers on her right hand. Paint was dripping off the canvas.

Ricky tried not to panic. He knew his grandmother would freak if any paint got on the couches.

"Mom, can we move these back a little? I need more room."

She turned to look at him and her smile faded for the first time. She focused on him a few seconds and smiled again.

"Yes, my baby boy, who isn't so little anymore."

She reached up and smeared some blue paint on his cheek.

Ricky moved the canvas back, as far away from the couch as possible. He could clean anything on the floor, but couches were a different story.

Myra looked at her big brother. He nodded. Myra smiled as she dipped her fingers in the yellow and joined her mom. Ricky hesitated, then went for the red and started painting.

Lori was running her fingers and hands onto the canvas in a frenzy as their combined work in progress became a multitude of color splashes, running everywhere, making no sense at all. Lori clapped her hands together, splashing some paint, then wiped her hands on her shorts and looked over her children's creation.

"That's beautiful! Keep going!"

Myra and Ricky kept on painting and then Lori sat down on the couch. Any worries Ricky had about protecting the couches were now moot. Lori put her painted hands on the arms of the couch and her wet shorts sat right on a cushion. Her head then fell in almost slow motion and she was asleep ten seconds after it landed on the arm of the couch.

Ricky just stared at his mother lying there, asleep.

It was good while it lasted. Myra turned and looked at her, the glow in her face fading.

"Go ahead and finish what you're doing, Myra," Ricky said. "Mom wore herself out."

She nodded and smiled at her big brother and returned to finish her painting.

Ricky walked to the kitchen and found a towel/rag. He wet it down and wrung it out before returning to his mother. He wiped down her arms and shorts and tried to wipe off as much paint as he could from the couch.

That's when the door opened.

Grandma Bea walked in with a bag of groceries in her hand.

"Hi, guys. How are..."

She stopped and her face went pale when she saw what was happening.

Myra's eyes got big. "I'm sorry, Grandma. I'll put this stuff away."

Bea sighed as she put her bag on the counter.

"It's okay. Finish what you were doing. It's not your fault."

Ricky helped his grandmother put the groceries away and then returned to try to clean off the rest of his mother.

"Do you think you can carry her?" Grandma asked.

It had been awhile, but he knew he could. She seemed to be thinner and thinner with every passing month.

They all knew waking her would be impossible for a few hours. When she crashed this hard, it was pointless to try.

Ricky lifted his mother and slung her over his shoulder, her head and limp arms falling to his back. He carried her back to her bedroom. Years ago she had the one main bedroom upstairs, but because of moments like this, Grandma Bea had switched her own downstairs master bedroom with Lori's since it was near the back door. Bea hoped this would encourage Lori to sneak in and out without disturbing the kids. She had slipped down the stairs trying to sneak in and out more times than anyone could count. However, most of the time she still came through the front door, defeating the entire purpose.

Ricky reached her room, stepped over a mound of clothes on the floor, and tried to ease her onto the bed. Bea came in.

"We need to get those wet shorts off her first."

When Ricky was younger, he would close his eyes when his mom would run around wearing little to no clothes in the house ranting and raving, but it had become so commonplace that it no longer fazed him.

Bea pulled her shorts off as Ricky still carried her and was relieved that she was wearing underwear, but the shorts got stuck on Lori's foot. As the shorts snapped back in Bea's hands, Ricky's weight shifted awkwardly and he dropped Lori on the bed. Her head scraped the headboard, but she never noticed.

He adjusted her legs and set her on her pillows. He started to place a blanket over her.

"Just leave her," Grandma Bea said. "I'll see if I can clean her up a little more."

Ricky moved towards the doorway as he and his grandmother switched places. He stood there a moment and watched Bea grab a towel to clean the rest of her daughter off.

"I'm going to change her into fresh clothes. Can you help your sister clean up the mess in the living room?"

Ricky nodded and closed the door. He felt an emptiness in his chest. He knew she was sick, but had never lost hope that she might get better.

He reached his sister, who was already putting away the paints and equipment.

"I'll get the easel. Good job, Myra. You're almost as good as Mom."

Lori was a talented artist. The walls used to be lined with her art that depicted beautiful and detailed buildings in Italy and France, others with people in different locations and some with horses running free. Most of that art was in the garage or long gone now.

"It was fun, wasn't it?" Ricky asked.

Myra smiled. "Yes, it had been a long time."

Ricky smiled. He would take a good thirty minutes with his mom once every few months rather than nothing at all, as long as it gave Myra some good memories to keep with her.

CHAPTER FIVE

THE WEEKEND AFTER FIESTA AND THE FAILED PAINTING PARTY, Ricky and Freddy were out on a Saturday, playing basketball with a few friends from the neighborhood. Freddy slipped and scraped his elbow and was still bleeding when the boys returned to Ricky's as the sun was going down.

They walked into a quiet house.

"Grandma! Myra! We're home!"

Grandma walked out of the hallway.

"Your sister is at Karen's house. She's going to spend the night. Karen's having a party tomorrow and wanted to have a sleepover tonight."

"And Mom?"

"I don't know. She hasn't been here all day."

She noticed Freddy's arm.

"What happened?"

"Freddy fell playing basketball. We're going to clean him up."

"No, no. Come here to the bathroom with me, Freddy."

She took him in, cleaned out the wound with water and a towel, and then took out a bottle of peroxide.

"That's going to burn, right?" Freddy said.

"Freddy," Bea said. "Would you rather feel the cut?"

"No," he whispered.

"She's trying to tell you nicely not to be a baby," Ricky said, smiling.

"Shut up," Freddy said.

He let out a hiss as Bea poured the peroxide on his arm.

"See, that wasn't so bad," Bea said. "Plus, I don't want you getting blood on my floors. I barely got all the paint off them from the Picasso Party."

Freddy nodded. Although he wasn't there, Ricky had told him all about it.

She put two Band-Aids on his scrape.

"That should do it. Put new Band-Aids and more peroxide or some Neosporin on after you take your next shower."

"That'll be at least a week," Ricky said, laughing.

Freddy moved to punch him but recoiled when he felt the scrape burning.

"Settle down," Bea said. "You're good now."

"Thank you," Freddy said.

"Okay, Grandma," Ricky said. "We're going to be in the room playing games."

"All right. Love you both to the moon and back."

"Love you, too, Grandma," Ricky said.

"Love you, Grandma Number Three," Freddy followed.

The boys went into Ricky's room as Grandma pulled some food out of the fridge.

Freddy sat on the edge of the bed and Ricky sat in his study chair, which he used more for gaming than studying.

He flipped on his television and pulled up the latest version of Madden football.

Freddy chose the Dallas Cowboys as usual, while Ricky picked the Houston Texans. They both loved each team, but Freddy won a bet giving him access to the Cowboys for a year. It was a close contest which he barely won, but he had used a cheat code while Ricky was in the bathroom. Ricky knew he had cheated, but at the time, Freddy was having a tough time with his parents divorcing, so he let it go.

They played for the next few hours into the evening. Lori hadn't returned, but the boys hadn't noticed.

The competition was fierce, and they were tied 4 to 4. It was almost midnight when they kicked into the tie-breaking game and were soon yelling as they traded touchdowns. Freddy was standing up as he'd just intercepted Ricky's quarterback in the final quarter when the game shut off.

"Hey!" Freddy yelled. "You did that on purpose!"

Ricky lifted his controller with both hands still holding it. He moved to check the TV when a loud whooshing sound flew by his ears. He looked back and both boys stared as the two window curtains flew up like they were hit with a heavy wind.

"You have the windows open?" Freddy asked.

Ricky's face went white as he shook his head and the curtains continued to dance.

Something moved and they shifted their gaze to Ricky's desk.

The sugar skull was looking right at them.

"Was that..." Freddy started.

"I put the skull facing towards my face when I sleep. It moved."

"Don't try to mess with me, Ricky. You know I'm not into scary."

The skull turned slowly, making a complete circle and as it stopped to face them again, the eyes glowed a dull blue.

The boys didn't hesitate. They scrambled out the door. Ricky was first but tripped on something and fell in the hall. The boys looked down.

Grandma Bea lay in a heap, her hand reaching out to nothing.

"Grandma!" Ricky yelled, the fear in his chest now compounding as he saw the woman who had raised him and his sister lying helpless.

She grunted and her hand moved in his direction.

"Freddy, call 9-1-1! Hurry!"

They heard a door creak across the house. They looked across the hall and saw the back of Ricky's mom's dress as she walked into her room and the door slammed behind her.

"Mom!" Ricky yelled. "MOM!"

Freddy stood there.

"What are you doing? Call!"

Freddy stood frozen another few seconds before he pulled out his phone and dialed. He ran to the living room to make the call and stuttered out the address.

"Ricky," Grandma whispered, her head still not moving.

Ricky bent down and put his face to hers.

"Grandma, are you okay? The ambulance is coming. What can I do?"

She opened her eyes and looked at him, then reached for his face.

"I'll always be with you. Take care of your sister. I love you."

"I love you too Grandma, but you're going to be..."

Her eyes closed as her hand fell. Her entire body went limp.

Ricky shook her. He yelled for his mother one last time before slumping down on the floor. He knew she was gone.

Ricky looked back into his room as he heard another sound. The skull's glowing blue eyes were pulsing now. It didn't move again, but he felt like it could see right through him and that it somehow knew the reason Grandma Bea was dead.

CHAPTER SIX

THE FUNERAL HOME WAS PACKED. GRANDMA BEA HAD MANY academic friends from the University where she taught Anthropology and Folklore for more than thirty years. Although she was officially retired almost seven years, she kept in touch with her fellow professors and still did some consulting work and guest lectures on a regular basis. She would spend much of her free time at the campus researching academic papers she was working on for potential publication or sometimes just to fulfill her current curiosities.

Ricky knew she had slowed down and retired early to help take care of him and Myra when Lori got worse. She always insisted she was tired of teaching, but he knew she had loved it. She was always trying to teach him, Freddy and his sister about unique cultures and the world outside their own. She did it by telling them stories about each culture's folklore, especially the good, the evil, the wars and internal battles, and the sometimes odd ways they dealt with them. It held their interest more than math or regular history.

Bea also had many neighborhood friends who she visited on Saturdays, especially the older ones who didn't leave the house much. She'd drive them to bingo in her SUV and sometimes helped them run errands. She enjoyed their company. Almost all of them were at the funeral paying their respects. Even Mrs. Johns, who was in her early nineties and only left her house to go to the doctor, attended. She moved slowly in her walker, but lost it once she reached the open casket.

Ricky, Lori and Myra were seated on the front pew of the funeral home. Lori sat in a zombie-like daze while Myra had her head dug into Ricky's side.

People came up to them to offer condolences. Myra said thank you, but Lori didn't acknowledge them. She stared off into nothing, looking numb.

As a group of professors paid their respects, one that Ricky recognized walked up to him.

"Hello, Ricky, I'm not sure if you remember me. I'm Jacqueline Baker."

The professor was a tall African American woman dressed in a black pantsuit.

"Yes, I do. Professor Jackie."

He turned to his sister. "Myra, this is Dr. Jacqueline Baker. Professor Jackie -- the one that Grandma always talked about. They were best friends. You haven't seen her since you were pretty small."

Myra looked up and the first thing she noticed was the necklace she was wearing. It had aqua stones and glittered in the light. Professor Jackie reached out to shake her hand.

"I like your necklace," Myra said.

"Why, thank you. This was a gift from your grandmother. It was given to her by a tribe in Tanzania. It's supposed to bring good luck to those who wear it. The day she retired, she gave it to me."

"I remember going with my grandmother to the college a few times to see you," Ricky said. "You were always nice to me. You gave me candy."

Professor Jackie smiled. "Yea, you were always a polite boy. You are both welcome to come visit me anytime."

"Thank you. I think I'd like to do that soon."

As the group got thicker, Ricky leaned into Myra's ear.

"All these people are here for Grandma Bea. She'd want us to greet them properly, and Mom's not going to do it. Can you help me? For Grandma?"

Myra nodded and wiped her tears. "For Grandma."

Ricky stood up and greeted some of the mourners, then moved from his pew and positioned himself a few feet from his Grandmother's casket after he saw the awkward looks towards his mother, who still wouldn't acknowledge anyone. He thanked everyone that walked by as Myra stood near him, nodding and shaking hands.

Freddy was sitting nearby with his mom, and Ricky motioned for him to help some of the older ladies struggling to get back to their seats. Freddy picked up on it and spent the rest of the time as a makeshift usher.

Ricky struggled not to stare at his mother. Her empty gaze made it worse somehow. Myra walked back to her pew for a few minutes to cry and gather herself, then rejoined him, still wiping at her eyes. Ricky would put his arm around her, but he had yet to shed a tear. The shock of witnessing her last breath of life was still inside, and his grandmother's last words were all he could think about when he wasn't distracted.

The day after Bea had died, Lori wouldn't get out of bed. Not that it was any different from the day after most nights when she showed up at 4 am, but they had things to take care of. Ricky had to be the one to meet with the funeral home and get everything arranged. Grandma had already pre-paid her funeral expenses years ago, and her insurance would cover any additional costs.

The service was nice. The University Choir, led by music

professor Charles Peterson, another old friend of Bea's, performed three songs. They were amazing. Even as they went into a heartfelt rendition of "Amazing Grace," making everyone in the room shed at least a single tear, Ricky's eyes remained dry.

Ricky looked toward the back of the room and saw his friend Ellie and her mother.

When the crowd dwindled as they neared closing time, she came up to pay her respects.

"I'm sorry, Ricky," Ellie said. "I know what she meant to you. She was always good to me. I still remember her always having snacks for us when we were little and how she would call and check on us all the time when she was working. I loved her, too."

Ellie. His first best friend besides his stuffed Pikachu when he was three. They were inseparable for many years until they hit eighth grade and the other boys started to notice what Ricky knew all along. She was an amazing girl. She was strong and a fierce friend, but something happened right before they went to high school. Ellie made the dance team and Ricky was in track and field. They started to separate after that, hanging with different crowds, and although their friendship stayed strong, it was different. They didn't just drop over to each other's houses anymore. They waved and sometimes braved a hug, but it was awkward for both of them. Neither knew why, but there was maybe still something there. Even after three years of this in high school, she still knew him better than anyone--even Freddy.

"Thank you, Ellie. I know you did. She always thought of you as family."

She smiled.

"We've always been family."

They looked at each other for a few more moments before Ellie's mom hugged Ricky and offered her condolences.

The family returned home. Ricky drove. Myra was in the back and Lori joined her, barely able to stay awake. No one spoke on the drive back.

THE FUNERAL THE NEXT DAY WAS BEAUTIFUL. THE SKY WAS overcast and a small shower passed as they rode in the limousine the funeral home provided. They followed behind the hearse to the cemetery. The rain eased by the time they arrived at the burial site.

The choir returned, singing some of Grandma Bea's favorite songs. Ricky, Myra and Lori sat in the front row on folding chairs under a large canopy. It appeared there were as many, if not more guests here than were at the viewing. It was 10 am, so he knew many of them had to take time off work to be there. His Grandma was loved by more people than he realized.

Once the funeral was over, Ricky wanted to stay until they lowered the casket and started to fill the grave. Ellie stood by him as they removed the straps and prepared the lowering device. He was trying to conjure up positive memories and remain focused when someone tugged at him. He turned around and saw Myra, still sniffling. She wrapped her arms around him.

"I don't want to see this."

Ricky knelt down and wiped her tears. "Why?"

"I just don't. And what's wrong with you? Why aren't you crying?"

The question caught him off guard. He hadn't realized it, even though many at the viewing and funeral did.

"I... I'm not sure, Myra."

"People grieve differently, Myra," Ellie said. "He's hurting. I can tell."

Myra nodded. "Can we please go? I don't want to see any more."

Ricky looked at Ellie and gave her a nod. He turned and hugged his sister.

"Of course. Let's go to the reception. Will you be there, Ellie?"

Ellie smiled as she nodded. Her eyes were still moist.

They drove to the reception hall at the church for a luncheon that Professor Jackie had put together. Ricky thanked them all. Lori sat at a table when Ricky noticed her making an odd face toward a group of professors.

He walked up to her.

"Mom, what's wrong?"

"These people. These academics. She chose them all over me."

Her voice sounded bitter.

"Mom, you know that's not true. She was always there for us."

"NO!" she yelled loud enough for a few people to turn their heads.

"Mom, please don't make a scene. Keep your voice down."

"I will NOT!" She stood up and her chair flew back, falling. Whoever hadn't already been staring turned their heads now.

"Mom, please. For Myra."

She looked at everyone staring at her.

"This is bullshit!" she yelled and stormed out.

"I'll go," Ellie said.

As she left, everyone turned and stared at Ricky.

Professor Jackie walked toward the fallen chair and picked it back up, tucking in under the table.

"Ricky, it's okay. She's hurting. Everyone understands."

Ricky's embarrassment calmed and he tried to fake a

smile. His chest felt empty like he hadn't eaten in days and was just starting to feel the hunger pains.

"Thank you, Professor Jackie," he said.

"No need to thank me. You made your grandma proud, and that makes me proud. She kept me updated on you and your sister all the time."

His smile turned genuine as the empty feeling subsided.

"Thank you. I never know what to expect from Mom, but you're right. We all grieve in our own way, I guess."

It made him think of his lack of emotion.

Ellie returned.

"She's in the truck. The windows are down, but it's warm out there. Do you have the keys?"

Ricky handed them to her.

"Don't let her take off, Elena Lee."

He didn't realize it was the first time he'd called her "Elena Lee" in years. It was a name her parents called her when she was in trouble, and he loved to tease her with it when they were younger.

"You get a pass on that one today," Ellie said, enjoying the reference. "Don't worry about your mom. I put her in the back. I'll just get the AC running and will stay in the driver's seat until you're done. Take your time."

He nodded. He waited for Myra to finish her food and waited another ten minutes before standing up and thanking everyone again, making sure he acknowledged Professor Jackie, Professor Peterson and the choir, and the University, that had donated money and secured the location.

After his speech, he thanked every person in attendance and shook their hand or hugged them.

He saved Jackie for last.

"I can't thank you enough, Professor Jackie. I didn't know what to do with my mom being... my mom."

"I understand, Ricky. You did an incredible job. I'm sure your Grandmother's smiling down on you."

He nodded and smiled. He enjoyed hearing that, but could still only picture her face just before she took her last breath.

"I'm going to get Myra and my mom home."

"You take care," Professor Jackie said as she reached into her purse, pulled out a card and wrote something down on it.

"If you need anything, or just want to come by and talk about what Bea was still working on after supposedly retiring, don't hesitate to call me. You may not have seen me in person for a long time, but I felt like I was right there with Bea. Like a surrogate grandma."

She handed him her business card. "My personal cell number is on the back."

Ricky nodded. He grabbed his sister's hand and then went to the truck with Freddy right behind him. He thanked Ellie and then switched places with her.

"Do you want me to drive you home?" Ricky asked.

"I would, but Mom and Dad are already waiting for me in our car," Ellie said. "I'll try to come by. I promise. It's been too long."

"I'd like that. And you're right. It has been too long."

Ellie backhanded him gently across his arm.

"That was for the Elena Lee crack."

She gave him a tight hug before she walked away.

"I may not be Ellie, but you want me to go with you?" Freddy said. "I'm not hugging you, though."

"Yeah, get in here."

"Good, because I already told my mom I was and she already took off."

Freddy jumped in and they returned home.

It had been a tough day for them all, and none of them

spoke on the drive until just before they got into the driveway.

"You good?" Freddy asked.

Ricky shrugged. "I just keep thinking what's life going to be like without her. I mean, what happens now?"

CHAPTER SEVEN

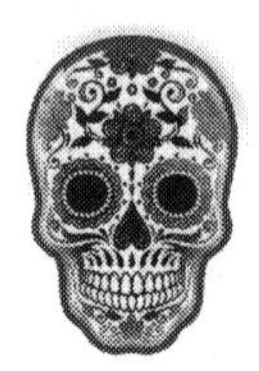

WHEN THEY ARRIVED BACK AT THE HOUSE, LORI WENT STRAIGHT to her room and shut the door. Myra stayed in the living room and flipped on the TV.

Freddy and Ricky went back to Ricky's room. He sat in his gaming chair and stared off into nothing.

Freddy moved toward the desk, saw the sugar skull, and instead walked to the bed.

Ricky hadn't thought about the curtains or the skull in the last few days. He kept picturing the entire scene with his grandmother, but the skull had kind of faded in the background. How could that be? Did the glowing skull eyes really happen, or was his mind just trying to process way too much information?

"Are you sure you're okay?" Freddy asked. "I mean, I've cried like ten times since she died and you seem kind of normal."

Ricky shook his head. "I don't know. I guess I'm still in shock, maybe?"

Freddy looked down. "You sure that's it?"

Freddy's head gestured toward the desk without him

actually looking at it.

"That did happen, right?" Ricky asked. "The curtains, the wind with the windows closed and the skull?"

Freddy nodded. "I don't really want to talk about it and now I'm scared to turn my head and see that thing, but yes. It happened. I had a nightmare that my curtains were attacking me. I pulled them off my window. My mom was pretty pissed at me cuz I tore one, but let it go. Figured I was just reacting to Grandma Number Three's death."

Ricky didn't say anything. He was thinking about it. There was something else. The wind. The curtains. The sugar skull. It all had to have happened at the same time his grandma had died. But there was still something else.

"Freddy, my mom. Didn't Grandma say she was gone that night?"

Freddy thought for a minute. "Yeah, she did. I guess she must have walked in while we were playing Madden."

Ricky remembered seeing Lori walking into her room and slamming the door as he was grieving over his grandmother. She didn't come back out of that room until after the coroner had confirmed Bea's death was by natural causes and the funeral home had removed her body. They had worked on her for a while, but he knew she was gone. He knew the exact moment when her arm fell that she was gone.

The doorbell rang.

Freddy stared at him. "I'll get it."

He left as Ricky took a look at the skull. Nothing. No movement, no eyes glowing. The curtains were fine, too. Had it been some kind of hysteria when she died? Her soul passing, maybe? But she wasn't dead yet when that happened. Maybe it was something coming for her. Death.

There was a knock at his open door. It was Ellie.

"Freddy left. Said he'd be back. Can I come in?"

He nodded. "Of course."

She took Freddy's place at the edge of the bed and stared at Ricky for a few minutes. He wasn't sure what to say.

"I want to ask if you're okay, but I know you're not."

He looked down.

"It's me, Ricky. I know things aren't exactly the same as they used to be, but nothing can change our history. We've known each other since we were three. Please talk to me if you need to. I'm not going anywhere. I was hoping you'd say something over the last few days. You were smiling and being yourself, but I know you're hurting. You don't need to shed tears for me to see that. When did you get so strong, anyway?"

He looked at her, surprised. "Strong? What do you mean?"

"I know you were being strong for your mom and Myra. I don't know how you've held it together."

He realized that's what everyone must have been thinking, but it just wasn't true.

"I don't know. I wasn't trying to be strong, but it's so much. It's too much. I had to arrange everything. I mean, we'll be seniors this year and I was so worried about what colleges I was going to apply to just a few days ago and now I don't know. I can't leave Myra here alone with my mom. I just don't want to think about it because I'm not sure about anything anymore. Grandma was the only reason I could still be a kid."

Then it hit him. Everything he had been holding in. He had been distracted making funeral plans that a responsible adult should have been doing, talking to the insurance company and worrying about his sister and his mom. Then trying to come to terms with whatever the hell it was that happened with the curtains and the skull and his grandmother. Even with all the chaos, it was the look on Grandma Bea's face that kept repeating in his head and it was there again. He tried to distract himself. His grandmother who had become the mother he and Myra never had. The mother they needed. The mother everyone needed. Grandma stepped in without hesitation, and he knew they were better off with her. She loved them and still took care of Lori, who had let her down over and over.

Then the memories he constantly tried to suppress about his mom's history invaded his thoughts. It started with Lori getting pregnant at seventeen by a thirty-year-old man she had just met and who disappeared as soon as he found out she was pregnant. Bea encouraged her to finish school and had arranged for sitters while she was at the University while Lori pursued her dream of being an artist, but less than two years into art school, she dropped out and left to spend eight months in Paris and Spain. She finally returned, but she was a different person.

Lori continued with her art but longed for more. She started to get sick. She looked lost, sleeping all the time and then disappearing for days. A few years later, she was pregnant again with a boyfriend she'd only been with for two months. They lasted about a year after Myra was born before he left for Australia with his band. They never heard from him again.

During all this craziness, Grandma Bea had always been there. As Ricky got older, Bea filled him in on the high-level history he didn't know or remember, never wanting to lie to him.

All of these thoughts came in a rush and his chest started to heave and his breath shortened. He wanted to yell out to his grandmother to come check on what was wrong, but she wasn't there. She would never be there again. She was just gone. She wasn't coming back. Maybe he thought this was an unexpected event, like a vacation that you hate but know you'll be back home soon to a normal, regular life. That wasn't going to happen, though. It was over. This part of life was over. He was going to have to figure things out, and soon. For the sake of Myra. For his own sake. What was he going to do?

Ellie reached out and grabbed his hand. The first tear fell as soon as she touched him and he just stared at her, lost in his own thoughts and fears.

"It's okay," Ellie whispered.

She wrapped her arms around him tightly. The dam broke. The tears kept falling and his entire body shook as he breathed in. He let out a big cry and squeezed her back. He couldn't stop and sobbed for the first time since he had broken his ankle when he was twelve, but this was worse. The pain wasn't on the outside, but all over. Ellie's warmth made it worse and better at the same time. She cried hard with him.

It was at that exact moment he realized he had always loved her, still loved her, and knew without a doubt that she loved him, too. No matter what the future held, there was no changing that.

CHAPTER EIGHT

RICKY MET WITH THE ATTORNEY TO DISCUSS THE WILL A FEW DAYS later. He went alone as his mom was still confined to her bed and had asked Freddy to hang out with Myra while he was gone.

He walked into the attorney's office and saw Professor Jackie already seated. She greeted him as he came in.

He wasn't sure why she was there.

Professor Jackie noticed the look on his face.

"I was summoned for the will reading," she said, looking embarrassed.

The lawyer walked in. His name was Thurman Cole. Ricky remembered his grandmother saying he was a brilliant lawyer and a good man.

"Hello, Dr. Baker and Mr. Luna," he said as he moved to shake their hands. "Dr. Bea was a wonderful woman and I'm sorry that she passed. I understand these are difficult circumstances, but it may be easier if we get right into it."

Mr. Cole opened his briefcase and pulled out some paperwork. He took a few minutes to get settled in. "We are here to go over Dr. Bea's Last Will and Testament. It will take a few weeks to process and get everything distributed, but Dr. Bea wanted me to get the details to you all as soon as possible to get everything filed promptly. She told me to make sure that you fully understood the process, Mr. Luna."

"Please, just call me Ricky."

"Okay. It's not overly complicated, Ricky. In a nutshell, she had a good-sized pension and insurance. She is leaving $10,000 to the college. Dr. Baker, she wants you to use that money for the Anthropology department."

Ricky smiled at Professor Jackie. "That was my grandmother. I know she loved her job and always wanted to give back."

"You will be in charge of the remaining money, Ricky," the attorney said. "Roughly $350 thousand dollars after all the outstanding expenses are paid."

Ricky coughed. "What? That much? To me? Why?"

"There are some stipulations. This money is to go to you, your mother and sister. However, you are the executor."

"What does that mean exactly?"

"You will have to decide how the money's distributed. $100,000 will go to you and your sister's college fund. Both of you are also the new owners of the house. The rest of the money is yours to do with as you please. You should get the initial amount in a few weeks and the rest after all the funeral and outstanding bills are processed. She left you a letter."

His eyes widened. "A letter? How?"

The lawyer smiled. "She liked to be prepared. She wrote three letters. One if you were still under 21, one if you were older, and then one for your sister in case anything should happen to you. She updated them a few years ago."

He reached in his briefcase and pulled out the envelopes.

"I'm going to give you all three and it's up to you when you want to read them, but for now I will ask that you please read the primary one for under the age of 21."

Ricky opened the envelope slowly. He pulled out two pages and saw a computer printed letter.

"Ricky. I have no idea if you are still a teenager or a young adult with a wife and kids as you read this (Since you're not 21 then I hope it's the former, but I hope you're happy). At the time of this writing, you are fourteen years old. I hope I left peacefully and have finished raising you and Myra and that you are both living productive lives or building your way to one. I want you to know I have no regrets. I loved my job and being a professor, but I loved you all more. That includes your mother, too. Take what you see in her life and what led her to this point. I truly hope she has defeated her demons and is a caring mother. She has made mistakes. We all make mistakes, most of which can usually be fixed or learned from, but there are some larger mistakes that are much more difficult to resolve. Prayer may not seem like it works, but it got me through the tougher times. My only concern was making sure you and Myra were safe, fed and loved. I know it's not easy, but someone else always has it worse. Remember to always appreciate what you have or what you had. I made sure you had a roof over your heads and a safe place to sleep at night. I also loved Freddy and Ellie. They are like family, regardless of what the present or future may hold.

My love of research drove me. I learned about different cultures around the world, and in all cases, love was key. In some villages in the most remote places on Earth, the inhabitants have to hunt for their food every day, but they are content. They have no air conditioning, television or video games that you love so much, but they are happier than many of my colleagues with big houses and luxury cars. I wanted to keep things simple for you both so you could find a middle ground. Work hard for what you want and please use your mother's example as a reason to work harder and love your family and those around you. First and foremost, love yourself and your sister. She will always need you and you will always need her, no matter how old you are. I know you love her and thank you for doing so much to keep her happy. Family is important and know that family may not always be the people who share your blood. I have friends like Professor Jackie that are more than family and hope you will, too.

I am leaving you as executor because I know you have a good head on your shoulders. You could have easily used your mother as an excuse when you were young to take the wrong path, and even though you sometimes fight with Myra, I know you are concerned for her and your mother. No matter that she wasn't there most of your childhood, I see love in her. She may not carry the responsibility, but she does carry the love. Forgive her. It will be easier for you to live every day without any kind of hate or resentment. You may not realize until you're much older, but as someone who has lived many years, I can tell you from experience that it's true.

There are days when I wish you were my own and I know in many ways you and Myra are my children. I'm grateful to have been a part of your lives. I do apologize for having to give you this responsibility, but who else could it be? Myra is still young and I don't know what she will be like when she grows up. She's more temperamental than you (and I say that with love, just an observation) ever were and maybe one day I'll make changes if time is kind and I have a better understanding of who she will be.

You gave me a sense of peace and accomplishment to my life. I felt I failed with your mother, but I also learned to forgive myself. Everyone--daughters, sons, significant others--reach a point where they make their own choices.

Those choices dictate what their future holds, and no one can blame themselves for what others may do. It took me many years to realize that. I still feel the weight of guilt, but I also know she made choices that were hers alone.
Remember that. When you come to a crossroads, try to make the right choice by thinking of the consequences they may lead to.
Please use this money to care for the family and to make sure you and Myra are educated, whether by trade or degree, so that neither of you ever has to depend on someone else. Also do your best to make sure your mother is safe. I trust you. I will miss you, dear Grandson. You made life rewarding. Thank you for making me proud again."

Since Bea's death, Ricky had only cried once with Ellie, but the tears flowed down his cheeks as he closed the letter. The lawyer gave him a sympathetic smile while Professor Jackie hugged him.

"She always talked about you both, you know that? You were her pride and joy."

He smiled at her and nodded. "Thank you."

Mr. Cole gave him some additional paperwork before he walked out. Ricky would have to use an account his grandmother had set up and would receive the details via e-mail later that day.

These are the type of situations where I always looked to you for help, he thought to himself as he headed towards the truck. *I guess this is kind of like a life final exam.*

Ricky felt the hurt inside and knew it would take time to heal. Even in her death, she gave a big piece of herself to make sure he and Myra, and maybe even his mother, had a chance at a future.

Thank you, Grandma.

Ricky didn't think about money or what he was going to

do with it as he headed home. He only thought of Grandma Bea and Myra.

Once he got home, he walked into the house and hugged his sister tightly, without saying a word. Somehow, Myra knew she didn't have to say anything. Her brother just needed that. So did she.

CHAPTER NINE

THREE WEEKS AFTER THE READING OF THE WILL, EVERYONE WAS trying to get back to normal. Lori would randomly appear from her room every few days but hadn't spoken a word to either of her children.

Ricky had to step up by making daily decisions and taking care of Myra with his mother checked out. His junior year had just ended and Ricky finished with A's and B's. All of his teachers gave him the option to skip finals, but he chose to take the one for Calculus so he could shoot for an A, which he had pulled off.

Myra was spending the weekend at her best friend Karen's house. Ricky and Freddy drove her over, and Ricky stopped cold as they returned to the house to find Lori was in the kitchen, chopping up tomatoes and onions.

Ricky walked up to her and took a breath before speaking. "Hey, Mom, what are you doing?"

She looked up at him with a blank stare on her face. "I have company."

"Company?"

"Yes, and I want you both to stay in your room. Or leave. He'll be here any minute."

She kept on chopping as she looked down, not waiting for a response.

It had been over a year since Lori had anyone over to the house. She typically left if she had a date or had made plans to go out with friends. Sometimes that one night turned into days.

"Okay," Ricky said, almost mumbling it out.

There was a knock at the door.

Lori put the knife down and cleaned her hands with a kitchen towel as she looked up and gazed directly at the boys.

Ricky wasn't sure what to read from that stare, but he motioned to Freddy and they rushed to his room.

Once they sat down, Freddy turned to him. "What was that all about?"

"Not sure. That's the most she's said to me since the funeral. Let's just play something."

Freddy sat on the carpet.

"You're gonna sit there?" Ricky asked.

"Yeah, I'm staying on the floor until you move that skull."

"Nothing's happened since that night. It must have just been a freak wind," Ricky said.

"Freak winds don't make fake skull's eyes glow blue."

Ricky ignored him. It had gotten easier to rationalize the events of that night with time passing. Ricky had been so concerned with trying to get back to normal that it was the last thing on his mind.

They flipped on the system and decided to play a fighting game. They chose their characters and were just about to start when they heard something.

It was yelling and moaning.

Ricky froze.

Freddy stood up. "Holy, crap, is your mom getting some right now with us in the house?"

Ricky listened. Once he heard a headboard hitting the wall, he knew Freddy was right.

"I guess... I guess so. I don't believe it. Turn the volume up."

"Dude, no way! Let's go to the living room and see if we can hear better!"

The thought of listening in on his mother having sex with a stranger wasn't on top of Ricky's list of anything ever. She had only done this once on a late night when she thought everyone in the house was asleep, but Ricky had been up studying for a test. He recognized the sound of her loose headboard from that night so many years ago, like a spider web of memories had just resurfaced.

"That's my mom, Freddy."

"Yeah, but she's gettin' some!"

"Sit down and play or we leave. I don't want to hear any more."

Freddy was still staring in the direction of the sound, wanting desperately to get in closer.

"What if that was your mom and dad?"

"Man, I don't think my parents have had sex since I was 8. Either that or they live in a soundproof room. Maybe that's why they got divorced. My dad always acted like he hadn't gotten any in forever. That's why he's a douche half the time. But yeah, probably would freak me out if I heard that with a friend in the house. Especially if it was Mom or Dad doing it with a stranger. Point taken."

He sat down and grabbed the remote to turn the volume up. They started fighting, but the noise grew louder and Ricky couldn't get it out of his head. Freddy beat him five times in a row and wasn't even trying.

"New record!"

"I'm distracted. This sucks. Let's just leave."

"It'll be louder when we go through the living room."

"Then we'll run."

The sound did grow louder, but just when they opened the door, it stopped.

"You hear anything?" Ricky asked.

"Nah. Nothing. Too bad. It was getting good. Better than hearing soft porn on cable."

Ricky closed the door as he heard his mother's open. The front door closed a few minutes later. Then the chopping noise returned.

They eased out of the room and back to the kitchen.

Mom had resumed chopping food like nothing had happened.

Ricky stared at her. He wanted to say something, but she was an adult. He was just glad Myra wasn't home.

"What?" his mom said, looking right at him, but continuing to chop as she grabbed another tomato.

She had opened that door, so he stepped right through it.

"What was that all about?"

"What was WHAT all about?"

"The guy. Who was he?"

"I don't have to answer to you."

"I'm not saying you do, Mom, but what if Myra had been here?"

"Well, she wasn't, was she?"

"Karen's mom called to ask if she could stay overnight just ten minutes before we left. So had you already planned on this guy coming over?"

She looked down and resumed cutting into the new tomato. She was pushing it down harder with each slice.

"I was in my room."

"And you think we're deaf and couldn't hear you?"

"This is my house and what I do is my business. I'm your mother, remember that."

"This was Grandma's house. And according to the will, it belongs to me and Myra now."

"Well, she's not here anymore, is she? I don't care what the will said. It's mine now. Unless you want to drag me out of here yourself, I think I'll do whatever I please."

Freddy looked down. Ricky wanted to stop this from continuing in front of Freddy, but that set him off.

"What about what I think?"

"You think I give a SHIT what you think? I'm a grown woman and your mother!"

This hit Ricky hard. She hadn't spoken to him like that since he was probably thirteen or fourteen when she was falling down drunk one night. She spent the next day, after waking up at five in the afternoon, apologizing.

"Yeah, the way you've treated us it doesn't surprise me you don't care. I'm concerned for Myra. Next time, let me know before you have some stranger you just met show up for a hookup."

She threw the knife down and it stuck on the wooden cutting board.

"You don't tell me what to do, you understand? Ever! I will do what I want whenever I want! You understand me, you ungrateful little jackass?"

"Everything I'm grateful for was because of Grandma. You should be grateful for all the times I had to carry you into your room when you were so wasted you couldn't even finish a complete sentence. Just because you screwed up your life and thought you were more important than your own kids, don't take it out on me."

She winced. She picked up her knife and walked around the kitchen island while holding the knife down. Ricky didn't move. He froze for a moment, not sure what she intended to do.

"You think you're the man of this house now? And what, I'm worthless?"

"I never said that. And I am the adult in this house now. Not like I had much of a choice."

She walked up to him and waved the knife under his chin, pointing the edge of the blade just under it.

"I am the adult here," she hissed. "Don't you ever question me or what I do, do you understand?"

"Or what?" Ricky said, his anger overtaking any initial fear he had. "You'll stab me?"

Her face looked enraged. She looked down at her hand with the knife in it. Her eyes widened, and she gasped as if she had just realized what she was doing.

She shook her head and her eyes watered. She let the knife fall and ran back to her room.

Ricky just stood there, panting.

"Come on, man," Freddy said. "Let's just go."

CHAPTER TEN

RICKY PICKED THE KNIFE UP OFF THE FLOOR. "NO, LET'S GO BACK to the room. I'm not leaving her here alone. Plus, I have to get you back. You've never beaten me five times in a row."

Ricky placed the knife on his bed and they got back to the game. He couldn't concentrate and Freddy beat him in back-to-back matches.

"Come on, Ricky. I'm enjoying kicking your ass, but it's okay."

Ricky stared back. "I'm fine. Another one."

There was still anger and bitterness in his voice.

This time, Ricky stared at the screen. Freddy chose an Amazon fighter, and Ricky thought of his mother's face on the fighter's body.

He got two perfect scores and won the best-of-three matches. He then chose to repeat with the same fighters.

"Hey, I wanted to change her!" Freddy said.

Ricky's stare made Freddy close his mouth and play. Another two perfect scores.

Ricky's face flushed with each punch, then threw in a fatality that made her head explode.

Then something moved.

They turned and saw the sugar skull's eyes glowing. The knife had moved from the top of his bed to the desk right by the skull. The knife was standing on its tip, spinning slowly for a few seconds, then lifted and flew across the room, landing on the corkboard on Ricky's wall with a big thump. It hit hard enough that most of the things pinned on the board fell to the floor.

Ricky looked back at the skull and it slowly turned. Its glowing eyes darkened, and a small bright hole burned in the center of each eye. It stopped and was looking away from him.

Ricky followed the direction the skull was facing. It seemed to be aligning with the corkboard where the knife had landed.

Ricky moved towards the board and surveyed it. Most of the pictures and notes had fallen or had shifted with the impact, but where the knife landed was unmistakable.

It was a picture from about 5 or 6 years before. It was a day when Lori was coherent and in the house. They were all sitting down for dinner and then decided to watch a movie. Ellie had taken the picture and it was all of them. Him, Myra, Mom and Grandma Bea.

The knife landed right in the middle of Mom's forehead, dead center.

There was a scraping noise behind him. Ricky turned back, seeing a silent Freddy pointing.

The skull's eye sockets were in full glow. Then it shook and moved halfway across the desk.

"That skull!" Freddy yelled. "It's possessed or something!"

Ricky couldn't believe what he was seeing. Whatever had happened with the skull when his grandma died was back.

"We need to break it!" Ricky yelled. "Grab it!"

"Hell no! I'm not touching that thing!"

Ricky wanted to run, but he stared into the skull's eyes and was captivated by their glow. The eyes seemed to gaze right at him.

He was overcome with a sudden realization that he had to destroy it right now.

He ran to the skull and threw it on the floor. It cracked, but didn't break. The eyes were still glowing. He pulled a pillowcase off one of his pillows and grabbed the skull, stuffing it inside.

Ricky held it like it was radioactive and then broke into a run.

He flew out of his room and out the front door with Freddy right behind.

"Where are you going?" Freddy yelled.

"I don't know! Just away from the house. I don't want it near me."

He kept running.

Freddy followed. Ricky had always been a little faster, but his adrenaline had him a full fifty yards ahead and he wasn't slowing down.

They flew past four blocks of houses and cars parked on the streets before they reached a grassy block where Stone Creek's lone water tower stood. Their high school cougar mascot, along with "The Stone Creek Cougars," was painted on the north and south sides of the tower. Its base was a concrete slab that jutted out in a rectangular shape about twenty feet on each side. The tower had a single attached ladder that led up 100 feet to a walkway that encircled it. Freddy stopped as Ricky kept running towards it.

"What are you doing?" Freddy yelled.

Ricky reached the ladder and shoved the pillowcase down his shirt. He used both hands to fly up each rung and didn't look down.

He and Freddy had only tried to climb it once when they

were freshmen, but they only got about halfway before they looked down and fear stopped them cold. They both closed their eyes and prayed as they took slow steps down and had vowed to never try that again.

Whatever fear that had held them years before was gone. Ricky was determined and didn't hesitate.

By the time Freddy reached the ladder, Ricky was more than halfway up.

Freddy put a foot on the first rung, looked up and stopped before taking step two.

He stepped back instead. He knew what Ricky was going to do and understood he had to do it alone. Plus, he had already decided unless Ricky was dangling from the tower and clinging for dear life, he had no intention of following.

Ricky reached the top of the ladder, running on pure adrenaline. He got to the thin walkway and pulled himself up. He looked down and saw Freddy waving at him, then took in a deep breath as he realized just how high in the air he was.

Don't think about it, he thought to himself.

He pulled the pillowcase out of his shirt and removed the skull. Its eyes weren't glowing and he didn't feel anything coming from it. He held it over the rail.

"No more. Whatever you are, no more."

He raised the skull over his head and threw it down so hard he lost his balance and slipped.

One leg fell over the rail. He landed on his butt, and the railing held, but he lost his grip on the pillowcase and it glided down after the skull.

Freddy jumped back as the skull landed a few feet in front of him and exploded into a white cloud as it shattered on impact.

Freddy moved up, afraid to step in the white ash it left. He eased his shoe onto it slowly, as if it were boiling lava.

"Is it gone?" Ricky screamed from above.

Freddy looked up.

"Come down and see."

Ricky took a moment to breathe and held his head down. He stood up and started down the ladder. A sense of relief held his adrenaline in check and once he got his feet comfortably on the ladder rungs, he found a rhythm and headed down in a steady, but nowhere near as fast as he had gone on his way up, pace.

He jumped off the last step and Freddy had moved away from the remains of the skull.

"That it?" Ricky asked.

"What's left of it. It exploded like a mini-bomb."

Ricky knelt down in front of the debris and ran his index finger across it. He grimaced as if he expected something to jump out of the ashes, but nothing did. He hesitated for another minute, looking around to see if any large pieces survived, but nothing. He didn't find the pillowcase, either.

After a few minutes, Ricky got up and looked back at Freddy.

"Why the water tower?" Freddy asked.

"While I was running, I just kept thinking about the best way to destroy it. The water tower seemed high enough to work."

"What do you think just happened at the house?" Freddy asked.

"I don't know. I just know it was something bad."

"It didn't throw the knife at us, at least. Maybe it has bad aim."

"It doesn't matter. Maybe that's why my mom was acting so crazy. Maybe something bad got in the house the night Grandma Bea died. Remember the little girl looking for her cat?"

Freddy nodded. "Are you kidding? I still have nightmares

about her. I woke up yelling just the other night. In my dream she showed up at my front door and had found her cat, then threw it at me and it tried to scratch my eyes out."

Ricky gaped at him. He'd only had one nightmare since that time. It was almost the same as Freddy's dream about the girl, except the cat was trying to scratch off the little girl's face in his version.

"You think that skull was possessed or something?"

"I don't know, but it's over. Let's go home."

They walked back slowly, calming down with each step.

"Maybe your mom's cool now," Freddy said.

"I guess we'll see. I wish my grandmother was still here. She'd know what to do with everything she knows about stuff that you can't explain. She saw a lot of unbelievable things."

"What do you mean?"

"You know she studied all different kinds of cultures and tribes that live in the most remote places on the planet. Remember the stories she'd tell us about spirits from Mexico and Haiti and how almost every place she'd visited had some kind of supernatural folklore?"

"Oh, yeah. When we were younger, around Halloween and Day of the Dead. I remember some of those stories scaring me."

"She might have known is all I'm saying, but right now, I don't want to know. I just don't ever want to see that stupid skull again."

They neared the house and the walk had finally calmed them both down. Ricky started wondering what it was about that skull that made him pick that specific one during Fiesta and if it was somehow his fault.

They got to the driveway when Freddy stopped abruptly and almost fell forward.

Ricky took another step before he looked up.

The skull sat on the second step of the porch, fully intact.

"What the hell?" Freddy whispered, his voice quivering. "I'm going home, Ricky. I'm going home."

He turned around and ran, leaving Ricky there alone, staring at the skull.

Its eyes weren't glowing anymore, and it wasn't moving. Ricky stepped towards it slowly, waiting for it to attack or do something.

Nothing. He was overcome with a need to grab it. He reached for it and flicked it off the steps with a backhand, knocking it onto the concrete walkway. He lifted his foot and stomped it with his shoe. It didn't resist and broke into large chunks. He fought his urge to lift the pieces and instead rushed inside.

His mother wasn't in the kitchen or living room. He rushed toward her room and her door was cracked open. He peered inside, and she was under the covers, breathing heavily and snoring.

He walked back to his room and opened the door.

The undamaged skull was on his desk again, as if it was waiting patiently for Ricky's return.

CHAPTER ELEVEN

RICKY STOOD THERE, MOTIONLESS, HAVING A STARING CONTEST with a skull that would never blink back. He kept thinking its eyes might glow again, or it could start flying across the room, but it just sat there.

Once the fear and frustration subsided, Ricky let out a big breath.

"What do you want with me?" he finally asked, hoping he wouldn't hear a voice but still somehow get an answer.

Another ten minutes without movement or an answer passed before Ricky finally broke his gaze.

"How about you chill out while I clean your mess up?"

His room was still trashed from the flying knife. He started to pick things up but didn't want to turn his back on the skull.

He tossed a handful of objects on his bed. His head jerked as he reached down to grab more and pricked his finger on a pin. It was the first time he looked away.

The pin had a green plastic head. It didn't stick in his finger but had gone in just enough to draw blood. Ricky instinctively put his finger up to his mouth and sucked on it. There was only a trickle.

His head snapped back at the skull once he realized he had lost sight of it. It still hadn't moved.

"Just stay there. Okay?"

He paid a little more attention to where his hands were reaching and looked up every few seconds for a sanity check. Once he picked up the last item and tossed it on the bed, he slowly turned back toward the corkboard. The skull would be behind him while he faced it.

The corkboard was crooked. It hung on the wall with screws from two saw tooth hangers attached to the back of the board, but one of them had come loose. It was only slightly off since the knife had penetrated straight through and into the wall, keeping it from spinning and falling.

Ricky looked back a few times at the skull, then went back to the corkboard. He reached to pull out the knife, then hesitated. He took a longer look at the picture where the knife had landed on his mom's forehead.

He held the corkboard and pulled the knife straight out. It didn't resist, but the picture of his family fell. Once the knife was out, the board stayed in place as he held it. He eased it up and down until the screw caught the hanger. He let go slowly just to be sure it was stable, then reached down to pick up the picture, still holding the knife in his other hand.

He went to his bed and sat down, making sure he didn't sit on the mess. He faced the skull as he stared at his picture with the new hole in it.

"Was this on purpose? Does this mean you're coming after my entire family or just my mom?"

He studied the picture as he ran through his memories of everything that had happened.

Grandma, what do I do? he thought to himself.

He calmed down as he thought of her and took in some deep breaths.

"You wouldn't be scared of this thing, would you, Grandma Bea?" he said aloud this time. "Not even a little. You'd say it was just a trinket that someone was manipulating and you'd do what you do to find out the truth."

He put the picture down and without thinking about it, snatched the skull up in his hands. He looked it over and tapped the knife against it.

"Why would you throw this knife around? What if I used it on you?"

He ran the knife around the skull's eye sockets, then scratched the blade across its face, leaving a scar.

"It's not like that'll stay, right?"

His phone dinged.

He put the knife down and pulled his phone out of his pocket. It was Freddy texting him.

"Sorry I ran. That was too much. Is it still on the front steps?"

"No, I'm holding it in my hand now."

The reply was almost immediate.

"WHY?"

"It won't leave me. I have to find a way to deal with that. I think no matter where I go or what I do, it will still be waiting for me somewhere in the house."

"Destroy it!!"

"I think we both know that's just not possible. Not without knowing more, at least."

Ricky decided not to tell him he had tried to stomp it. Considering a water tower toss wasn't enough, he didn't see the point.

"I'd come over, but I just can't tonight. I'm still shaking. I asked my mom if I could sleep in her room and she told me to quit watching scary movies."

"Seriously? What scary movies? *The Nightmare Before Christmas* still freaks you out."

"Hello! It's a psycho skinny skeleton who's in love with the Bride of Frankenstein's cousin. Anyway, she told me no, but as soon as she's asleep I'm sneaking in with my pillow and blankets to sleep on her floor."

"You can always come over. I don't think I'll sleep tonight."

"Not happening. I'd rather sleep under my bed than go to your house tonight. No offense."

"You're good. I get it. Hopefully the Pumpkin King won't be under there with you."

"Not cool. Still, try not to let the skull kill you or anything."

"I'll try."

Ricky put the phone down and looked back at the skull.

"You have Freddy terrified. I'm scared, too, but if you refuse to leave, I guess I have to find a way to get used to you."

He put the skull back and went to his closet. He reached into a bin that was labeled "School." His grandmother had made him get organized his sophomore year to keep his room clean enough to study in.

He rummaged through the bin. He pulled out a rally towel with a Cougar mascot on it. As he placed the towel over the skull, he wasn't surprised the scar he had just given it was already gone.

"Even if you survived that water tower, I can at least leave you a reminder. I hope you were scared on your way down before exploding."

He knew it wasn't likely, but he still hoped.

Another text alert dinged on his phone.

"How about we hang out at the creek tomorrow?" Freddy typed. "It's been a long time since we've been out there. Something to keep you distracted."

Ricky sent back a thumbs-up emoji. Distraction sounded like an excellent idea.

CHAPTER TWELVE

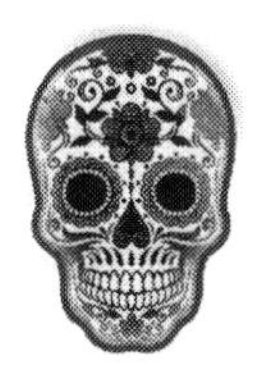

FREDDY CAME BY THE HOUSE IN THE LATE AFTERNOON. HE knocked on the door to the room but didn't want to enter.

"It's okay, Freddy," Ricky said. "The skull and I have a truce."

Freddy stuck his head in slowly.

"How do you make a truce with a flying skull?"

"It let me clean up my room last night. I talked to it."

"Did it talk back?" Freddy asked as he started to leave the room.

"No. You can come in."

Freddy stepped fully in but left the door open, staring at the skull that was still covered in the Cougars rally towel.

"It didn't talk back to me, but I covered it up and tried to get it to react. That towel's been on it all night and it didn't try to move or shake it off. Unless something happens, I'm hoping it'll be calm. At least for a little while."

"You don't seriously believe that, do you?"

"No, I don't, but I'm trying to convince myself that it's enough so I can sleep."

"Is it working?"

"I don't know. I slept maybe four hours, but I don't know if it's because I felt like nothing was actually going to happen or my body just gave out on me."

"How about we get to the creek?"

"That sounds like a good idea."

The boys left, walking through the neighborhood toward the creek.

The house where Ricky had spent his entire life was in a neighborhood where the homes were spaced out twenty feet or so from each other with connected fences.

It was the East side of town; a neighborhood made up of six streets that ran to the East/West over seven blocks, with Stone Creek, the actual creek the town was named after, bordering to the north and one main highway to the South. Each street's name was water related. The southernmost street was Aqua, followed by Tide, Rain, Water, Wave and Stone Creek Street, which was the last street where each house's backyard merged into a ten-foot hill that led up and then down thirty feet into the actual creek. Ricky, Freddy and Ellie all lived on Rain street.

The bottom of the creek extended 150 yards then rose again, serving as the border to the north side of town. A train bridge connected these two sides of the creek. The houses that bordered both the creek and the railroad track ended up with an extra almost acre of land. The homeowners had used Ricky to mow those acres for years since he had a sitting lawnmower that belonged to his late grandfather. The wild grass, especially near the tracks, grew fast, so Ricky always had a nice chunk of money by the end of each summer.

When Ricky was still in elementary, the creek was filled with water, roughly ten feet below the highest crest of the hill. Many years of drought had changed that. It was now more of a stream but gave the kids a much larger area to play. The city was responsible for mowing that grass, and it sometimes stood up to five feet tall before it was taken care of. His grandfather always told him to leave it to the city in case anything happened.

This creek ran through several miles of town and some spots were a favorite hangout for kids, especially teenagers. When Ricky was younger, he and his neighborhood friends liked to hang out near the railroad bridge, which was strictly prohibited by his grandmother and mother when she was coherent. Of course this meant they spent most of their time crossing or playing around it, ready to run when they heard the train heading through. That was never a major issue since they typically had at least a few miles and minutes of warning. It was hard not to hear the train in the desolate area a few miles before hitting their neighborhood.

The boys reached the creek and threw some rocks into the shallow water, talking about the last time they had been there and some of the stupid things they had done back when they were in middle school.

"How about a middle school repeat?" Freddy said as he ran up the hill. Ricky followed until they were about twenty feet from the bridge.

"What?" Ricky asked.

"Time to make the ants rain!"

Ricky laughed at the memory.

"So where's the enemy nest?" Ricky asked.

Freddy pointed toward the ground. "There."

Ricky looked down and saw a small hole in the dirt with raised soil. It was an underground anthill with no central mound. Large red ants entered and exited the flat hole.

Freddy reached into his pocket and pulled out a small item with a fuse.

"A Black Cat?" Ricky asked.

"Yes, check this out!"

He pulled out a small box of matches he had taken from his kitchen drawer.

He stuffed the firecracker in the ant pile hole then lit the fuse.

He smiled a devious smile and then stepped back about five feet. Ricky followed.

"You think we're far enough back?" Ricky asked. "Remember last time?"

They took a few more steps back. Ricky closed his eyes. The Black Cat exploded.

"Awesome!" Freddy yelled as he jumped up.

Ricky ran to the mound. The hole was a little bigger and the ants were swarming. Then he felt a sting on his arm.

Around the same time, his best friend yelled.

Ricky looked up and saw that Freddy's back was crawling with red ants. Then something stung his head.

They stared at each other, realizing they hadn't moved far enough.

"They're all over you!" Freddy yelled.

They did a manic dance, jumping up and down and sweeping their fingers through their hair. Ricky ran back to the thick grass and threw himself on the ground, rolling to get the ants off him.

"What are you doing?" Freddy asked.

"Getting them off me!"

Freddy was getting stung more and followed Ricky's example. As they rolled around like madmen, a high-pitched voice laughed.

Ricky looked up. It was Ellie.

"What exactly are you two doing?"

She covered her mouth with her hand, trying not to laugh out loud, but she couldn't help herself.

"I smell fireworks. Did you idiots try to blow up an ant mound?"

"How... how did you know?" Freddy asked.

She looked down. "My brother did that last year. I was smart enough to run."

"We thought we had moved away far enough this time," Freddy said.

"This time? Meaning y'all did this before and were dumb enough to try again?"

They stood up. Ricky couldn't feel any more stings, but even if one or two bit him now, he probably wouldn't notice. "Hi, Ellie."

"Hey, Ricky."

Before the funeral, it had been at least three months since he and Ellie had a meaningful conversation, and now he had seen her three times in just a few weeks.

"What are you doing out here?"

"I was at home, wondering how you were doing. I walked to your house, but no one answered. I figured you were close since Grandma Bea's SUV was there. Decided to try the creek and saw y'all doing something once I got closer. Figured I'd come check it out."

"Glad you did," Ricky said.

"I guess some things never change. Remember when we were in third grade and you tried to catch that lizard?"

Ricky looked down. "You always have to bring up the lizard."

Freddy looked at them both. "How come I don't know about the lizard?"

"Do I tell him or do you want to?"

Ricky sighed. "Go ahead. I know you're dying to."

"So, we were playing over here by the creek, not too far from where we are now. A lizard jumped on my foot and I screamed. Ricky tried to be brave and pull it off me, but it ended up biting his finger and wouldn't let go. So he shook it and started yelling. Well, not yelling so much as shrieking louder than I did when it scared me in the first place. So he shook his finger and ran around in circles. I know he wanted to cry, but he kept yelling. So I reached over and grabbed the lizard and threw it off. The tip of his finger was red for days."

"Not my finest moment," Ricky said.

"I know who the brave one is," Freddy said. "Too bad that's not on video anywhere."

They all laughed, then a loud bristling sound echoed behind them. They all turned toward the tall weeds.

"Did you hear that?" Freddy asked.

"Yes, I did."

They looked over. It was a still, windless day, but a portion of the grass was pressed down, then raised back somewhat, and another piece pressed down.

"Is that a dog?" Freddy asked.

Ellie and Ricky stared at each other. "Dog or rabbit?"

"I pick rabbit!" Ellie yelled.

"What?" Freddy said.

Ellie and Ricky took off toward the sound. They had played this game when they were younger, before the rigors of high school and cliques and hormones had altered their friendship.

Freddy followed.

The three of them moved toward the grass as whatever they were chasing made more steps and more patches of fallen grass. The trail went beyond the patch of weeds near the bridge and into the hill of the creek. They kept running.

"No barking! It's not a dog!" Ellie yelled. "I win!"

"Doesn't count until we see a rabbit!" Ricky yelled.

They chased it as it ran in a circle. The unseen target moved faster, but they stayed right behind.

Then the path shifted and stopped. They stopped, too, and looked around. The grass started to fall around them. The invisible movement was suddenly everywhere and then a larger, almost perfect full circle of grass came down at the same time, forming around them in an instant.

"That's not a rabbit," Freddy said.

"No, it's not. Never seen that before," Ellie said.

Her voice was shaking as dusk settled in.

"What is that?" Ricky asked.

The circle around them rose and fell two more times, each blade of grass in unison, as if being conducted to follow music.

Then it darted away in a fast line.

Ricky felt a strong sense of heat in his chest. He didn't know what it was, but was overcome with a need to find out.

He ran.

He chased the path left by the unseen animal with Ellie right behind him. Freddy stood frozen in his tracks.

They chased it up the hill. The tall weeds thinned out as they neared a patch of brown grass that hadn't grown most of the summer, but still yielded to the invisible pressure.

There were footprints. They both stopped and kept looking down and the steps slowed down, then turned and ran towards them. They didn't have time to react as the footsteps turned to their right, heading over the hill and into the now dark creek.

"Have you ever seen that before?" Ellie asked.

"No. I don't know what just happened. But you saw what I saw, right?"

Ellie nodded. "Footsteps. From something that wasn't there."

"No dog or rabbit. The grass looked like it was being stepped on."

Ellie's eyes were moist. "I'm scared, Ricky."

He reached over and grabbed her hand. "It's okay. I am, too."

"You think the creek's haunted?" she asked.

"Have you even heard of something like that ever happening?" Ricky asked.

Ellie shook her head. "It didn't hurt us, whatever it was."

Freddy jogged over.

"Where were you?" Ricky asked.

"Sorry, man. I don't play ghosts."

"You think it was a ghost?" Ellie asked.

"I don't know what else it might be." He reached up and pointed a finger. "Either of you notice there was no wind before, and there's no wind now?"

Ricky and Ellie looked at each other. They hadn't realized it, but Freddy was right.

There had been no wind other than what hit their faces as they were running.

"I don't know what just happened," Ellie said. "But ghost or not, something was definitely there."

"I know who'll be the last to die if that ever happens again," Freddy said. "Me, because I ain't chasing a thing. You'll both be the curious ones who get to be Victims 1 and 2."

CHAPTER THIRTEEN

"COME ON, RICKY. IT'LL BE GOOD FOR US."

Freddy had been wanting to go to the carnival all week, but with everything going on, he hadn't brought it up to Ricky until he came by his house this particular afternoon. After the creek incident, Ricky spent the next few days home with Myra and it had been relatively quiet. The carnival was only in town for another two days, but it turned out to be an odd day with his mom.

Lori had woken up in a good mood and tagged along with Myra to hang out with Karen and her family and go to dinner. It was a first. Ricky was in the living room most of the day, avoiding the skull and thinking about calling or texting Ellie, but never gathering enough nerve to do it.

"I guess Myra will be fine as long as they're with Karen's family," Ricky finally said. "She's supposed to spend the night again, but I told her to text me if anything changed or if Mom got out of hand. I do need to get out of the house. Let's go."

"Yes!"

Ricky had an emergency stash of money for whatever he and his sister needed in his room. Most of it was in the bank, but he used that lawn money when he needed it. He had received an initial payment from his Grandmother Bea's inheritance but hadn't used it for anything yet. Today seemed like a good time.

Ricky pulled out some cash. He took a quick look at the skull that remained covered with his rally towel without incident.

"Behave yourself while I'm gone," Ricky said.

He waited a moment and happily received no reply. The boys moved out to the truck. They were excited, but Ricky turned the key and nothing happened. The truck wouldn't start.

"What's going on?" Freddy asked. "This truck always works."

"I don't know. I guess we can't go."

"We're not giving up that easy," Freddy said. "The bus stop is right down the street."

Ricky was frustrated, knowing he had to get the vehicle checked. His grandma had a friend that had been her regular mechanic for over 15 years. He lived just a few streets down and she always said he was reasonable. Ricky figured he'd call him tomorrow.

He locked up the truck and they headed toward the bus stop. It was about three blocks away in front of the only gas station within about five miles.

They got to the stop and waited for the bus that went to the carnival area on the outskirts of town, near the baseball fields where Ricky played when he was little. His baseball life lasted two seasons before he realized it wasn't his game.

The bus finally pulled in and there were about seven people waiting. They got in and it was almost full. It would have taken them about 15-20 minutes going by car, but the bus made several stops and it took almost 45 minutes to get there. They didn't say much during the trip.

Once they were near their destination, the evening carnival lit up the entire sky. The lights of the Ferris wheel and the Zipper stood out as they looked like the tallest rides there until they got close and saw a bungee cage shooting a victim up in the air much higher than either one.

"That looks cool!" Freddy said, although Ricky knew his friend didn't have the stomach for it.

They ran to the ticket booth and as Freddy walked toward the first window, Ricky stopped him.

"I got it," he said.

"Mom gave me money, but I'm not going to say no," Freddy said as he backed away from the booth.

"Consider it a gift from my grandma."

Bea had taken them to the local carnival almost every year. As the boys got older, she would stay with Myra while the boys went off on the bigger rides.

They went straight to the Zipper and rode that first. For the few minutes that the ride took, spinning its individual cars in complete circles and back as the entire Zipper moved along its zippered shape, Ricky felt free. He didn't think about his grandmother, the skull, Myra or his mother. He just felt the exhilaration of being thrown up and down and screaming with his best friend like they always had in the past. It was a rare, worry-free moment, compared to the last few weeks.

As soon as it was over, he wanted to ride it again, but Freddy said, "Nah, this one's cooler. Let's go bungee!"

They moved toward the bungee, which was on the opposite side of the Zipper, and they heard a voice say, "Hey, guys!"

They turned and it was Ellie. She had walked away from a group of friends, most of them dancers. It was the same crowd she had been hanging out with since high school started.

"Hey, Ellie," Ricky said. "Good to see you."

"It's good to see you out of the neighborhood, Ricky."

"My first time in a while. Freddy made me."

"Yeah, I'm pretty pushy," Freddy said.

Freddy turned to the right and saw another group of people he recognized.

"I'm gonna go say hey to Charlie."

Ricky nodded as Freddy walked off and left them alone while Ellie's group looked on, waiting for her.

"How are you doing? I went by yesterday, but the truck was gone."

"Yeah, I took Myra to get something to eat. Been watching her the last few days, but she's out with a friend tonight. Didn't realize you came by."

"I can always go by again. Not like you live far."

"Why didn't you call?"

"Well, hadn't heard from you in a few days so I wanted to surprise you. Is everything okay at the house?"

Ricky knew she wouldn't ask that without reason. "I guess. Why would you ask?"

She smirked as her eyes shifted left. "Just checking."

"Ellie," he said. "You did the lie face."

She let out a breath. They both knew when the other was lying from years of observing each other.

"Okay. Freddy told me some weird stuff had happened at the house. Weirder than what happened at the creek the other day. He told me he was worried about you."

Ricky shook his head. "Freddy needs to learn to keep his mouth shut."

"You know he's only looking out for you. I know he's your best friend now, but he wasn't always."

He looked down as he laughed. "Yeah, we had a great friendship for a long time, didn't we?"

"What do you mean had?" she asked.

"You know what I mean."

She did. Even with their strained relationship over the last few years, neither one of them had ever had a steady boyfriend or girlfriend that lasted more than a few months, and no other friendships, not even Freddy's, had been stronger than what they had growing up.

"Yes, I do. Sucks that we have to get older, but even if we don't hang out often, it hasn't changed our trust of each other, has it?"

"No," he said. "I think my waterworks the other day proved that."

"Then why are you hiding this from me?"

Ricky looked around at the crowd waiting for her and Freddy talking to their other school friends.

"Fine. Freddy's right. Some weird stuff's been happening, and I'll tell you everything. Freddy's too scared to talk about it much and I haven't even told him things that have happened when he wasn't there because I'm afraid he may not come back to my house anymore. Just somewhere else. Come by tomorrow if you can."

Someone from her group yelled, "Ellie, we're going to the House of Mirrors. Come on!"

She turned back.

"I'll catch up with you in a few!"

Ricky was surprised. "It's okay, Ellie. Don't change your plans because of me."

"Shut up, Ricky. Come on."

She grabbed his hand and led him to the Ferris wheel. They stood in a short line before getting on.

They sat across from each other in the car. As soon as the wheel started moving, she leaned toward him with a serious face.

"We'll talk tomorrow, but right now, just tell me how you're doing without Grandma Bea. I know it has to be hard.

Whatever's happened, I'm here and I plan to always be here."

Ricky looked at her. "I don't know. Everything's changed. It's... just different."

She stared at him as he tried to keep his guard up.

"Who have you talked to about it?"

He shook his head. "Freddy's there. He's seen some of the things that are going on. I just wish Grandma was still here."

"She always will be in spirit. It feels odd being in the house and not hearing her voice."

"I really miss her. I took so much for granted. I'm having to worry about money and Myra and my mom now."

He stopped.

"What about your mom?"

"That's part of the other stuff that's going on."

"Forget about tomorrow, just tell me Ricky."

He hesitated. "Something strange happened the night my grandmother died."

He told her about the skull and his final moments with Grandma Bea, but stopped before telling her how he tried to destroy it and couldn't do it. He hoped Blabber Freddy hadn't already said something.

Ellie hesitated.

"You don't believe me, do you?"

"If you were anyone else, I probably wouldn't, but after what happened at the creek that night and talking to Freddy, I believe you. That's scary, but there's more to it, right?"

He nodded. "There is, but I'll tell you more another day. I'm actually enjoying this."

She nodded.

"Thank you."

"For what?"

"For not treating me differently. For just being there."

His eyes glossed over as he met her gaze.

"It's okay. I know what she was like. I know what your family life has been like."

She reached over and gave him a hug, a big one. As she moved back, she looked right at him.

"You know you're an idiot, right?"

It caught him off guard. "What do you mean?"

"I mean, it's here. The signs, the moment. A Ferris wheel and we're all alone. I just gave you a super hug."

Ricky just stared at her and didn't know what to say.

"I guess a girl's gotta take matters into her own hands sometimes."

"What do you m--"

Ellie grabbed his face and kissed him.

He almost squealed from being caught off guard, but let it happen and kissed her back. The kiss was gentle and they both had their eyes closed. Ricky felt himself shaking, but felt her shaking just as much. It was the best kiss either had experienced and they were both lost in every second.

After finally releasing, they stayed staring at each other.

Ellie broke the silence first. "I'm shaking."

He grabbed her hand. "So am I. Ellie, that was..."

"Perfect," they both said.

They stayed holding hands as the ride ended. Before exiting their car, she hugged him again.

"I have to go. I came here with Joanna and promised my mom I'd go back with her, but I will come see you tomorrow, okay?"

He just smiled. "Okay."

She ran off to catch up with her group while he walked around aimlessly, feeling a little dizzy.

"Hey!" Freddy yelled. "There you are. Where'd you go?"

"Uh, Ferris wheel."

Freddy's eyebrows furled. "With Ellie?"

He couldn't hide his smile. "Yes."

"Dude, something happened, right? You look like you just threw up."

He just smiled. "It was nice, that's all."

"Lying Jack. I'll let it go for now. Let's go get on the swings!"

They spent the next two hours on rides, but never ran into Ellie or her group other than seeing them in the opposite direction.

They ate too much and had a great time. It got later and they joined the group of friends Freddy had spoken to earlier. They had more fun with the larger group, especially on the bumper cars. As expected, Freddy lost his junk food on the bungee ride.

As the carnival came to a close, one of the boys named Joey asked them if they wanted to go to his house for a video game fest. He lived in the same neighborhood, just a few more blocks down.

"Let's go!" Freddy said, but Ricky, still reeling from his encounter with Ellie, who he hadn't been able to stop thinking about, didn't want to.

"Nah, I'm okay. Go ahead without me."

"Joey brought his car, so we're going to go. We can drop you off at the house, I'm sure."

Ricky thought about it.

"You know what, I'm cool. I think I want to just ride the bus back so I can think."

"Think? No video games and you want to think? Man, Ellie did a number on you. I'll get it out of you later. All right, if that's what you want to do, I'll see you later."

They slapped hands and Ricky said his goodbyes to the group before heading to the bus stop.

CHAPTER FOURTEEN

THE BUS LINE WAS FULL AND HE HAD TO WAIT FOR THE THIRD ONE to finally get on. He moved to the back, seated with a young boy whose mom and younger brother were in the seats in front of him.

The boy was mad because he had to leave, even though Mom kept telling him the carnival was already closed.

"Did you have a good time?" Ricky asked.

The boy gave him a look with his arms still crossed.

"My friend Freddy puked on the bungee."

The boy started laughing. "Really? Did it get on you?"

"No, it flew in the other direction but I'll bet pieces of it fell in someone's drink and they slurped it down good!"

The boy started laughing. "Ewwww."

The boy then started talking about the Zipper and other rides he had ridden.

The mom tapped Ricky on the knee and mouthed, "Thank you."

The family got off at their stop and the bus was down to ten people. Ricky kept thinking about Ellie. The bus finally arrived at his stop, but he was so caught up in his thoughts he missed getting off. He finally came to his senses a little while later after realizing how quiet it was.

He stood up. He was the only one left on the bus.

"Hey, I missed my stop!"

The bus driver looked in the rear-view mirror. "Which one?"

"The Stone Creek East gas station."

"No worries. I'm heading downtown and will eventually loop back around. It'll be awhile, but I'll get you back."

Ricky thanked him and returned to his seat, even though he had the entire bus to choose from. He didn't think about it and welcomed the extra time. Time to think about Ellie. It was nice. First time in weeks he had gone this long without worrying about his mother or sister, although he hoped Lori hadn't found a way to ruin her time with Myra.

He saw downtown approaching and stared out the window.

The bus stopped.

Ricky didn't hear anyone get on the bus. He looked out at the empty downtown street. Nothing much was lit up this late in the three block stretch of downtown, just the lonely streetlights and a few stores with signs on that never turned off. He had been focusing on the appliance store in front of him and realized they had been stopped a little too long.

He stood up and looked toward the front of the bus.

The driver was gone.

Ricky eased out of his seat and moved forward, wondering if the driver was picking something or someone up and he just couldn't see him. He checked each row, but no one was there. He finally reached the front row and still no sign of the driver. The bus door was still closed and he never heard it open, but he had been distracted. He looked back down the aisle of the empty bus. Something creaked. The door was opening. He stared at it until it reached its full open position. Still, no other person was inside or outside the bus door.

He eased down the big steps and stepped off.

He was at the far end of the downtown blocks. Behind him were the darker streets near the post office, but nothing lit them up. His only destination was forward. There were no cars parked on either side of the street, which was unusual. Typically, at least 4 or 5 cars were there from the bar patrons a few blocks east or west of downtown, but not tonight. It was just three empty blocks before him and the streetlights. There was a thin fog outside that seemed more ominous with the store and streetlights reflecting off the haze.

"Hello?" he called out.

There was no reply. Ricky saw a motion to his right and turned to look, but it was just a flashing neon "Closed" sign in front of the locally owned Miss Pepperoni's Pizza House, which was one of his favorite places to eat. Nothing was there, but he saw something move in the reflection of the store's front window. He turned back but didn't see anything behind him. He looked across the street toward the music store, but only saw himself in that window. He looked back at the bus and saw something bright streak across its tinted side windows.

It was a thin flash of green light, almost like someone was running a laser pointer across it.

Ricky felt his heart start to pound as he took a few steps further down the block. The fog seemed to be thickening.

Behind the lamppost to his left, something was definitely there.

He froze. He tried to stay quiet but his heart was crashing against his chest. Something wet slithered across the back of his neck.

He flipped around. A black shape was just inches from

him. It seemed human for the most part, with thin, sickly arms. There was no face, just blackness, like a shadow come to life. Its head tilted a few times, and a pink tongue came out of its mouth, licking Ricky across the chin.

"Ugh," he yelled and jumped back. His breath quickened as his eyes bulged.

"What are you?"

The thing replied with a hiss. He moved back faster and it didn't give chase.

The shadow thing was about seven feet tall and its legs hinged the wrong way. They seemed to move backward as the knees craned forward, as if its lower torso was reversed.

It crept towards him. He walked back towards the pizza joint with its bright window display. For some reason, he thought that light from the closed sign might protect him a little more.

He upped his pace, but the figure didn't speed up. He looked back to make sure he wasn't going to run into the window and saw his reflection staring back at him. He was pale. And just behind his reflection, another face appeared in the window. It had two slits for a nose and dark glowing eyes like the sugar skull. Its face was thin and surrounded by musculature without skin. Ricky turned back and the shadowy figure was only a few steps away. He flipped back to see the other creature's reflection and then took off running towards the bus. He looked to his side and the muscled creature was running with him, its reflection moving along each storefront window and keeping pace with every one of his steps.

It kept moving. Ricky stopped to see what would happen and the reflection stopped, too.

Ricky turned back and the shadow was still taking its time, but coming right at him. His breathing was heavy and he could feel the sweat on his neck. It had turned humid and he could feel his clothes sticking to him. He ran faster towards the bus and saw that the door was still open.

He darted through and tried to glance at the side of the bus to see if there was another reflection there, but he was moving too fast to tell. He shut the door and ran to the back of the bus to the last row.

Ricky scrunched down on the last row of seats. He could hear his loud breathing. He was having trouble catching his breath. He leaned over the seat in front of him and glanced forward, not knowing what to do. Then he saw the streak on the inside left windows. The reflection was back. It was staring right at him, smiling, revealing a set of sharp, gnarling white teeth. The bus door opened.

He turned toward the front. A wave of nervousness rose from his groin through his stomach and finally up his throat and around his entire skull. This was a terror he had never felt before. The shadow creature emerged from the bus step and moved down the aisle, never taking its eyes off him. In the bus it looked bigger. It had to bend slightly to avoid hitting its head on the ceiling. The arms and legs looked like they had tattered strings of clothing around them, but he saw no actual clothes. He looked closer and with the help of the bus lights, he saw what it was. Torn pieces of black flesh hung off various parts of its body. Its eyes were large empty sockets, but he knew they were fixated on him.

"What do you want?" he was finally able to yell. Still no response. The shadow kept moving and the reflection kept staring.

The reflection moved to the window closest to Ricky, but another image floated on the opposite right window. Then another in the next. The same image filled every individual window on the bus. Each face was the same and they all stared at him with glowing eyes and a wicked smile like they were ready to devour their prey.

Ricky looked away from the windows and the shadow creature stood before him, then leaned its head forward, only inches from his face.

Ricky was too scared to move. He couldn't look away and he couldn't get up and run. He felt his heart beating in his throat.

The shadow opened its mouth and it widened, revealing a gaping hole. It was like it was devouring blackness. Its gap widened even further as the creature in the reflection shrieked with a piercing laugh. The bus lights blinked and then shut off.

In the middle of the shadow something emerged. It was a smaller shape, but familiar. It took a step forward and reached out with its small, but human hand. It was the little girl in the bathing suit. She looked exactly the same. She had her head tilted and looked straight into his eyes. She put her hand on his shoulder.

"Kitty," she said in almost a whisper. "I found you."

The reflection shrieked again. Ricky felt like his ears might burst and the fear overcame his entire being. He reached up to cover his ears as the shadow stepped forward and the little girl disappeared back into its body. The shadow raised its head and brought its gaping mouth over Ricky's scalp, preparing to devour him. Ricky's eyes blurred. He was covered in darkness as the shadow consumed him.

He blacked out.

Ricky woke up with the bus driver shaking him.

"Hey, kid. At your stop. You okay?"

He stared. He was in the same spot, drenched in sweat. He had no idea how much time had passed.

"What? What happened?"

"I don't know. We had a few folks we picked up and dropped off on our way back to your stop. Once we got here, I never saw you get up. I only saw your feet and for some weird reason the lights wouldn't turn on, so I came back here to check on you. You were laying on your side. Thought you were asleep, but you were talking. Mumbling more like it. You yelled when I first tried to wake you. Scared the living crap out of me. So thanks for that."

Ricky turned to each side, taking a second to gather himself.

"So we never stopped downtown? I mean, you didn't leave the bus?"

He chuckled. "No sir. I can't leave the bus unless it's an emergency. We did go through downtown. Only had one customer, but he was pretty drunk and crashed in the front seat. Everything else was normal."

Ricky looked at the windows.

"So you didn't see anything? I didn't get off?"

The driver laughed again. "Did someone spike your punch or were you doing a little drinkin' at the carnival? You don't smell like it, so I'm guessing no. Take anything at that carnival?"

"What? No. I don't do drugs, if that's what you mean."

"Well, any chance someone slipped you something? You sure are acting like you're on something. Or maybe you got on the House of Horrors ride?"

"No, no. I'm fine, I think. Maybe I was just more tired than I thought. Thank you. I'll go."

He got off the bus, still disoriented. He still had to walk to his house.

He started cautiously, looking around as he moved down the streets. Had he just fallen asleep and gotten spooked? It didn't seem likely. He had been thinking about Ellie and then suddenly he was downtown, being chased by these two freaky creatures and the little girl. He couldn't figure it out. Nothing like that had ever happened to him before, but then again, nothing that had been happening recently had ever happened to him before, either.

CHAPTER FIFTEEN

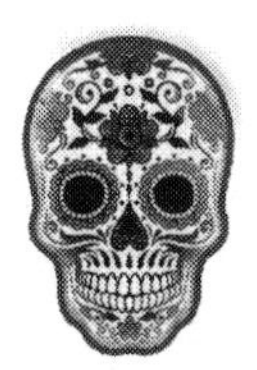

RICKY REACHED HIS HOUSE. HIS HANDS WERE STILL SHAKING AS he opened the door. He just wanted to get to his room and calm down, but he noticed something in the kitchen that he couldn't make out. He focused. Lori was sitting there with all the lights off. The microwave and coffee maker were the only things illuminating the floor.

Lori was slumped in a chair that was pulled back from the table with her elbows on her knees. An orange light glowed as she puffed on a cigarette.

"What are you doing?" Ricky asked. His voice quivered.

"What does it look like I'm doing?" she said without moving.

"You're not supposed to smoke in the house, Mom."

"That was your grandmother's rule. Not mine."

He wanted to push but was still too shaken from what had just happened.

"Fine, Mom. Do whatever you want. Where's Myra?"

She didn't answer. He knew Myra was supposed to stay with Karen, so he let it go and started towards his room.

"You know what's so screwed up?" she asked, whispering.

He didn't want to answer. He had no idea what condition she was in but didn't want to fight.

"I never wanted you," she said, not waiting for him to engage.

"I never wanted your sister, either. You ruined my life. I just wanted to go to Paris and to paint and to do whatever I wanted. I never had the chance."

His temperature shot up. "You did go to Paris. You abandoned me. You left me with Grandma."

"Yeah, she was good for that. But I never wanted to come back. I wanted to stay there forever, but I had to."

"Maybe you should have stayed. You just gave Grandma someone else to take care of."

She still didn't move. She just took another puff of the cigarette.

"She was a bitch. So sanctimonious. A professor. What did she ever do with that?"

"She did plenty. She taught students who wanted to better themselves, and she traveled the world. She could have done more but had to adjust her entire life to take care of her grandchildren since her daughter was such a colossal disappointment."

It hurt him to say it, but his instinct was to protect the memory of his grandmother. He loved his mother, but realized at this exact moment that he'd always loved Grandma Bea more.

"Yeah, she was better than me. Better at everything. I'm just a lost whore, is that it? She ever tell you about the men she was with when she was younger? I didn't fall too far from the tree."

"Even if that's true, she grew up, married a good man and made something of herself. You're in your thirties now. So what's your excuse?"

"Who exactly do you think you are? A seventeen-year-old

little shit that can't take care of himself. You know nothing about life."

"I'm the person who Grandma trusted to take care of you and Myra, that's who I am. And I'm having to do it alone since I've had to be the parent instead of you."

"Yeah, that old bitch left you in charge of the money. How horrible is that to do to your own daughter?"

"She knew what you'd do with it. We'd probably be broke in a year."

"Self-righteous little prick."

Lori's voice never raised. She said each word calmly and clearly.

"I'm your mother no matter what. I want you to give me a few grand."

"What are you going to do with it?"

"None of your business. I'm an adult, no matter what your precious grandmother thought of me."

"Yeah, I'm not giving you a damned thing. We'll live and eat and I'll make sure Myra is taken care of."

"Then you're going to leave."

"What do you mean? I'm not going anywhere."

"You're a senior, aren't you? You're going to go to college since that's what Grandma had weaned you for. A little pussy college boy."

Ricky's anger overshadowed the hurt. He tried to tell himself that she was just drunk or high and arguing was pointless, but he was beyond the point of caring.

"I'll never leave Myra. I'm not you. You left us both a long time ago. I can't even trust you alone with her. I have to make sure she's at a friend's house if I'm late. Even she knows what you are."

"Is that so?" Lori asked, "And what exactly am I?"

"Worthless. You're not a mother and you weren't a daughter. You're just concerned with where you're going to get your next dick and your next fix so you can stick it up your arm or snort it up your nose."

His voice cracked on the last words. He'd had these thoughts hundreds of times in his head when he was angry, but it hurt him to say them aloud. He tried to stop himself, but the odd relief of what he'd said opened a long dormant door.

"We'd be better off if you just left. Maybe walk off the creek bridge when the water's shallow."

He started sobbing uncontrollably.

"Are you crying?" she asked, turning her head and finally looking up.

"You're the big man trying to talk about me, but you still cry like a pussy? The pussy your grandmother raised. I'm glad you're crying. You want to act like Mister Bigshit, in charge of the house and the money, but still cry like a baby. Get the fuck out of my face. You're just like me, you know. A colossal disappointment. I would have been better off aborting you and your sister. The flesh they pulled out would have been worth more in the trash somewhere instead of what's standing in front of me."

Ricky couldn't take it. She had never said anything so cruel before, not even on her worst days, but he had pushed back. His sobbing became uncontrollable.

"I'm sorry, Mom. I'm... just sorry."

"I know you're sorry. The sorriest excuse of my life."

He ran to his room and threw himself on his bed. The skull was there, still covered.

He cried for almost ten minutes straight before he could control himself. His fear mixed with the pain his mother had just inflicted and the guilt he felt from his words to her. He knew she had been sick for years. Sick. That's the word Grandma Bea always used. He was around thirteen when he finally realized what that meant. Drugs, drinking and men.

Grandma Bea had always been their shield. He only remembered Lori cussing at him once or twice, but never like this. Grandma Bea was the buffer. She would send him and Myra to their rooms and walk Lori to bed, letting her take out everything on her. Grandma Bea had always told him it was a losing battle to argue back, but tonight he couldn't stop. The things she said about him. About Myra.

He really needed his grandma right now.

Once he finally calmed down and only a few tears were left, he looked up at his desk. The skull wasn't there anymore. The towel lay flat on the desk.

He raised himself up and felt his elbow hit something.

The skull was on the bed next to him, its eyes glowing bright.

The desk started to tremble. His computer flipped on, the screen flickering on and off. The dresser drawer flew open. Balled socks jumped out, then his briefs and boxers flew across the room.

The doorknob started to turn and his corkboard fell.

The curtains whooshed up and were flying in mid-air violently, like a gale force wind had blown through the window. Ricky picked up the skull and threw it against the wall. It fell with a thud but didn't break.

His lamp tipped over, putting the room in darkness. He heard everything around him moving, then silence.

Ricky moved around frantically and the only light was a dim hue coming from the floor beyond the foot of his bed. He crawled over and looked down. The skull was facing up and its eyes were glowing brighter than he had ever seen them. It pulsed several times, and then everything in the room came on at once. The lamp, computer and TV lit up. His clothes drawers flew open and more items were flying across the room, hitting him all over. It was a chaotic symphony until his drawers were empty. He felt like something punched him hard in the chest, leaving him breathless.

He fell off the bed and then nothing.

When he woke the next day, he was still on the floor with his clothes everywhere. The bulb in his lamp was broken, but everything else seemed fine.

The skull was back on his desk like nothing had ever happened.

Ricky looked at his clock, but it was blinking from having been thrown across the room.

He looked at his phone. It was 10 am. He had been out for hours.

It took a minute for some of his memories to return and he quickly ran his hands over his body, checking to see if he was hurt or bleeding.

His chest felt a little sore, but he was okay.

He remembered the rest. The bus, the fight with his mom and the skull going crazy in his room.

He was trying to get settled when his phone went off. Ellie texted. She was coming over in 20 minutes. Everything else went out the window as he thought about the best part of the night before. Ellie and the Ferris wheel. He wasn't sure what he was going to tell her.

Ricky ran to the bathroom and washed up as fast as he could. He put most of his clothes back in his drawers, then kicked the last pile under his bed. He put the corkboard back on the wall but stuck some of the items in his desk since he didn't have time to put them all up. He was ready in fifteen minutes when the doorbell rang.

As he walked to answer the front door, he decided he was going to tell Ellie everything.

CHAPTER SIXTEEN

ELLIE WALKED IN, PAUSING TO LOOK AT HIM. LORI WASN'T IN THE living room or kitchen area. Ricky felt relieved and figured she was asleep.

"What's wrong?" she asked.

He gave her a half smile.

"Come in. I'll tell you."

She walked in and sat on the couch.

"Let's go to my room. I don't want my mom to hear anything. I'm not even sure if she's here."

Ellie thought his mother was probably in no condition to eavesdrop even if she was there, but didn't protest.

They went to his room. Ellie moved to sit on the desk chair, but Ricky stopped her.

"No! Don't sit there."

"Okay," she said, moving to the bed while her forehead scrunched.

"You'll thank me after I tell you what's going on. I promise."

"What is it, Ricky?"

"Everything started after I bought that skull."

She looked back at the desk and pointed at the skull. "That *calavera*?"

He nodded. "And things have gotten weirder since that night my grandmother died."

He spent the next half hour telling her almost everything. He didn't leave much out, other than the crying part.

Ricky ended with the bus and mentioned he had gotten into an argument with his mother the night before. He didn't give all the details. It hurt him to think about it again, so he kept it to himself.

Ellie sat there with her mouth open, staring at him, but didn't say anything right away.

"You're saying everything in this room was flying around?"

"Yes, I know it sounds insane, but it's happened more than once. Freddy was here the first time it happened, so he knows, but he's too scared to talk about it."

She looked at him, studying his face.

"Do you believe me?"

She nodded slowly. "I know when you're lying, remember? But we also have to consider that you've been through a lot lately. It's been horrible for you. First Grandma Bea and now your mom acting the way she is. I believe you believe everything, but any chance it's from lack of sleep or the anxiety of all this pressure?"

He shook his head. "No. I understand why you'd say that, but like I said, Freddy was here. If he hadn't seen it, I'd agree with you. In fact, I wish it was just anxiety making me lose it. It would be better than what's going on."

"Freddy is kind of gullible."

"What about the other night at the creek? Are you saying all three of us didn't experience whatever was out there?"

Her eyes flickered as she remembered that. She had tried

to rationalize that, too. But the vivid memory of it flooded back.

"Yes. Yes, we did. That wasn't normal, but we didn't actually see anything, so I guess it's easier for me to think it was still a freak wind. But this. This is a whole other level."

Ricky pointed at the skull. "That thing flew across the room and I can't destroy it."

He slashed his hand across the air to emphasize how it had taken flight and the skull responded. It darted off the table and into a curtain, following the same direction as his hand.

Ellie jumped.

"Oh my God! Did you just do that?"

He looked over. "No."

But when he moved his hand, he had felt something.

"You saw that, didn't you?"

She stood up.

"Yes, I saw that."

"See, it's not just me."

Ellie moved toward his desk. She checked for something that might have launched it and thought maybe Freddy was behind the curtain or under the bed pulling a string in some kind of elaborate set up.

She checked under the bed and then pulled back the curtain where the skull had landed.

"No one's behind the curtain, Ellie," Ricky said.

She turned red as she looked back at him.

"I know you just as well, remember? I get it. It's not like Freddy and I didn't try to trick you all the time. I think you only fell for it once. You were always smarter than we were."

Ellie looked down where she had moved the curtain, and the skull was on the carpet. She picked it up and studied it.

"So you can't destroy this thing?"

"No, haven't been able to yet."

"Well, maybe I can."

Ellie let it fall to the floor and lifted her foot and crushed it. It cracked with just one strike. She looked under her sneaker and scattered the debris around with her foot.

"Not coming back together now," she said.

"Just wait."

He moved towards her. As they stared at the skull, the pieces and dust that remained melted and seemed to absorb into the carpet. It was gone.

Ellie jumped back. Her heart was racing now.

"What--what just happened?"

"I don't know. I've never been close enough to see it disappear before."

They looked around the room and the skull was sitting in its normal place on the desk.

"It's not Freddy," Ellie said, her voice shaking. "It's real."

"I thought you believed me."

"I told you I believed that you believe it, but you're not losing it. It's there. What do you think it could be?"

"I don't know."

"This all started the night Grandma Bea died, right?"

"Yes."

"Was there anything odd that happened before that day or even recently that you're leaving out? Some kind of sign?"

He thought about it. "I don't know. My mom was weirdly nice to me and Myra one day. It was one of those rare times where she was actually here, if you know what I mean."

She did. She had been around a few times when Lori had one of her episodes.

He told her about the movie and manic way she wanted to hang with them. It had happened before, but her come down was fast.

"It's nothing new, but that was the only strange thing I can remember."

Ricky realized there was one important thing he hadn't mentioned yet.

"Well, there was the little ghost girl looking for her cat."

"What ghost girl and cat?" Ellie asked.

"A few days before Fiesta, a little girl came to the house looking for her cat. She was in a bathing suit and it was after midnight. Neighbors think it was the ghost of a girl who died a long time ago in a house a few streets over."

"And you don't think that's important?" Ellie asked.

"No, it was freaky, but I never saw her again until the bus last night. I've only really thought about that once or twice. It's almost like I'd forgotten."

"Maybe you blocked it out. That is pretty terrifying. She could be important. Anything else you might have overlooked?"

"No, I don't think so."

Ellie thought as her breathing settled. "Maybe it's the house? Some kind of spirit in here?"

"You believe in that?"

"I still remember all the stories Grandma Bea told us and all the weird things she saw and accepted as fact. Spirits, ghosts and other planes of existence."

"Yeah, I was just reminding Freddy about that. So do you think any of that is real and could happen here?"

"For someone who took an alternate reality trip on a bus last night and has a skull he can't break in his own room, you're oddly pessimistic."

Ricky thought about it. She was right. How could he not consider anything after what had been happening?

"I don't know. Why does it matter?"

"Well, if you can figure out even a little bit of what's going on, you might be able to tell if it's bad spirit or maybe it's your grandma still hanging around or something."

"It can't be my grandma. When this all started the first

time with the wind and the skull's eyes glowing and moving on the desk, it was right before she died."

"So why couldn't it be her?"

"She was still breathing. If this is a spirit or whatever, it was already here. Maybe the skull caused everything."

"What about the little girl?"

He wasn't sure. "The little girl looking for her kitty showed up before I bought the skull, but I don't know. I just don't know."

"It's too bad Grandma Bea's not here. She'd probably be able to tell us something. Do you know anyone else that can help? Friends of hers?"

Ricky's eyes popped wide as he remembered Dr. Jackie.

"Yes, Professor Jackie. She's the Dean of the Anthropology department. She and Grandma studied and traveled together researching a bunch of books and articles they worked on."

"I remember Grandma Bea talking about Professor Jackie. Do you know how to get a hold of her?"

Ricky stood up and reached into his back pocket, struggling to get a grip on his wallet.

"Yes, she gave me her card."

He pulled it out. "Here. It has her personal number on it. She said to call her if I ever needed anything."

"Then what are you waiting for?"

He took out his phone and dialed the number. It rang three times before going to voicemail. He hung up.

"Why didn't you leave a message?" Ellie asked.

"I panicked. I'm not sure what to say and I'm not going to leave an incoherent voicemail."

"Just don't go into detail. Keep it general and say you just want to meet with her."

He nodded and exhaled as he dialed back. It rang and went to voicemail again.

"Uh, hello Professor Jackie, this is Ricky Luna, Bea's

grandson. I kind of need to talk to you. It's about stuff you and my grandmother worked on. Please call me back when you get a chance. Thank you."

He hung up quickly, afraid he would ramble on.

"Okay, it's done. Hopefully she'll call me back soon."

Ellie smiled. "See, that wasn't so bad. I hope she has information that can help."

"Yes, this is good. I at least have somewhere to go for help or advice, assuming she doesn't think I've lost it."

"I'll come with you to tell her what I saw if you'd like."

"Yes, I'd like that. I guess we'll see how it goes, but what do I do in the meantime? I'm still freaked. Right now I'm more worried about this whole thing with my mom acting worse than usual."

Ellie took a long look at the skull.

"What about *Dia de los Muertos*?" she asked.

Ricky shrugged. "The Day of the Dead? What about it?"

"I mean, it's a sugar skull."

"I don't get you, Ellie."

"What's the meaning of that day?"

Ricky's face was blank.

"Ricky, think about what your grandma showed us. The sugar skulls are part of the altars--the *ofrendas*--used for Day of the Dead. Does she still have the one in her bedroom? The one she keeps for your grandfather?"

Ricky clicked. "Yes, last time I checked."

"Then instead of sitting around waiting, grab the skull and let's go check. Maybe it's connected somehow."

Ricky's face flushed as he wondered why he hadn't thought of that before. He reached for the skull, but hesitated.

"You need it, Ricky, and I'm never touching that thing again."

He took in a breath. "Stay chill, okay?"

"Are you talking to the skull?"

"Yeah. I know. Helps me deal. Usually."

He swiped the skull before he could think about it too long and headed toward the stairs with Ellie behind him.

Ricky hesitated at the top of the stairs. There was an open area with couches where Bea used to sit and read whatever she was working on. Sometimes she read to him and Myra. There were two rooms, one on each side of the reading area. One was his grandmother's room with a large bathroom connected to it, the same room where his mom used to live. The other was Grandma Bea's office.

Ellie put a hand on his shoulder. "How long has it been since you've been up here?"

"Not since a few days after she died to get her clothes and important papers for the funeral."

Ellie grabbed his hand and held it.

"It's okay. We'll walk in together."

Ricky turned his head to look at her and her smile was all he needed. He took slow steps through the sitting room to his grandmother's bedroom on the left. Ellie squeezed his hand a little tighter before letting go so he could open the door. The skull was in his other hand.

They entered. Grandma Bea's bed was a mess. Ricky had put several outfits and papers on it when he was gathering her things and wanted to get out as fast as he could, so he had left things as they were. There was a long dresser on the right side of the room and a large walk-in closet towards the back left side. Ricky walked past the dresser. To the right was Bea's nook with a vanity that held a round mirror with lights all around it. It was positioned before the bathroom door and just across from it was a small table in another nook that was only visible if you were heading to the bathroom.

This was where Bea had created her makeshift altar to remember her late husband.

"Wow," Ellie said as she flipped on the lamp. "She kept it going all this time."

"Yeah, I actually hadn't seen it in a few years. I would usually just come in to get something or talk to her without coming into this part of her room. It's nice to see a picture of my Grandpa Leo."

The altar held three pictures. One of Bea and Leo on the day they were married, one taken the same year he died, and then one of Leo in his Army uniform. A small bottle of Jack Daniels and a shot glass were off to the side and in the center was another sugar skull, smaller than Ricky's and fairly plain. It was all white with blue coloring on the mouth and eyes with one green flower on the top.

"It's not as fancy as last time I remember seeing this," Ellie said. "Then again, it was years ago."

"Yeah, well, when the Day of the Dead was closer she'd add marigolds and decorate it more with salt crosses. She always picked up two new mini-bottles of Jack. One to take to his grave and then she'd down the one they had here all year and replace it."

"Your grandpa looks so handsome in his uniform. You look like him."

Ricky tried to hide his reddening cheeks.

"Thanks. I guess we should try... something?"

He lifted the skull and looked into its eyes. "This is your element. Maybe this is what you want."

He picked up the *calavera* on the altar and handed it to Ellie. He eased his sugar skull in its place. It was a lot more menacing than the one that had been there all these years.

"I think we need a newer picture," Ricky said. "Hold on."

He pulled out his wallet and the plastic picture holder. He thumbed through it and passed a picture of him and Ellie when they were younger.

"You still have that? That was summer before second or third grade, right?" Ellie asked.

"Yes, one of my favorites."

"I carry one in my purse. The classroom pic from Kinder."

Ricky smiled as he pulled out the picture he was looking for. It was one of just him and his grandmother that Myra had taken just two years before. His grandmother had given him this one. He added the picture to the altar.

"Need some candles, too."

Ricky moved toward the closet and pulled out three stacked bins that were at the end of it. From behind their original location, he pulled out a trunk.

"This is where she keeps the cool stuff she's collected over the years."

Ricky opened the trunk. It contained a single divider and was stacked to the top with items. He pulled out some cloth bags and then pulled two candles with bases from them. He returned to the altar and set them on each side.

"Oh, need some flame."

Ricky turned back toward Bea's vanity, opened a drawer on the bottom left and pulled out a red butane click lighter.

"There we go," he said, lighting each candle.

He turned off the lamp. They both stared at the altar with its new skull and candle illumination.

"What do we do now?" Ellie whispered.

Ricky shook his head. "I don't know."

He looked into the flames and then to the skull.

"Okay, freak skull. You have an altar and candles to draw whatever's in you closer. I don't know how you can come any closer since you have no problem flying around my room. What do you want?"

Nothing. Just the flame and an unmoving skull.

"Are you here to hurt me? What do you want?

Another few minutes of nothing. Ricky slapped his hand on the table and Ellie jumped.

"Hey, it's okay," she said. "We don't even know what we're doing."

"No," Ricky said. "This thing destroys my room and flies around, then when I want it to do something, it just sits there? I don't think so."

He banged his fist against the table and the candles moved with the impact.

"Say something!" Ricky yelled. "I'm here! TELL ME WHAT YOU WANT FROM ME!"

The flames shot up and out on each side, throwing heat in their faces. The flame held for several seconds before descending back down. The candles burned out with a pop as the skull rose in the air and spun in a circle. Its eye sockets exploded with fire, which then engulfed the spinning skull until it burst. The falling embers disappeared before landing on the altar, but the skull was gone.

Ricky and Ellie were both so scared neither one had moved. They stayed staring at the altar and then looked at each other.

"Are you okay?" Ricky asked, reaching for Ellie's face to make sure she hadn't been burned.

"Yes, just in shock."

They looked back at the altar.

"What just happened?" Ellie asked. "Where did it go?"

"I think it was telling me not to mess with it," Ricky said. "Like a warning."

"Where did it go?"

He already knew.

"I'd bet money it's back in my room. If this wasn't what it wanted, that's where it always ends up. If this was some kind of spirit, it doesn't want to tell me why it's here."

"We'll figure it out, Ricky. Let's go make sure. I want to

come back and help you get her room back in order when the time's right. How does that sound?"

Ricky was distracted, but this brought him back to the moment. "Yes, that sounds good. Let's go."

He grabbed his picture before they walked out, and he closed the door behind him. They ran down the stairs and back into the room.

As Ricky expected, the skull was on his desk. He sighed and sat on his bed.

"I need to find out what's going on. Professor Jackie has to be able to help. I can't keep doing this."

He didn't realize his hands were shaking. Ricky felt lost, but now he had a purpose with Dr. Jackie, even if it was a short-term one.

Ellie grabbed each of his hands and guided them around her. She hugged him tight. He hugged Ellie back and just as he was enjoying the moment, the phone rang and vibrated in his front pocket as their bodies pressed together.

They both jumped.

"Sorry," Ricky said.

She turned red.

"Hello? Yes, hi Professor Jackie. Thanks for calling me back. Tomorrow? Sure. What time? Okay, I'll be there."

Ellie pointed to herself.

"Oh, and I may bring a friend."

He hung up. "Tomorrow at 2pm at her office. She's working but has a free hour when she can meet us."

"Then we'll be there tomorrow. Are you going to tell Freddy?"

"Yes, I'll see if he wants to come, too. I'm not sure if he will, but I won't blame him if he doesn't."

"Why? He's your friend."

"Yeah, but asking your friend who can't even watch

Ghostbusters without covering his eyes to come to the next Amityville house every day might be too much."

She smiled, then laughed.

"Then I'll see you tomorrow. I need to go home, but call me if you need anything."

He nodded.

"I mean it, Ricky. You don't have to do this alone."

"I will, Ellie. I promise."

She grabbed his hand and slowly let it go as she walked away.

After he heard the front door close, he turned back to the skull.

"Why can't you be making things better for me instead of worse?" he asked. "Like making the phone ring five minutes later."

He shook his head as he looked down. "I should have kissed her."

The skull stared back at him as if it was silently judging and agreeing that yes, he should have.

CHAPTER SEVENTEEN

RICKY LAID BACK ON HIS BED FOR THE NEXT TEN MINUTES, thinking about what he should have done differently with Ellie, what would happen when he met with Dr. Jackie and what else the skull could mean. With his family and his sanity at stake, it was Ellie he thought about most. His regrets about her and thinking of all the opportunities in the last few years he never took that might have helped them get closer. He tried to shake it off and did another involuntary check on the skull. It hadn't moved, but something dawned on him.

The skull.

Did I do something to make it fly, or did it do that on its own?

He thought he felt something when it happened, but wasn't sure what it was.

He got up and stood in front of the skull, concentrating.

"Move," he whispered.

The skull stared back at him, but didn't budge.

"Move!" he yelled.

Ricky pointed his hands at it as if he was going to shoot lightning like a superhero, but the skull sat there staring right back.

"Well, crap. I guess it was just you. I wish you'd get out of my room!" He flung his hand across like he was air slapping it and the skull flew in the direction of his swipe.

This time he definitely felt it. It was a shock wave that started in his fingers and shot up his shoulder, almost like when he'd banged his funny bone before. He stared at his hands.

He tightened his fingers and squeezed them into his palms, forming a rigid fist. He focused on the pillows in front of him. He threw his hands to the side, but they didn't move.

He edged closer to one pillow and stared at it. Again, he tightened his hands and then felt the electric shock go up his arms and into the back of his neck and down his spine. The pillow shot upward into the ceiling and as it fell, he stepped back and the pillow fired back in his direction, hitting him softly in the chest.

It had moved with his body. He took a breath, feeling winded and dizzy.

He walked to the other side of the bed nearest his windows where he had thrown the skull. It was on the floor, unharmed.

He faced his desk on the far side of his room. He didn't raise his arms, but squeezed his fingers and hands. The sensation of electrical discourse in his body was more pronounced this time. It shot faster and more sharply in a fiery streak down the same spinal path as before. He concentrated on his lamp with the broken bulb and raised his head. The lamp mimicked his movement and flew in the air, but before it could hit the ceiling, he held his stare and the lamp hung in mid-air.

He moved to the left and the lamp turned and dangled horizontally on its side. He tilted his head and the lamp moved up 45 degrees, still floating in the air. He got dizzy again and exhaled as he felt like he couldn't breathe. The lamp fell to the floor and he put his hands on the nearest windowsill to hold himself up. A strong sense of vertigo overcame him and he eased himself on the bed, panting.

How am I doing this?

He slowly reached down and picked the skull up, meeting its gaze and taking in big breaths.

"What did you do to me? What do you want?"

The skull stared back. Its eyes didn't glow. It looked like any regular trinket you'd buy at a store to decorate for Halloween or *Dia de los Muertos*. Nothing special about it, except that it was indestructible and possibly giving him the ability to move things with his mind.

He stretched out on his bed, trying to contemplate what had happened, but his head was still spinning. When he woke up almost an hour later, the skull was sitting on his chest.

CHAPTER EIGHTEEN

RICKY WAS WORN OUT THE REST OF THE DAY BUT THERE WERE NO further incidents after he screamed a little and returned the skull from his chest to his desk. The next morning he got ready to meet Dr. Jackie and was about to head out the door when he turned back to the skull.

"I don't know exactly what I'm going to tell Professor Jackie, but maybe you need to come with me. Just behave yourself, okay?"

The skull ignored him while he opened his computer desk drawer and retrieved the Cougar rally towel, which he had stopped using. It made him more nervous not to see the skull's face than having it covered and wondering if it was actually still there. He wrapped it around the skull and put it in a smaller drawstring backpack with the Dallas Cowboys' star logo on it.

"Stay there," he whispered as he pulled the strings closed.

Ricky went out to the truck to see if it might turn on and it started without issue. He had warned Ellie they might need to take her mom's car since it hadn't worked the night of the carnival, but would pick her up if it was fine.

He drove down the block to get her. She wore a short summer dress and for the few seconds it took her to walk to the car, he thought of nothing else.

"Hey," she said as she got in the truck. She had a journal in her hands.

"What's with the book?"

"Were you planning on memorizing whatever Professor Jackie tells us?"

He opened his mouth and then closed it. It would be Ellie who thought ahead.

"I hadn't even considered that."

"Of course you didn't, that's why you have me. Do you think it might be a good idea to show her the skull?"

"I thought about that before I left my house. It's here," Ricky said as he pointed to the Cowboys bag on the console between them.

Ellie let out a breath.

"I know it's a good idea to show her but I'd be lying if I said it didn't freak me out that it's in the truck with us."

"That's why I'm not leaving it in the backseat. I want to keep an eye on it."

She pulled away a little so that the bag wouldn't touch her.

"Where's Myra?"

"I got Karen's older sister Theresa to babysit. They know more or less what's going on with my mom. Theresa picked her up earlier and they were heading to the park and pizza after. I didn't want them staying at the house anyway in case my mom decided to wake up and cause trouble."

Ricky reversed out of the driveway.

"I take it Freddy's not coming?" Ellie asked.

"Of course not. I texted him and he said he might come by later to get caught up. He'd eaten too much junk food at the carnival the other night and ended up coming home sick from

Joey's house the next day. Said he was still sick to his stomach but feeling better."

"How much of that do you believe?"

"I know he got sick, but I'm sure he was good enough to go with us if he wanted."

They spoke about Myra and summer, but neither one mentioned what had happened the night before or anything about their shared moments over the last few days.

South Texas University at Stone Creek was located just outside Stone Creek on the outer borders of the city, one of four locations throughout South Texas. They arrived in about thirty minutes. Ricky drove into the parking lot and thoughts of Grandma Bea overwhelmed him. He had come with her about a year before to gather some books for research she was working on, but hadn't seen Dr. Jackie since she was traveling at the time. He always enjoyed coming to the school with his grandma.

They walked into the Anthropology building and took the elevator to the second of four floors. Professor Jackie's office was still in the same place and when they walked in, a secretary sat at the main desk. He remembered her face, but not her name.

"Hi, Kayla," Ellie said. "I'm Elena."

Ricky looked at her.

She motioned to the desk and her nameplate, and he rolled his eyes, feeling stupid.

"Hello, Elena. Good to meet you," Kayla said. "And hi, Ricky. Great to see you again and my condolences on your sweet grandma. She was a wonderful woman. I'm so sorry I wasn't able to make the funeral. I was on a family vacation."

"Thank you, Kayla," Ricky said. "I appreciate that."

"Dr. Jackie's expecting you. Go right in."

They walked into the office and Professor Jackie was sitting at her desk. She stood up to give him a hug.

"This is Ellie," Ricky said.

"Oh, yes! Ellie! Bea mentioned you over the years. I saw you at the funeral. Good to put a face to the name. Please have a seat."

She motioned to the roomy leather chairs in front of her desk. Ricky set the backpack on the floor in front of him.

"So," Professor Jackie said. "How can I help you?"

"Uh, I'm not sure where to start. And I'm not sure if you're going to think this is way out there and I'm losing it."

She smiled. "Over the years, your grandma and I saw many things that I'd consider 'out there.' I know she shared some stories with you. She loved to tell me about your reactions when she did. Even so, we've kept most of the unexplained phenomenon to ourselves. Being academics, there's a certain line of disbelief that can discredit you rather quickly. There's always another academic who would love to see you fail to further their own career and get their hands on your grant money. I doubt anything you tell me will shock me."

Ricky looked down, hesitating.

"The night my grandmother died," Ricky said, still not looking up. "That night something was going on in my house."

Professor Jackie's eyes narrowed. "Going on how?"

"I was in my room with my best..." he turned to look at Ellie. "With one of my best friends, Freddy. Something came into the room like a gust of wind, and the electronics went crazy. Within minutes Grandma was on the floor and died right after."

He stayed looking down.

"There is obviously more to this, Ricky."

"Are you saying you believe me, just like that?"

"Ricky, you've been through a traumatic experience. Being one who has seen the look of doubters in my time, I'll give you the benefit of the doubt. You're already here, so please go on. You've felt compelled to come here and I will give you that level of respect."

Ricky sighed.

Ellie grabbed his hand. "Tell her everything you're comfortable with, Ricky. I think there's stuff you still haven't told me, but it's okay. It can't hurt."

He looked up. "I don't know what anything means or if they're tied together. A little girl came to the house a few days before, looking for her cat in the middle of the night. Grandma said she talked to the neighbors and they think the girl died over thirty years ago in a house fire somewhere in the neighborhood."

He gave her as many details as he could remember, including how his mother had reacted the night Grandma had died.

"So your mother just went into her room?" the professor asked.

He nodded. "But that's not unusual. I think there could have been a tornado ripping the house apart and if she was out of it, she would go to bed like nothing happened."

He told her about the skull and how he couldn't destroy it. Her eyebrows raised high at this comment.

"It's true," Ellie said. "He showed me yesterday. It breaks, but keeps coming back."

He left out the tale on the bus and the squeezing to move objects around the night before. He just thought that was too much to believe and even now he wasn't sure if the bus incident was a nightmare or if his ability to move things was real or just his mind playing tricks.

"If I had to guess and all this you've told me is true, it seems like something has invaded your house. Maybe through that skull or something else controlling that skull."

Professor Jackie stood up and went to her bookshelf. She pulled out a book and flipped through some pages.

"This book was one your grandmother and I collaborated on about twelve years ago. We went to East Africa and visited some obscure villages. One thing we always learned on these adventures was each village or tribe's folklore. Sometimes they aren't just stories, as we've been witnesses to many inexplicable events and rituals. In one village, we saw a man in a hut that floated about six inches off the ground for five days straight. I wanted to film it but they considered it sacrilegious, so we respected that but kept notes. He was as flat as a board and they allowed us to run our hands around him, but nothing could explain it. His eyes would open every so often and they were white. You couldn't tell he had pupils."

"What was wrong with him?" Ricky asked.

"They had a type of Shaman. He claimed he was trying to cast a dark spirit out of the floating man and that he had been possessed by evil. The victim had always been a bad, spiteful man, but had started acting worse and more strangely for months. He eventually tried to rape a young woman in the village. Fortunately, the girl's family caught him before anything happened and they beat him. They took him to the village elders and when they questioned him, he spoke in someone else's voice and the floating started. The Shaman came in but only received meaningless gibberish as a response while the man remained airborne."

"Did he die?"

"On the fifth day the Shaman got him to drink some kind of concoction of goat's blood and herbs he had put together. The man looked like he was throwing up, but no food came out. Then the Shaman looked up and so did the elders in the room. They recoiled, but not in fear. Their heads moved like in a tennis match, like they were seeing the same thing moving in the same direction."

"You mean you couldn't see anything?" Ricky asked.

"No, but they could. Your grandma and I tried to look in

the same direction. We saw dust move within the hut and shift direction, but whatever it was, we were blind to it. The man fell to the ground and grunted. He coughed and coughed until his eyes returned to their normal color. The hut's front flaps flew open and dust jumped out like a freak windstorm had blown through. Everything was calm after that."

"What do you think it was?" Ellie asked.

"The Shaman told us the bad spirit that had taken him over was expelled. This spirit enjoyed torturing the young girls and women of the village and used the man to do its bidding. Since the man was already evil, it was easy to convince him."

"You think that's happening in my house?" Ricky said.

"I can't know for certain. It could also be a spirit tied to the house or the skull. When we visited a village in Spain, there was an obsidian stone with an almost perfect circle in the center that everyone in the small town feared. They tried to throw it away and destroy it, but somehow it would appear in the oddest places. They believed the circle was an evil eye and brought bad luck and death to whoever possessed it. It would appear in different locations or attract a child who didn't know what it was and take it home. We recorded three cases in just the two months we were there where members of the families who possessed the stone became extremely ill. Most were said to have died or came back a different person."

"Like the skull. It keeps coming back."

"It could be related to an object like the skull, or just a person possessed and affecting things around them. There are evil things in this world that we can see and sometimes can't see. There are evil people who live and breathe that are bad enough alone, but that can open doors into their hearts. A spirit or demon or whatever you want to call it always looks for a way in to fulfill whatever their special desires are."

"Like a Jedi can take over the weak-minded?" he asked.

Professor Jackie looked at Ellie and back to Ricky.

"It's a Star Wars thing," Ellie said.

The professor smiled. "Yes, I'm familiar with the plight of the Jedi and that's a brilliant example, but instead of a weak-minded person, it can be someone whose soul is weak or is already evil, inviting them in. It could be many things. I can do a little more research, but I need you to keep me in the loop."

They nodded.

"Now, with that being said, I do have to ask, have you been to a doctor?"

He looked at her with a scared look.

"I don't mean go tell your doctor what you told me. They may just commit you. We feared we'd be committed if we ever went public with some of our experiences, but I want you to know your grandmother and I only told that story to one other person before today. We thought we could trust them, but they laughed us off and avoided me for a few months. I know what it's like to fear being marked as crazy. I know what I know, and I've spoken to others in our field who have hinted at some of the things they've seen and I know there's more to many of their stories they're holding back. We respect that in our field and are careful where the lines of plausibility and believability cross. Your grandmother and I were together when these things happened, and we shared our experiences only with each other. I'm not aware of her telling anyone else about this."

"She told us a few things, but never in that much detail."

"Yes, that's the way to go. I think you should go to a doctor and just let them know you're tired and want to know if it's just stress. I've seen tribes take herbs similar to peyote, and they saw flying unicorns with fangs blowing fire. Now THAT was explainable. Your mind may just be trying to compensate for your sadness and sudden thrust into adult responsibilities."

"I understand. If I think it's getting too bad, I'll make an appointment.

"Also, there's one more thing."

"Yes?"

"It may be a big ask. It would be helpful if I could see the skull. Would you be willing to bring it by?"

"Actually, we thought that might be a good idea. I have it here."

Dr. Jackie's eyed widened. "Show me."

Ricky reached in the bag and unwrapped the skull from the rally towel. He raised it and held it in his palm over Dr. Jackie's desk.

The professor used both hands to gently lift it from Ricky's grasp.

"So this is the troublesome sugar skull you bought at Fiesta. I admit, it stands out from most of the designs I've ever seen."

She looked it over, then took a picture with her phone.

"Would you mind if I keep it to study? I can return it to you tomorrow or you can come by to pick it up."

Ricky thought for a moment and glanced at Ellie.

"Sure, Professor. I'm not sure if it'll stay, but if there's any way you can help, please. Study it. If you need it for a few more days, that's fine, too. I can come by and pick it up when you're done."

"I'll be out the rest of today but depending on how much progress I make, plan to come by tomorrow afternoon or the next day after 2 pm. I'll let you know for sure. Do me a favor. Will you interact with it?"

She handed it back to him.

"Do you want me to try and destroy it?"

"For now, just hold it and walk around the room. Try to pretend like Ellie and I aren't here."

He felt awkward as he stood up and moved around the room with the skull in his hand. There was no way for him to pretend like they weren't there. He tried to concentrate on the skull.

"I know you feel odd, Ricky. How are you with it at home when it's just you?"

Ricky realized this could help, so he tried to let the awkwardness go.

"Are you going to do anything?" he whispered to it, now almost hoping it would. "I know I told you to behave, but a little glowy eyes action might help."

He thought about trying to make it fly across the room, but he wasn't ready for that. That might scare off Ellie and Dr. Jackie for good. Nothing happened for the next ten minutes other than his feeling more awkward with every pass.

Dr. Jackie was scribbling on a legal pad.

"That should be enough, Ricky," Dr. Jackie said as she put her pen down.

"Should I try destruction now?" he asked.

"Yes, go ahead. Just try not to break anything in here. Some of these items are priceless to me."

"I'll keep it simple. Watch your eyes."

He tossed the skull up and let it fall to the floor. It bounced off the carpet harmlessly.

Ricky stomped on it once and as expected, it shattered, leaving pieces and white residue on the carpet.

They all stared at the spot for the next minute.

Nothing happened.

"Should be disappearing any second," Ricky said.

Another thirty seconds.

"I saw it, too, Professor," Ellie said.

Nothing.

Professor Jackie picked up the pen and jotted down more words.

"I'm sorry, Professor Jackie. I'm not sure why it's not doing anything."

"It's okay, Ricky. I'll sweep it up and keep the remnants with me. It didn't need to be whole for me to investigate."

"You don't believe me now, right?"

"I am still reserving any judgment. I've learned not everything can go as planned when you don't really know what you're dealing with."

"I can sweep it up."

"No, it's okay. Go ahead and leave it. Part of the process. I do have to get to an afternoon class so I'll let you know about coming by."

"Okay, Professor Jackie."

"I'll see if I can find any more references this evening after work. Also, please give me updates if anything else happens while the skull is with me. Call or text me at any time. I will get back to you as soon as I can if I can't respond right then and there. Maybe we can narrow it down to see if it's something you should worry about and what we might be able to do."

He shook his head. "I hope nothing else happens. I need to keep Myra safe."

Professor Jackie looked at him. "Safe from this or from your mother?"

His head jerked.

"I know what your mom's been through and her past. Bea was my best friend."

"We just got into a couple of big fights. She's the same some days, but with Grandma gone, she's been... uglier, I guess."

Ellie's head turned toward him when he said this.

"If you think she is a danger to you or your sister, you need to let me know," Professor Jackie said.

"I will. I think she's fine. It's just my grandmother's always been there and I think it's just stressing us all out. My mom probably just expected Grandma to always be there to take care of us."

"I'll let it go for now, but do expect you to tell me if it gets worse."

The professor turned to Ellie. "I'm going to trust you to call me if he won't."

She handed her her card. "Please keep my number on your phone and give me yours, if you don't mind."

Ellie nodded and jotted her number on a post-it.

Ricky and Ellie stood up.

"Thank you, Professor Jackie," Ricky said. "I thought you'd figure I was just crazy."

"I can deal with crazy," she said. "But I don't sense that from you. Whatever it is you're keeping to yourself, just make sure you talk to someone about it. It's a lot better when you can get things off your chest."

They walked out of the office and said goodbye to Kayla when they heard Professor Jackie yell.

They ran back in the room. Professor Jackie was standing by the spot where Ricky had crushed the skull. The debris was gone.

"I saw it," the professor said. "It just faded away."

"Maybe it's back in my room," Ricky said.

"No," Professor Jackie said as she pointed to the chair where he had been sitting.

They couldn't see since the chair was facing away from them but walked over and the skull was sitting there, waiting.

"I haven't been startled like that in a long time," the professor said.

"Do you still want me to leave it?" Ricky asked.

"Yes, now more than ever."

"Good luck. I hope it behaves itself."

The professor had calmed down and put the skull on her desk.

"This is fascinating," she said.

This time they finished saying goodbye and walked to the truck in silence.

Once they got in, Ricky took a second to process what had happened.

"I hope she finds something," he said.

"So do I, Ricky. One thing I want to know. What is it you're still not telling me about your mom? You made it sound like it was just a normal argument. I saw your face when you said it was ugly. There's more to that, isn't there?"

He took in a deep breath.

"That fight with my mom wasn't normal. It was beyond ugly. She was cruel. Said some horrible things about my grandma and even..."

He looked down.

"She said some awful things about you, didn't she?"

He nodded. "And Myra."

She put her hand on his shoulder. "You don't have to tell me the details. If it hurt that much, I can only imagine how bad it was. What else? Is there more?"

He thought about his ability to squeeze his body and control some of the items in his room. He looked down at his feet. A small wrench had been there for weeks since he had to tighten the battery terminal one morning. He stared at it. He tightened his fingers and hand muscles and moved to raise the wrench to his hands.

Nothing.

He tried again, squeezing harder. The wrench didn't move.

"What are you doing? What is it?"

He contemplated telling her when his phone rang. It was Professor Jackie.

"Ricky, I was about to head to my class and the skull disappeared from my desk. Right in front of my eyes, as clear as day. Is it with you?"

The phone was loud enough for Ellie to hear what she had said. She grabbed the Cowboys backpack while Ricky checked around the car, but there was no skull.

"Nothing here, Professor, but I'd bet money it's sitting on my desk at home."

"Okay," the professor said. Her breath was coming in quick spurts. "You'll let me know?"

"I will."

They hung up.

"This thing just keeps on surprising," Ellie said. "Just before the professor called, what exactly were you trying to do? Are you still leaving something out?"

"No. That skull just has me freaking out a little, I guess. I'm just worried."

She ran her fingers through his hair. "Yeah, me too. I'd like to come over the next few days, just to make sure you're fine. If that's okay with you."

He nodded as he leaned closer and gave her a quick kiss on the mouth.

"Wow," she said. "That was unexpected."

"I, uh, I'm--"

"Ricky, it's okay. I meant it was unexpected in a good way. You're such a boy sometimes. Just drive."

CHAPTER NINETEEN

Ellie and Ricky headed straight back to his house. It was quiet as they entered, and Ricky had no idea if Lori was home or not. He was more concerned with getting to his room than finding out what his mother was up to. They rushed in and as expected, the skull was sitting on his desk in its usual spot.

"Were you homesick?" Ricky asked the skull. "I guess I should thank you. At least the professor believes me now."

"I'll text Professor Jackie to let her know it's here," Ellie said. She was already tapping out the message, then lifted her phone to take a picture before hitting send.

"No matter what happens, it keeps coming back to the house. Even when I'm not here."

"Maybe it's connected to you and your room," Ellie said.

"Or maybe it just didn't want to be studied. To keep its secrets hidden."

Ellie's phone dinged.

"It's the professor. She said thanks and that this may actually help her narrow down her research. She thinks it's either tied to you, the house or maybe even your family, and will let us know when she has more information."

Ricky took a moment. "I wish there was a way we could help. What do we do in the meantime?"

"Just keep trying to live each day as normally as you can," Ellie said. "But maybe we can do something. Did Grandma Bea have any of her research books or notes here at the house?"

"Yes," Ricky said. "In her closet where I found the candles. Some of those bins have her personal journals and some books, and the bookshelves in the reading area upstairs have a bunch more of her books. I had to take some of that stuff to her at the University a few times when she was in the middle of something."

"You want to see what we can find? And would you be okay letting me read through the books?"

"That's a good idea. I'm here alone way too much, and I keep having longer and longer conversations with that skull. How about you read the books and I'll check out the journals?"

"Sounds like a plan. Let's go."

They headed upstairs to the reading room first.

"Here, on the back wall. These are all her work books."

Most were hardcovers, but there were also some bound editions specific to some of her classes. Ricky and Ellie started thumbing through them. Most were historical from places all over the world and many still looked new.

"Here's something," Ellie said, pulling out one of the bound textbooks. "Papua New Guinea, Tribal Folklore. Written by Dr. Beatrice Luna and Dr. Jacqueline Baker." She thumbed through a few more. "There are a few here. More folklore in South America, Africa, and Europe. Your grandma wrote or co-wrote a bunch of these."

They gathered nine books.

"This is a good start, Ricky. Let's go check on her journals."

They put the books on the floor and headed into Bea's still messy bedroom.

Ricky moved toward the closet and pulled out three bins and placed them on the bed. They each took one and started rummaging. Most of the journals were simple classroom journals, but a few were leather-bound. Bea put large headers over different sections and Ricky saw "Shaman Healing" and quickly flipped to the next few headings. "Folklore" and "Wards" caught his attention. They continued on and found three journals that looked promising.

"I guess that's it," Ricky said.

"It's plenty for now. How about I help you clean all this up? We just added more to the mess we left when we came in earlier."

"Sounds good. Grandma would be pissed at me if she knew I brought you in here with it looking the way it does."

They spent the next half hour putting everything back in its place and tidying up Bea's bed and closet.

"This looks better," Ellie said. "You want to go downstairs and get started on these books and journals?"

"Might as well. Are you hungry? I can order Chinese delivery. Chicken fried rice still your favorite?"

"Yes," Ellie said as she laughed, "I can't believe you remember that."

"Come on. Every time Grandma let you pick what you wanted, you always picked Chinese. Even when you knew I was dying for pizza. And it was always the same order."

"But it's been years. It's nice you remember."

They grabbed the books from the reading room on their way downstairs and stacked the books and journals on the kitchen table.

Ricky grabbed his phone and was about to start dialing.

"Ricky, is your mom here? Should you order her something?"

Ricky had no idea and didn't want to find out.

"It's okay, Ricky. I know things have been rough. Think of it as a peace offering."

"What if she makes a scene?"

"I've seen her at her worst, remember?"

"You've seen her out of it. Never as bad as what I've seen recently."

Ellie didn't reply but looked at him impatiently.

Ricky shook his head and headed to Lori's room. He knocked twice.

"Mom? Are you awake?"

No answer. He looked back at Ellie and shrugged. She motioned her head sideways and her eyes bulged.

"Fine," Ricky said as he turned the knob. It was open.

He peeked in and Lori was in the bed with her back towards him.

"Mom. Ellie's here and we're going to order some Chinese food. Want something?"

"Egg rolls," Lori whispered without moving. "Four."

Ricky waited to see if she was going to say anything else, but she didn't. He returned to the kitchen.

"She wants egg rolls," he said as he dialed and placed the order.

Ricky picked up the first journal with the "Shaman Healing" and thumbed through it as Ellie grabbed the first book on the stack.

She jotted down some notes in the journal she had taken to Dr. Jackie's. Ricky noticed and walked to his room to pull out a spiral from his desk drawer and a pen.

They continued doing research until the doorbell rang forty-five minutes later.

"Food's here," Ricky said, jumping out of the chair.

He set the bags on the table and grabbed water and soda from the fridge.

"Mom!" he yelled. "Food's ready!"

He grabbed some paper towels and put the drinks on the table.

"Maybe she didn't hear you," Ellie said just before the door to Lori's room opened.

Lori walked out. She was in a black and red lace top with matching underwear. Her hair was uncombed and covering part of her face.

"Mom, can you put on some clothes, please? I told you Ellie's here."

Lori smiled as she looked up at Ellie.

"Hi, Ellie. She's seen me wear less, son. Remember my string bikinis? I think she'll survive."

"The beach trips," Ellie said, smiling. "It's okay. I'm the guest and you're right. The bikinis were way more revealing. I think I can take it."

Ricky wanted to protest but didn't say anything. He was just happy she hadn't lashed out and had at least been friendly.

Lori sat at the table and Ricky placed her foam food container, chopsticks and a glass of water in front of her. He did the same for Ellie as she moved the books out of the way.

The three sat and ate for a few minutes without saying a word. Lori finished her first egg roll, and as she picked up her second one, she looked back and forth at Ellie and Ricky. She was obvious enough that they both noticed and stopped eating at the same time, but didn't want to glance at her directly.

"So," Lori said. "Are you two finally--"

Ricky closed his eyes and mumbled, "Please don't."

"Finally what?" Ellie asked, trying not to show concern.

"You know," Lori said as she grabbed the end of the egg roll and wiggled it from side to side and then let it fall between her fingers, catching it midway.

Ellie spit out her food and started laughing while Ricky dropped his chopsticks and buried his face in his hands.

"Come on, you're both practically adults now. I'm sure you've heard worse. Would you rather I have said fu--"

"NO!" Ricky said. "The visual was fine. We get it."

"And no," Ellie said after composing herself. "The answer to your question is no. Not playing with egg rolls or peaches. Just a little sugar."

"Somebody kill me," Ricky said as he reburied his face. "Please. Anyone."

"Stop being so sensitive. I've heard you and Freddy talk worse. Are you embarrassed? Come on. You've both been friends forever. Why aren't you bang--"

"Mom!"

"Sorry. Why aren't you playing with each other's food?"

Ricky shook his head and Ellie kept on laughing.

"Hmm," Ellie said, looking at Ricky squirm. "Let's just say I haven't been invited to his restaurant."

Lori lowered her egg roll and let out a sharp breath, then looked back at Ricky.

"You still haven't taken your finger out of your ass?" Lori asked. "What are you waiting for? She's beautiful and knows you better than anyone."

"Mom, please stop," Ricky said without raising his head.

"Ellie, do you like him?"

"Stop!"

Ellie smiled as she took another bite of her food. "Yeah, he's all right. Maybe we're both a little scared. Ricky, so why haven't you yanked your finger free?"

She laughed even louder and doubled over as Ricky slapped his hands across his forehead. "Make it stop, please."

"Look at me, Ricky," Lori said. "You know what happens to people who don't take chances?"

Ellie looked back up and Ricky opened his hands enough to reveal one eye. "I don't wanna know."

She held the egg roll up high, brought it up to her lips, puckered to kiss it, then tossed the entire thing over her shoulder and it landed on the kitchen floor.

"You throw away something good and fresh and your food never gets kissed, touched or eaten." She snapped her teeth together. "That's what happens."

Lori picked up her last two egg rolls, grabbed her drink and got up and left. She stopped and eased her foot on the egg roll on the floor and pressed down until the insides of the roll oozed out.

"Limp and useless. What a shame," she said as she lifted her foot and headed back to her room.

Ellie had fallen off her chair and was laughing so hard she started to choke.

She took a minute to compose herself and then got up on the chair, wiping away tears.

"I'm glad you enjoyed that," Ricky said.

"Who doesn't love dinner and a show?"

Ricky's hands were still covering his face. Ellie got up, still giggling, and walked up to Ricky and gently pulled his hands apart, revealing his red cheeks. He kept his gaze sideways.

"Hey," Ellie said as she cupped his face. "She has a point, you know. We're running out of time. I'm scared. Scared to lose you. But after this year, we might both be going to different places for college. What have we got to lose?"

His eyes finally met hers.

"I know. I know you're right. My mom just humiliated me, but I know she's right, too. We can't talk about this seriously right now. Not after that."

"You got totally burned by your own mom. I almost wish Freddy was here to rub it in."

"Oh, please. Please don't tell him."

"I agree this may not be the time or place, especially with everything going on, but how do you feel about me?"

"I l--" he paused. "I like you, too, Ellie. I'd like to see what we might have. When the time's right."

"You mean after all this is hopefully done and not halfway through our senior year?"

Ricky's embarrassment finally subsided. "Yes."

Ellie lowered her head and kissed him.

"The time may never be right, Ricky, but you need to be ready. I won't wait forever. I hope you know that."

Ricky nodded. "I know."

"I'll end the pain of your humiliation. How about we finish this food and get back to reading?"

They finished and got back into the research for the next few hours. Lori never returned and as it got later, Ellie got a text from her mother.

"I have to go. I'm taking my mom to San Antonio tomorrow for a doctor's appointment and we're going to stay overnight with my aunt for a visit. She wants to go shopping for a late birthday gift for my cousin. She's on her way to pick me up. I'll take the books with me."

"Okay," Ricky said. "Thank you for coming with me today. Thank you for everything."

"Why don't you tell Freddy to come over tomorrow? I don't want you to be alone."

"I will. I'll read what I can until you get back."

"No, you won't," Ellie said. "Not once Freddy gets here."

"You're right. Then I'll think about reading it."

There was a loud honk outside.

"Gotta go."

Ellie gathered her books and gave Ricky a hug and a kiss on the cheek. "Let me know if anything happens, okay?"

He nodded. She opened the door to leave and then turned back.

"While I'm gone, do me a favor?"

"Of course. What is it?"

"Lay off the egg roll."

Ricky's mouth stayed open as Ellie cackled on her way out. He finally laughed, resigning to the fact that he'd never live this one down.

CHAPTER TWENTY

KAREN'S SISTER THERESA DROPPED MYRA OFF EARLY THE NEXT morning. She was excited about her sleepover with the girls and was telling Ricky all about it.

Ricky struggled to keep his eyes open. He had been up all night thinking about Ellie, the kiss, what Dr. Jackie might find and even read a little out of the journals, but he couldn't concentrate. His mind kept wandering and he couldn't fall asleep. He even turned to the skull to ask it what he should do about Ellie.

The skull gave no response and didn't fly around. By the time Ricky's body had given out, it was almost 3 am.

Ricky made Myra breakfast as she continued to tell him about how Karen had laughed so hard at dinner she snorted out her drink from her nose over the slices of pizza on her plate and then ate them anyway.

"I'm glad you had a good time, Myra. I'm going to try and get a little more sleep. Freddy might come over later."

He had texted Freddy the night before and he was planning to come over by noon. Ricky tried to get back to bed, but it was no use. Myra was too wired up and had the TV blaring and his mind continued to wander. An hour passed and Ricky decided to go shower and then hung out with Myra for the rest of the morning.

Freddy came over at noon on the dot. He joined them to finish a movie, and then the boys headed to Ricky's room to play games. Freddy noticed the stack of journals on Ricky's bed.

"Summer homework?"

"No, research."

"How did the meeting with Professor Jackie go?"

Ricky caught him up, leaving out the egg roll fiasco.

"So the skull disappeared from Professor Jackie's office and reappeared here? Any more flying around since that night at the water tower?"

Ricky didn't want to lie, but he wasn't sure he wanted to share how he had controlled the objects in his room.

"No, the skull hasn't flown around on its own. It's been behaving itself for the most part."

Ricky sensed Freddy's relief.

"Do you want me to help you do some research?" Freddy asked with a groan.

"No, I think I'd like to forget about everything for a day. Besides, Ellie will read enough for both of us."

"I'm glad she was able to go with you."

"Me, too."

Freddy stared at him for a moment. "Everything good with you two?"

"I think so. Maybe we have a shot at some kind of future."

"All right!" Freddy said, raising his hand until Ricky gave him a high-five.

"How about we play?" Ricky asked.

They spent the next few hours playing Madden. About three hours in, Freddy got a text.

"Hey, it's Joey. They want to get an online game going."

"I'm in," Ricky said. "Living room?"

"Oh, yeah."

They grabbed the game system and moved. Although they usually stayed in the bedroom, the living room had the bigger TV and a better sound system. Grandma Bea let him do this now and then when Myra was there, as long as they let her play some games.

"Myra, a bunch of us are going to play Call of Duty. We want to use the big TV."

"I get to play!"

"Tell you what, Myra. These games take long. Let me and Freddy play online for a couple of hours. We'll play dealer's choice later and you can pick the first two rounds. What do you say?"

"Okay, I wanted to play on my tablet and chat with Karen anyway. We'll play later. You promise?"

"I promise. Thanks, Sister. Have you seen Mom?"

"She left earlier. Said she was going on a date."

"Okay." Lori hadn't mentioned anything, but it was nothing new.

The boys sat down and started playing, and the next few hours flew by. Even as tired as Ricky had been, he welcomed the change of pace and concentrating on getting a kill streak instead of skulls and monsters.

Eventually, a few of the boys had to drop off and Myra returned.

"I'm ready. I pick twice!"

The boys groaned. Myra loved the dance games, even though the boys claimed to hate it. Still, they did it for her and both enjoyed it, even though they'd never admit it.

It was almost midnight when a key rattled the door and Lori walked in. It was early compared to some nights, but she was alone. She stood and looked at them for a long time.

"Keep it down," she mumbled as she headed to her room.

They did. They continued playing the game for another few rounds.

"Okay, now it's our call," Freddy said.

Myra crossed her arms and threw herself on the couch.

"Come on, Myra. You know the rules. Thirty minutes and we get to switch playing. Whatever the next person wants. Freddy gets to pick."

She looked at Freddy and her face softened.

"Freddeeeee..."

"Nope, Myra. Not gonna work tonight," Freddy said. "Your brother and I have a grudge match from earlier. We tied last game and it's tie-breaker time."

She pouted but didn't complain. She got up to get something to drink.

The boys put in Madden and quickly went at it. They started yelling until they heard knocking from Lori's room. They quieted down.

"Been awhile since she did that," Ricky said.

"Yeah, I know. Usually we don't wake her up. We'll have to whisper-yell."

They mouthed curse words and "No!" as they played back-and-forth.

Ricky was about to beat Freddy for the win when Myra screamed.

They both jumped. Ricky turned back, expecting to see the skull floating over her head, but she had dropped her drink and pointed down.

There was a cockroach on the floor.

Grandma had pest control, and it had been a long time since they'd seen an insect in the house.

"Get it!" Myra screamed.

Freddy and Ricky looked at each other. Ricky got up and grabbed a magazine from the mail tray they kept in the entryway. He stepped cautiously towards the roach. It was moving but slowly like it couldn't decide where to go. He lifted the magazine and was ready to strike when the worst thing imaginable happened.

The roach took flight.

It jumped in the air and headed straight toward Ricky's head.

He shrieked louder than Myra had, and Freddy jumped behind the couch as Myra ran behind the kitchen island.

The roach flew around their heads and they scrambled, all three yelling so loud the neighbors could hear them.

There was a loud sound as Lori came out of her room. She was wearing a thin nightgown, her hair was a tangled mess, and she came out yelling.

"I have a headache! Why the hell are you screaming?"

A small hand popped out from behind the island and pointed up.

The roach was near the ceiling light of the kitchen, moving around, deciding on its next move.

"That's why you're screaming? Just kill it!"

She rushed back to her room and came back with a sandal in her hand. She threw it and it landed dead center on the roach, crushing it, leaving a dark streak as it fell to the floor dead.

"It's just a damned roach!"

She was heading to her room when Myra yelled again.

Lori turned back. "What?"

She pointed at the wall. Another roach was crawling across it.

"You big brave high school seniors. Can't you do this?"

She picked up her sandal again and moved to the wall and struck it down with one swift slap.

"There! Now shut up or go to sleep!"

She moved down the hallway and stopped. She turned around slowly and shuffled her bare feet back into the kitchen. She had a dazed look in her eyes, one Ricky had seen so many Saturday nights before.

"What's wrong, Mommy?" Myra asked.

She opened her mouth and a roach's feelers emerged from her lips and flew out.

Myra screamed but Freddy and Ricky stood there in shock as another roach emerged, crawled on her face and then took off from her forehead.

Myra went hysterical. "What is that! What is that?"

"Run to your room!" Ricky said.

He was more terrified than the night the skull floated.

Myra didn't hesitate. She took off and closed the door, throwing herself under the sheets.

"What's going on Ricky?" Freddy said, his voice trembling.

"Mom, are you okay? Are there more?"

She looked at him, still dazed.

"More?" she asked, and as her lips opened, a flood of roaches rushed out of her mouth and spread over her body. She looked down, as if she had just realized what was happening and started screaming and swiping at the moving swarm covering her.

Ricky was frozen. Roaches flew around him and he was afraid to move, but his mother needed him. He moved towards her and a wall of roaches formed a few feet in front of where he stood, flying in a crazed circle, preventing him from moving any closer. He was paralyzed.

"Freddy, help me!" Ricky said.

Freddy had his head covered with a couch pillow.

"Can't... can't move," he mumbled.

Lori was on the floor. Roaches were coming out of her hair and moving under her nightgown. She kept swatting and slapping them away, with pieces of what she had already smashed stuck between her fingers.

Ricky looked around for something and focused on the

sink faucet. He ran to the sink, picked up the attached sprayer and turned the water on. He aimed it at the wall swarm and pressed the button as hard as he could. The rush of water hit the wall and it broke apart enough to give him an opening.

Ricky ran near his mom and almost threw up as he saw the roaches crawling all over her. He gagged and then jerked back when the sprayer ran out of hose. He aimed it and pressed. The water stream hit her and some of the roaches cleared off.

Lori sat up, drenched, and looked at him. Her eyes were bulging, but he didn't see fear in her face anymore. He kept shooting the water at her but she raised her hand for him to stop.

"Are you trying to drown me?" she yelled, as if there weren't hundreds of winged vermin flying and crawling all over her.

Ricky stopped pressing and then Lori shook her head and snapped out of it.

"Stop this!" she yelled, but the roaches kept coming. The swarm that had broken up in front of Ricky then moved towards her and thickened like a brown coat shifting all around her body.

She reached down with her hand and grabbed a handful, crushing them, and then raised her hand to her mouth and shoved them through her teeth, crunching loudly and swallowing each bit.

A moment later, all the roaches flew up in a steady pattern. The front door flew open and the swarm shot outside in a buzzing line and the door closed behind them.

Freddy puked in the snack bowl and Ricky ran back to the sink where he lost it. They looked back up at Lori, transfixed by what had just happened.

"Mom?" Ricky asked.

Lori was sitting on the floor with pieces of roach on the

side of her mouth like she had taken a bite of a big sandwich and dark mustard was still on the ends of her lips. Ricky had to struggle to look.

She looked up at him, still in a daze.

"Can you all be quiet now?" she said in a whisper.

He nodded. "I think our roach problem is taken care of. I'll call pest control tomorrow and see if they can come in."

She nodded and eased herself up.

"I think I need a shower," she mumbled as she headed back to her room.

CHAPTER TWENTY-ONE

IT WAS LATE AND RICKY WAS TRYING TO HAVE A NORMAL MOVIE night with Myra. It had taken more than an hour to calm her down the night before, and Ricky explained a bunch of roaches had just gotten in through an open window and pest control was coming in the next day. Ricky was happy she had missed the rest of it. He couldn't shake the memory of the event and hoped that nothing like that would ever happen again.

Freddy was reluctant to hang out, but Lori was out of the house again, so he joined them.

Although it should have been Ricky's turn to pick the movie, he let Myra take his turn. She wanted to watch one of her long list of Disney movies, which was about as normal as it could get.

Once the movie got going, Myra was laughing with the boys who would never admit to enjoying watching this for about the twelfth time. They had gone through two rounds of popcorn and Myra was almost done with her big bag of marshmallows. Ricky even caught Freddy singing along with the Princess.

The door opened and they all turned.

It was Lori. Myra got off the couch to go greet her but stopped just as she was about to break into a run. A man they didn't recognize followed her in. He had long hair in a pony-tail, wore a jacket that probably hadn't fit him in about ten years, and it looked like he hadn't showered in days.

Lori smiled at them, but she didn't introduce the man and they walked straight to her room.

Myra looked at Ricky, but he wasn't sure what to say.

"Who is that?" she asked.

"I don't know, Myra," but he feared what sounds might come out of her room next.

"Why don't we go watch this in my room?" Ricky asked.

"Why? We already have everything here."

Ricky and Freddy started picking up the drinks and snack bowl when they heard the first headboard smashing the wall sound.

They all froze. Myra had a questioning look on her face.

Ricky grabbed the remote and switched the TV to a news channel and turned it up.

He grabbed Myra and led her to his room.

"Is Mom okay?" Myra asked.

"Sounds pretty okay to me," Freddy said.

Ricky gave him a dirty look and he closed his mouth.

They moved to the room and he got the movie going again.

They took a few minutes to set up and could still hear the banging of the headboard and to their horror, loud moaning.

He tried turning up the TV even more when they heard the man yell, "Yeah, girl! Just like that!"

The boys tried to pretend that they didn't hear anything, but the banging was too loud to ignore.

"It's okay, Myra," Ricky said. "They're probably just watching a movie."

"Ricky," Myra said. "It's okay. I know they're having sex."

He dropped the remote and it knocked the popcorn bowl down.

"What? How the heck do you know that?"

"I'm in 5th grade, Ricky. They told us about this last year."

After the shock wore off, Freddy started laughing. "Classic."

"Shut up, Freddy."

"You don't have to lie for Mom," Myra said. "I know we don't talk about it, but I know she's sick and she has sex with her boyfriends."

Ricky wanted to say that was no boyfriend and neither were the other men who she had been out with, but this was the first time she had brought someone home while Myra was there, even after their last argument.

"I forgot my marshmallows!" Myra said.

"I'll get them, Myra. Just wait here."

"No, Ricky. I can get them."

She rushed out of the room.

"She'll be fine," Freddy said. "It'll take like five seconds."

A door opened from the other side of the house.

Ricky knew it was Lori's and rushed out of his room with Freddy right behind.

The man and Lori were walking out of the room. He was tucking his shirt in and they saw Myra as they entered the living area.

"You never introduced me. Who is this?" the man asked as the boys walked up.

He pulled out his wallet and put some money on the table.

"That should cover it," he said as he was still looking at Myra. "A little tip in there, too, but tell you what. You throw her in for another round and I'll pay double."

Ricky felt the heat rise in his head and he stared at his mother.

Lori just smiled. "She's a little girl."

"That's why I'm willing to pay extra. Hell, I'll triple it."

Mom just looked at the man but didn't reply, making Ricky's head get hotter. Myra would have to pass the stranger to get to her own room, and Ricky didn't want her one step closer to him.

"Myra, go back to my room," Ricky said.

She ran without questioning, and the man kept his gaze on her the entire time.

"Where you going, little lady? Come party with your mom and me."

Ricky couldn't wait.

"What the hell do you think you're doing? She's ten, you sick bastard."

The man looked back as Myra closed the door to the room.

"You need to watch your mouth young man, before I close it for you."

He felt the anger in his neck and head. He felt dizzy, but composed himself. He didn't want to pass out with this asshole around.

"Mom? Say something! He's talking about Myra!"

Lori looked down.

"Your mom knows what's important. Money talks, right?" he said as he slapped her butt.

"Get the hell out of my house!" Ricky screamed.

He rubbed Lori's bottom. "Nah, I think I may just go one more round."

Ricky stepped forward, "So what, another three minutes? Or more like two since I'm sure you needed time to get your clothes back on and off."

"I'm gonna break your fucking neck!" the man said as he rushed past Lori.

Ricky stared at him but didn't step back. He knew this enormous man could kill them all, but he didn't care.

"I said get OUT!"

A fork from the kitchen table flew in the air and landed directly into the man's crotch. He yelped as he fell to the floor.

He looked down and blood was coming out of the front of his jeans.

"What the hell?"

Ricky was almost shaking with rage. The utensil drawer opened and a steak knife jumped out and hit the man on the shoulder.

"Aaah!" he screamed. "What the fuck? How are you doing that?"

Another knife flew out and landed in his thigh.

He leaped up and limped his way out the door, yelling.

Ricky was still shaking as the door slammed shut. Freddy put his arm on his shoulder and Ricky felt himself calm down.

Lori grabbed the money off the table and turned back to her son.

"What is wrong with you?" she snarled. "That man will never come back now!"

"What?" he yelled. "Why would you want him back? He wanted to hurt Myra!"

"Yeah, well, that money would have been worth it."

Ricky fell back like she had struck him with a bat.

"How can you say that? It's your ten-year-old DAUGHTER!"

"Maybe it's time for her to start earning her keep."

A fork flew up in the air between them. It pointed at Lori, then flipped around and pointed back at Ricky. He wasn't sure what was going on. He wasn't controlling it. At least he didn't think he was, but he could feel his face pumping with anger.

The fork fell.

"I don't ever want another man like that coming into this house while Myra is here, do you understand?" Ricky screamed at her.

"It's my house."

"No, it's OUR house! Mine and Myra's! I get to say who it belongs to and you do anything like that again I'll throw you out, do you understand?"

She laughed. "I don't think so. I'll be here as long as I need to be."

Utensils leaped out of the drawer and fell to the floor.

"You can't touch me," she said coldly as she went back to her room.

Ricky and Freddy just stared at each other.

"Calm down, man," Freddy said, breathing hard. "I don't know what just happened. Did you do that with the fork and the knife, or did she?"

Ricky's temperature started to lower as he tried to process what had just happened.

"I don't know. I thought about stopping that bastard and there was no way I was going to let him get to Myra. I wanted him dead but I'm not sure how much of that was me, how much was her or if it was that skull."

"Man, I'm shaking," Freddy said, looking at him with fear in his face.

"This can't go on," Ricky said. "She's stronger than I am."

CHAPTER TWENTY-TWO

MYRA STAYED IN RICKY'S ROOM FOR THE NIGHT AND HAD gotten up early to go watch tv the next day. Ricky was up and stretching on his bed when there was a knock at his door.

"Come in," he said, expecting to see Freddy.

After the night of flying utensils, Ricky had been too shaken up to talk about anything and told Freddy it would be better if he went home. Freddy didn't hesitate, but Ricky had already texted him to come over if he was up for it.

It was Myra who stuck her head in.

"Mom's making lunch," she said.

"For herself?" Ricky asked.

"No, she said she's making lunch for all of us."

"Sandwiches?"

"No, she's cooking."

He typically heard pots and pans banging when Lori did try to cook, although she almost never finished a meal, but it was quiet this time.

"Okay, how is she acting?"

"Mom seems fine."

He knew Myra was happy anytime that Lori was in a somewhat normal mood.

"Keep an eye on her. I'll be right there. Yell if she does anything."

Ricky hadn't even started his day. He brushed his teeth and went to the kitchen.

There were some items cooking on the stove. Smelled like meat of some kind.

Ricky was still thinking about the night before, but decided to approach cautiously to keep Myra calm. "What are you making?"

Lori looked up at him. She squinted, revealing dark patches under her eyes. "Food," she snarled. "And you will eat it. Is that other boy coming, too?"

Ricky nodded. "Freddy should be here soon."

"No-good kid," she mumbled. "He stays here half the time, now I have to cook for him, too?"

Ricky looked down. "Then don't bother."

"Too late," she said. "Already on his way, right?"

On cue, Freddy knocked after trying the doorknob.

"So comfortable he can just walk in," Mom said again under her breath but loud enough for Ricky to hear.

Ricky let him in, but before he did, he whispered, "She's cooking, but she's angry. I don't even know if she remembers last night. Just warning you."

Freddy nodded.

He came in and they moved to the living room to watch TV with Myra. Ricky kept looking back as his mother was cooking. Lori looked back at him a few times with a stare of hate. He half-expected she would throw the pan of food at him.

About ten minutes later she said, "Come and eat."

They moved to the kitchen.

She served them each a plate. It was supposed to be a

chicken burger, but Ricky saw that the meat was overcooked and burnt. There was bacon on top, but it looked like it had expired six months ago. She made a small side of pasta, but the color was wrong. It was dripping with sauce of some kind, but he had never seen that color before. It was a mix of dark green and orange.

Myra was about to dig in.

Ricky put his hand across her fork to block her.

"Let her eat," Lori said through her teeth.

Myra gave him an odd look and dug in. She took a forkful of the pasta and eased it in her mouth. The ends of each piece look like they were dripping with gunk and looked rotten to him.

He turned to his side and Freddy was already halfway done with his chicken burger.

"What are you doing? Is it good?"

"Of course it's good," Lori said.

She was able to hear what he thought was a whisper.

"He's almost done. For a little bastard, he sure does eat a lot. You gonna want more?"

Ricky wanted to lash out at her. She'd never said a bad thing about Freddy and couldn't believe what he heard.

"Are you gonna eat?" Lori said looking at her son, holding up her fork with a menacing face. "I spent the last hour getting this shit together."

He stared her down, but with Myra and Freddy both eating away, he didn't want to ruin it, no matter how she was being.

He lifted his burger and took a bite. He couldn't breathe for a second after swallowing the first piece. It was dry and made his throat feel like it was going to close.

He coughed up what he had eaten.

"What's wrong?" Freddy asked.

"How can you eat that?" Ricky choked out.

"What are you talking about, man? It's good."

Myra nodded in agreement and she took the last bite of her pasta.

Mom had purposely given him rotten food. The others looked like his, but something was different. He couldn't even swallow a small piece.

"What's your complaint now? Just because I made it? Ungrateful kid."

He put the burger down and started on the pasta instead.

It was worse. The pasta felt like moving worms in his mouth. They were slimy without much texture and whatever the sauce was he didn't want to know.

It was one of the worst things he had ever tasted, and his eyes watered as he took a full bite.

"This is disgusting," he said.

Lori grabbed his plate and eased it over to Freddy.

"You have it, freeloader. If he's just going to complain, then someone should enjoy it."

Freddy looked at him and then reached down to take some pasta since he had already finished his.

He took a forkful in his mouth and ate it. Then took another. He finished it and then picked up the rest of the burger. Freddy took a big bite and kept on going.

Ricky was staring at him in disbelief.

"How are you eating that? It doesn't taste awful?"

Freddy shook his head and took another bite.

Ricky turned to Myra, who was slowly eating her burger.

"Myra, does your food taste fine?"

Her mouth was full, but she raised her thumb and mumbled, "Good."

Ricky couldn't believe they were enjoying it.

"They're not looking for a reason to be an asshole," Lori said looking at him. "Just adding more to the disappointment of having you."

He looked from side to side, but neither Myra nor Freddy seemed to care how she was talking to him.

"Even this little bitch likes it," Lori said as she motioned toward Myra.

Ricky stood up. It was taking everything he had not to rip into her, but he just walked away.

"Where are you going, Ricky?" Myra asked.

"To my room. Not hungry."

He sat on his bed, letting his anger subside. It wasn't working.

"How could they even fake eating that food out of just courtesy?"

Freddy came in the room a few minutes later. "I was helping clean up. What's up with you, Ricky?"

Ricky's eyes bulged. "What do you mean what's wrong with me? After all that crap she said about all of us?"

Freddy scrunched his forehead. "What are you talking about?"

"She called you a freeloader!"

"When did she say that?"

"You were right THERE!"

"Are you kidding me? Your mom was the nicest I've seen her in years, and that was the best meal she's ever made. I know it's weird after the last couple of nights. I checked my food for roaches before I took a bite, but it was fine."

"She called you a bastard? She said it loud enough to hear!"

Freddy stared at him, dumbfounded. "I don't know if you slept on the wrong side of the bed but I never heard that."

"She said, 'For a little bastard you sure do eat a lot.' How did you not hear that?"

"Dude, I heard her ask if I wanted a little mustard and she was glad I ate a lot since there was plenty of food."

Ricky wanted to slap him across the face. "What? I heard

her clear as day! And she kept giving me that same evil look. She called me an asshole!"

"You were kind of being an asshole, but I never heard that, either."

Ricky stood up. "She looks like she hasn't worn make-up or showered in days."

"Now you're really freaking me out. Your mom has her hair brushed and is cleaned up. That's the best I've seen her look in days. Figured she was trying to make up for last night. She was actually looking like a normal mom. I thought you'd be happy."

Ricky didn't know what else to say.

Finally, he yelled, "Myra! Come here!"

Myra ran in.

"I'm helping Mom clean up."

"Close the door and come here real quick."

She did. "What?"

"During lunch, did you hear Mom call me any ugly names or cuss at all of us?"

She looked at him as bewildered as Freddy had.

"Ricky, Mom was normal for once. She's dressed all pretty and smells nice. She made excellent food. That was almost as good as Grandma's food."

Ricky paused. "So you didn't hear her call you a bitch?"

Myra's head snapped back. "Ricky, why would you say that? No, she wouldn't call me that. But you just did! She started to walk out."

"Myra, I'm sorry. I thought I heard her call you that and say other bad words to me and Freddy."

She stopped and turned around. "I think you just want to cause problems because you're still mad at Mom. I know she did some bad things, but this means she's really sorry. You're supposed to forgive people when they're really sorry."

She walked out.

Freddy was still looking at him.

"So what exactly did you hear and see?"

Ricky described the looks and the hair and how she had cussed at all of them.

"You aren't messing with me? You really didn't see or hear that?"

Freddy held his finger up. He left the room and returned a few seconds later.

He held up his phone, showing a picture of Myra and his mom cleaning. It was from behind, but Lori's head was turned to the side.

She looked normal. Her dress was pink and clean and her hair was pinned up but looked nice. She looked beautiful, like the mom he remembered and had lost hope of ever seeing again. Her face was made up and she looked fresh. That wasn't what he saw at the table.

"What's wrong with me?" Ricky asked, his voice filling with fear now. "That's not who I saw in the kitchen. And the food? Your food was really good?"

"Yes, it was. I tell you, I think yours tasted better than mine. The pasta was incredible. Not sure what that sauce was, but it was good and I was hoping to take some home but I didn't leave anything to take."

Ricky sat back on his bed. "I must be losing it," he said. "What if all the stuff Mom told me was just in my head and I told her all those awful things and I was totally wrong? What do you remember about the last two nights?"

"I remember everything," Freddy said. "The roaches, the man it looked like you somehow stabbed with your thoughts."

"So that did happen?"

"Yeah, all that happened."

"Then what is going on today? Why did I see and taste things so differently?"

"I don't know, man. Maybe whatever mental fight you had against her last night messed with your senses."

Ricky walked to the door and stuck his head out. Lori looked just like she had in Freddy's phone picture. He knew there was no way she would have had time to change and get cleaned up in the few minutes he had been in his room. Something was wrong with his head. Or something was making him think there was.

All he knew was he needed to figure this out soon or he might completely lose his mind.

CHAPTER TWENTY-THREE

Ricky woke up to an early text from Ellie, who had just gotten home from her trip with her mother. Normally he was a heavy sleeper and a text wouldn't wake him, but he struggled all night worrying about his sense of reality and every creak had kept him on edge.

"I just got back. Did some reading. Can I come over? Everything okay while I was gone?"

Ricky took a moment to reply.

"Yes. Give me 20 minutes. Want me to go get you?"

"I'll drive. Be there soon."

Ricky got ready and went to check on Myra. She was in her room, drawing on a canvas.

"Where did you get that?"

"Mom said I could use it. Lent me some of her drawing pens, too."

She had a half-drawn picture of what looked like an Amazon warrior. Myra was definitely the one who inherited Lori's artistic talents.

"Looks good. Is Mom here?"

"She left earlier after she brought me the drawing stuff. Didn't say where she was going."

"Okay. Ellie's coming over."

Myra nodded as she went back to drawing.

Ellie showed up and brought in some books and a notepad. Ricky already had the journals he was supposed to read stacked on the kitchen table.

They sat and Ricky caught her up with what had happened while she was gone. Ellie gagged at the roaches story and couldn't believe that they went from a night where Lori was willing to give Myra up for money to her being a perfect mom the next day.

"You think it was just guilt from the night before?" Ellie asked.

"I don't know, Ellie. Myra and Freddy were both there, so I know that happened, but yesterday... yesterday I was seeing and hearing things that weren't real. I don't know if it was a trick my mind was playing on me, if she or the skull were somehow manipulating me, or if I'm truly just losing my sense of reality. I don't blame Myra for being so accepting right away, but I think she's just trying to find a way to cope with it. Freddy was just glad my mom was being normal. But I never saw that normal. Not until after I went to my room."

"I read what I could during my free time, but I don't remember seeing anything like that. Not yet, at least."

"There's something else."

He told her about the knives and utensils flying around and how the knife stabbed the stranger trying to hurt Myra.

"Was it something you did? Or was it the skull or your mom?"

Ricky felt he had something to do with it, but wasn't sure.

"I don't know, Ellie. I really don't."

"Maybe it's time to tell Professor Jackie. The more information, the better, right?"

"I think I'd rather wait until we see her again. This sounds insane enough in person, but I want her to see my face when I tell her. Do me a favor, though. Before I call her, text Freddy. I want you to double check my story with him just to be sure my mind is straight today."

"Why isn't he here?"

"Joey invited us over. I told him to go ahead without me. I think it's good to give him a break from me. Even though things were good yesterday, the two nights before were insane. I know it's still freaking him out."

Ellie nodded and texted Freddy. He replied almost immediately, and they went back and forth a few times.

"Freddy said everything you said was right. He never saw Lori do or say the awful things you heard. He said he doesn't want to see another roach for the rest of his life. He also said he knows your mom tried to pull Myra in with some guy that paid her for--."

She hesitated.

"It's okay. Sex. Even Myra said that word, which I hope I never have to hear her say again. We all know what my mom is, was and can be. No point in hiding it."

Ellie nodded. "Okay. You want to call Professor Jackie now?"

Ricky dialed. The professor picked up on the second ring.

"Ricky?"

"Hi, Professor Jackie. I know you're still researching but wanted to check how long you think it might be. I have some new information, but I'd rather tell you in person."

"I haven't found anything solid yet. I think this new information would help, but I understand if you're not ready to share. I need a few more days for sure, but I'll contact you as soon as I'm done. Stay safe, Ricky."

Ellie had her ear near the phone and heard the entire conversation.

"I still think you should have told her."

"I'm afraid she'll make me go to the doctor. I want her to keep researching, and maybe I'm not ready to admit I might be losing it. Let's see how the next few days go and I promise I'll tell her when we see her."

"I'm sure she'll find something," Ellie said. "Maybe we will, too. I didn't read anything that was exactly like what you're going through, but I'm not done. I should have plenty of time today."

"Yeah, maybe more research will help. Might help keep my mind off all this. I'm still not sure how to process it all."

They read on, finding a few items here and there that were interesting and hinted at supernatural events, but nothing that came close to what had been going on.

Ricky had finished skimming a journal, and Ellie was in the middle of a book.

"Break?" Ellie asked.

"Yeah, I think we need one."

He grabbed some drinks and checked on Myra, who was still enjoying her drawing time.

"Ricky, can I ask you something?"

"Of course."

"That night with your mom and the stranger. I know Lori used to do that kind of stuff before, but has it been going on all this time?"

"She rarely brings anyone to the house. She usually goes somewhere, but this is the second time it's happened since Grandma Bea died. The first time Myra wasn't here, but this time, she just didn't seem to care."

"It couldn't have been easy to hear that. If a violent man ever threatens you or Myra again, please promise me you'll call the police. The whole knives thing. That could have gotten way worse. Why didn't you just call the police, anyway?"

"I didn't even consider it. It didn't get dangerous until that man talked about Myra and then it escalated so fast there wasn't time to think."

"Maybe the trauma of everything made you see and hear what wasn't there yesterday. Your mind trying to rationalize that she's not capable of being a regular mom."

Ricky sighed and slumped in his chair. "That's possible, I guess. I'm just lost. Hearing my mom have sex with a creep while one of my best friends is getting excited about it is beyond traumatic. Then to do it again with Myra here. It's sad when you have two high school boys in a house and the only one getting any is your mother."

Ricky's face strained like he had eaten a sour lemon.

"Ugh, just saying that out loud grosses me out. Makes me sad, too."

Ellie hugged him. "You know, if you'd take some motherly advice maybe she wouldn't be the only one with somebody."

Ricky looked at her and hugged her back. "I get it."

"Do you?"

He looked down but thought about his mind and control. Was she really wanting to get together or was his mind just playing with him again?

Ellie tapped him gently on the cheek.

"How about we get back to research? We have early registration tomorrow, so can't be up too late."

"Registration? But we just finished classes a few weeks ago!"

"Didn't you get the e-mail?"

"I automatically ignore the ones from school. It's summer."

"Well, it's tomorrow. Maybe me, you and Freddy can go together."

Ricky nodded. They returned to their research until they finished reading everything. Neither one found anything significant, but by the time Ellie left, Ricky didn't care. All he could think about was a potential future with this amazing girl.

CHAPTER TWENTY-FOUR

Ellie and Freddy showed up to Ricky's house early. Registration Day. They would get to register first since they were now seniors, so the earlier, the better. They left in Grandma Bea's truck. Ricky kept thinking of it as Bea's truck, even though he knew it was now his. It made him feel better, knowing there was a direct connection to her.

"This is our last time," Ellie said. "No more registrations or signing up after this summer."

"I don't know why we have to do this so early," Freddy complained. "We shouldn't have to see the school for another two months!"

"Come on, aren't you even a little excited?"

Ricky was. It was a good distraction. He wasn't sure what the next year might bring, but it had to be better than the last few months. Other than Ellie, it had been mostly all bad.

They arrived at school and moved to the cafeteria where the registrations were happening, separated by last names. They huddled in a small group, waving to a few friends.

"You ready to do this?" Ellie asked.

"Senior year!" Freddy said.

"Yeah," Ricky said. "I guess it's time to get it done."

Ellie Cruz and Freddy Fernandez went to the A-G line, and Ricky moved to the H-N line on his own.

The line was long, and he ran into Gerald Krause, a friend since middle school. They spent their time catching up. Ricky just told him he had been busy, but didn't bring up the death of his grandmother. As the conversation went on, Gerald offered his condolences. Stone Creek may be a small San Antonio suburb with only one high school, but it held almost four thousand students between kinder and high school and most people knew each other well enough to hear about big events such as marriages, births and deaths.

Ricky felt someone tap him on his shoulder. A tall, lanky guy Ricky had never seen before was looking at him. He was wearing a red shirt with the silhouette of a surfer on it.

"Hey, bro," the guy said.

Ricky took a second to see if it was a friend he just hadn't seen in a long time or had changed their look drastically. "What's going on?"

"Just wondering about that girl you were talking to when you walked in. Is she your girlfriend?"

He caught Ricky off guard.

"Who? Who are you?"

"Sorry, bro. I'm Corbin. Corbin Brock." He shook his hand. "I'm new. Gonna be a junior this year, just moved from California. What's your name?"

Ricky stared at him and mumbled, "I'm Ricky."

"So, the girl? Is she your girlfriend?"

Ricky looked over at Ellie in her line. "You mean Ellie?"

"If that's the hot girl you walked in with, yeah."

Ricky's first thought was to immediately punch Corbin California in the face and saying yes, that Ellie was his girlfriend, but even with the move in the right direction, he knew nothing was clear with them and didn't want it getting back to Ellie he had lied.

"Friends. Good friends. One of my best friends."

"Cool, man, cool. You think you could introduce me? I'd like to get my hands on that."

Ricky gave him a scowl.

"No offense, bro. I know she's your friend, but you gotta admit, she's smokin'."

Ricky couldn't argue with that. "Yeah, she is."

"So you gonna help me out?"

He thought for a moment. "No, man. Sorry. We've known each other almost all our lives and try to stay out of each other's way when it comes to stuff like that."

"Aw, man, uncool. Well, it was good to meet you anyway."

Corbin walked away without saying anything else or getting his registration done. He wasn't a senior, but Ricky guessed he had come in as a transfer. Ricky moved up the line and looked around for him, but lost him in the crowd of students. He glanced over at Ellie a few times, but didn't see Corbin approach her.

He felt sick to his stomach. What right did he have to keep anyone away from her? She was beautiful and everything he wanted, so why wouldn't someone else recognize that? It bothered him when she dated Paul for a few weeks the year before. He was a mutual friend they had both known since elementary and was now one of the star basketball players for the school. As much as that had bugged him, for some reason this Corbin bothered him more. Maybe it was just him. Ricky knew he and Ellie were still reconnecting, but he also knew he hadn't asked her to be his girlfriend or made any significant move. They only discussed a potential future after all this mess was sorted out.

He got to the end of the line and got his registration information.

Freddy ran up to him. "Let me see your schedule."

"Hold on. Let's wait for Ellie and we can compare them together."

"Uh, okay. You could just do it twice, you know?"

He looked up and Ellie had just grabbed her packet. As she stepped away, Corbin was standing there and they started talking.

"So come on, show me."

Ricky pulled out his schedule and held it out, looking past Freddy at what was going on.

Freddy compared their classes. "Hey, we got Advanced Cal together! Man, I was already thinking of dropping that as soon as I saw it, but I'll keep it now."

He saw Ricky looking past him and turned around.

"Whoa, that guy moving in on your girl?"

"You know she's not my girl."

"Well, maybe if you'd take your finger out of your ass, that could change. You've seen her more in the last few months and I know there's something there. What are you scared of? Better do it this year before guys like that do it first."

"Unbelievable. My mom said the same thing about my finger in front of Ellie."

"We all see it. Maybe we need to get shirts made that say 'Ricky, take your finger out of your ass - signed, Friends and Family' for inspiration. Maybe I'll start a petition."

"We just got to get past all this craziness," Ricky said. "Anyway, things seem to be okay with us right now." He wasn't ready to share the more intimate details and discussions of what had happened with Ellie. Not yet.

"Guys are going to keep on hitting her up, man. Don't wait too long."

Ellie finally left and moved towards them.

"So how are your schedules looking?"

Ricky looked at her up and down. Her cheeks were red.

"Who was that?" Freddy asked.

"Oh, new guy. Corbin from California."

"What's he like?"

"I don't know. Just asked who I was."

"And if you had a boyfriend?" Ricky asked her, almost accusingly.

She smiled. "Yes, he did ask me that. How do you know?"

"Because he asked me the same thing."

She shrugged as if it was no big deal. Guys hit on her often, so she was used to dealing with it.

Ricky wanted to stop himself from saying what he was dying to say, but knew he couldn't hold back.

"So what did you say?"

"You know I don't have a boyfriend," Ellie said, almost staring him down.

He looked down and didn't say much else.

Freddy moved into Ricky's ear. "Maybe if someone would learn how to..."

Freddy waved his finger and made a popping noise with his mouth. Ricky punched him on the arm.

"Shut up!" he said through clenched teeth.

Ricky pulled out his schedule to change the subject. They compared classes and then moved together to greet a few of their friends. Corbin was gone and they didn't see him again. And Ricky was looking.

They went through a few of the club and organization tables, grabbed some snacks that the PTA had laid out and finally left. Ricky was still thinking about Corbin on the ride back and trying to hide it as they spoke.

They got near the neighborhood.

"Ellie, am I taking you home or you want to come hang out at the house?"

"I'll hang out. Just stop at my place so I can leave my stuff."

Ellie had accumulated two bags of items from the various tables. Ricky pulled into her driveway and parked. He turned down the radio and heard rumbling behind him.

"I'll be right back," she said and opened the door.

She got halfway down the driveway and turned. She started talking.

Ricky looked back. Corbin was sitting on a motorcycle and talking to her.

"Stalker alert," Freddy said.

Ricky didn't hesitate and got out of the vehicle.

"Hey, Ricky!" Corbin said. "Good to see you again, bro."

"Did you follow me?"

"How else was I gonna find out where this pretty lady lives?"

Ellie was smiling but had a look of concern on her face.

"It is kind of odd that you followed me."

"Sorry, no worries. I just wanted to see if you might wanna go out. Or did you lie about not having a boyfriend?"

She turned to look at Ricky. "No, no boyfriend. Maybe a potential, but he hasn't asked yet."

Corbin smiled and Ricky looked down.

"Then how about we just grab some lunch, even if it's just to wake this potential idiot up. Not an official date, but I don't know anybody but you and Ricky here. Just moved a few days ago."

She smiled, still looking at Ricky as if she was waiting for him to say something, but he wouldn't make eye contact with her. Her face turned red and she turned back to Corbin.

"Why not? Just lunch. Nothing more. Tomorrow?"

"Sure, I'll be here to pick you up."

"She can meet you there," Ricky said, trying but failing to stop himself.

Corbin looked at him.

"He's right. My mom won't let me go on a motorcycle with someone I just met."

"No problem. Give me your number and we'll figure it out."

She moved towards him to save his number on her phone and then sent him a text with her name on it.

Ricky returned to the truck.

"Man, you gonna do anything?" Freddy asked.

"You heard all that?" Ricky asked.

"Lowered my window down as soon as you jumped out of the truck. Intense. You pissed?"

Ricky was, but thought about it. "I don't have a right to be pissed. She's right. Things may be better, but I've never asked her to be my girlfriend. I haven't even asked her on a proper date."

"How blind are you? She was almost begging you to. See the way she was looking at you when she said that? You are a dense man and I am deeply ashamed to call you my friend right now. One year left. She's giving you so many signals and you're like a blind puppy about to walk over a cliff. This California dude just got here and he's already made more moves than you have your entire life."

Ricky was still questioning everything with Ellie. Even though she had never lied to him, the fear of rejection over the years was still strong. Plus, he wasn't sure if he could trust himself after what happened with his mother during lunch a few days before.

Ellie returned to the house and then back out to the truck.

"I'm ready."

Ricky was steamed, but he was more mad at himself.

He pulled out of the driveway, half hoping the motorcycle was still behind him so he could "accidentally" dent it, but Corbin was gone.

They went into the house and to Ricky's room. He hadn't said anything since they left Ellie's.

"Ricky, are you mad at me?" she finally asked. She didn't believe in holding things in.

He shook his head. "No, I just didn't get a good vibe on that guy."

"He's harmless," she said. "Just new."

"So it's not a date?" Ricky asked.

"If almost anyone else was asking, I might not answer, but since it's you, no, it's not a date. Not yet."

Ricky let it go and held his jealousy in.

Ellie sensed he was struggling and changed the subject.

"So what do you think senior year's going to be like?"

They spent the next few hours talking about school and friends they'd seen, with Ricky working hard not to think about or mention Corbin again. His insides still felt awful.

And of course, all he could think about the entire time was Corbin.

CHAPTER TWENTY-FIVE

OVER THE NEXT FEW DAYS, ELLIE AND CORBIN HAD GONE ON two non-dates. Freddy, Ellie, and Ricky were chatting online one morning, planning on what they might do later when a "stud49" popped into a conversation.

"What up, bros?" the person typed. Ricky already knew who it was.

"How did you get into our chat?" Ricky typed.

"Ellie just added me."

"He asked to join us. Wanted to say hi."

They had a group conversation for the next ten minutes. Ricky tried to ignore him, but he kept interrupting with funny comments that Ricky wanted to laugh at but struggled to hold it in, keeping his "LOLs" to himself.

When Freddy typed, "You're a funny dude, California!" it was too much.

Ricky left the chat, then spent the next 15 minutes focused on the screen, obsessing over what they were talking about.

Ricky moved to his bed and laid down, covering his eyes and face with his hands to try to calm down.

He thought about Corbin Brock not existing and moving

back to California, but he knew he was being a jerk. This guy hadn't done anything to him. He did what Ricky was afraid to. He asked Ellie out and he liked her, but could he blame him? He knew Ellie was a rarity. A beautiful person, inside and out. Anyone would be lucky to be with her and he hadn't done anything to further their relationship, even after that kiss.

He was just calming down when his computer pinged.

He looked up.

"Stud49" had sent him a private message.

"Dude" was all it said.

He hesitated, then typed back.

"Yeah?"

"Man, I'm so glad you're not her boyfriend. She talks about you a bunch, but I get the friend zone vibe. Just want you to know I have a short-term plan for her."

"What do you mean?"

"I'm gonna sweeten her up before I take her juice, bro. I figure it'll take me two weeks at most."

Ricky's nostrils flared.

"You really think she'll give it up that easy?"

"I have my ways."

"Why are you telling me this?"

"Cuz I can tell you're into her. Who wouldn't be? Just hope you don't cock-block me. You and Freddy are the only buds I have right now, so wanted to let you know."

Ricky got an odd sense.

"So you're telling me as a friend or is that your way of telling me to back off?"

"I'm trying to be easy, but I'll be straight since you don't get it. You've had your chance. Hell, seems like you've had years of chances, but if you haven't moved yet, I think they're done. Just stay out of my way."

"What if I told her everything?"

"That's a puss thing to do, no matter if we're friends. She'd think you were being a jackass if you did that. What girl respects a guy that would rather break a bro-code than ask her out? Think about that. Back off. I'll only tell you once."

"You're not my bro. And what if I don't?"

"I guess you can wait to find out. Just stay out of the way and we're cool."

Ricky started to type, but the chat session closed and Corbin was offline.

So much for thinking it was just him. He didn't intend on telling Ellie, at least not now because he knew one thing Corbin was right about. He'd come off as a tool if he squealed and still didn't even try to ask her out and see what might happen.

Ricky still took screenshots, just in case.

CHAPTER TWENTY-SIX

FREDDY TEXTED RICKY EARLY. A STREET FOOTBALL GAME WAS happening and Freddy wanted to be sure Ricky would be there. This was something their mutual friends did every few weekends during the summer, but it had been awhile since Freddy had participated and with everything going on with Ricky, it would be his first time playing this year.

Ricky looked around his room. He had gotten into a daily habit of checking if something was off or out of place. He glanced at the sugar skull, which had been quiet for over a week, then got up to check on Myra. She was in her room playing on her tablet. Lori had been fine the whole week. He stopped at his sister's door.

"I'm going to go play football with the guys just down the street. Is that okay? I know mom left earlier, so I'm going to lock the door. Call if you need anything, but just in case I can't hear my phone, you come get me. You got it?"

Myra nodded, still paying attention to whatever she was doing on her machine. "Okay, Ricky. I might go see you."

"Just stay on this side of the street if you do, okay?"

"Okay."

He left and picked up Freddy in the truck, even though it was walking distance. Once he got there and met up with the neighborhood gang, he saw Corbin standing with Ellie, dressed to play.

Ricky walked toward them with Freddy by his side.

"What's he doing here?"

"He wants to play. I wanted to introduce him to some of the guys."

Corbin reached out to shake his hand. "What's up, Ricky? Good to see you again." He winked at him, but Ricky didn't say anything.

They joined the crowd and played street football. It was a regular game, but Ricky was wound up and when the first pass came his way, it hit him on the temple since he was looking at Ellie.

"Damn, are you a senior from Texas or from the Pre-K class?" Corbin said, making everyone laugh.

Ricky was even more mad and dropped the next ball thrown his way.

"Pre-K, come on!" Corbin yelled.

Then it stuck. For the rest of the game, it was, "Throw it to Pre-K!" and "Good job, Pre-K!"

Ricky caught a touchdown and everyone was laughing as someone screamed: "Pre-K with the score!"

It was harmless fun, but the fact that Corbin had instigated it made it worse. Ricky was huffing and puffing.

Corbin caught the ball and Ricky jumped to cover him. They were playing two hand touch football, but Ricky led with his fists and popped Corbin in the hip.

Corbin went down and grunted.

"Dude, what the hell, man?"

"Sorry, California. It gets rough down here in Texas sometimes."

The guys looked at Ricky and laughed. A few of them patted him on the back. He glanced up and saw Ellie frowning at him.

At that point, Ricky didn't care. It was worth it to shut him up.

"Come on, Pre-K, that's not cool," one of the boys said. "Even if he is a Cali hippie."

Corbin limped up and kept going.

Right before the next play was called, he said, "It's okay. Pre-K's just mad cuz I'm moving in on the girl he wishes was his. Too bad he was still acting like he's in Pre-K and didn't do anything about it."

The play started and Corbin rushed at him and threw his shoulder into Ricky's side. He felt a sharp pain as Corbin broke free and caught the next touchdown.

The boys threw in some "oohs" and "aaahs" as Ricky stared Corbin down. He knew his friends joining in was just part of the smack talk but all he could think about was Ellie watching and Corbin getting all his friends to laugh and call him "Pre-K" within just a matter of minutes. Plus, his side hurt.

They kept on playing, but Ricky walked back casually to his teammates.

Freddy walked up to him. "Come on, man. Let's get him back together."

Ricky smiled. They were on the same team as usual. They had tried being on opposing sides before but it always ended up in a big argument and they wouldn't talk for days.

They kept on going and were on offense. Freddy looked at Ricky and pointed out a pattern on his hand, then pointed to Ricky and back to himself.

Ricky nodded.

They both took off for a pass and moved to cross each other. As expected, Corbin went after Ricky and right as they intersected, Freddy checked him, knocking the wind out of Corbin as Ricky caught the ball and made a touchdown on the first play.

"Pre-K TD!" Ricky yelled, owning his new moniker.

The boys laughed.

Corbin stayed on the ground for a minute.

From that point, the game went on without incident. Ricky's side hurt and so did Corbin's, so they avoided each other the rest of the contest.

The game ended with Ricky and Freddy's team winning by two scores. All three boys walked to Ellie after shaking hands with everybody.

"That got a little rough out there, didn't it?" she asked.

"Yeah, your buddies here decided to play hard," Corbin said.

"You kind of deserved it with that Pre-K shot, Cali-boy," Ellie smiled.

"It was just a joke," Corbin said.

"You seemed to be a little fired up there, Ricky. What was that about?" she asked.

"Just had a Hall of Fame moment," Ricky said, not making eye contact.

"Let me go get you both some water."

"I'm thirsty, too!" Freddy said.

"I'll get you some, Freddy, but you don't seem to be hurt."

"I'm hurt that you didn't want to get me water."

She walked towards the ice chest that the boys typically shared during their games to grab some bottled waters. Corbin, who was bent over catching his breath, said, "Do shit like that again and this is going to get way worse than a football game."

Ricky looked at him, "Are you serious?"

"Keep it down, unless you want her to hear. Didn't think you were a wuss."

Ricky lowered his volume.

"You're seriously threatening me?"

"Bet your ass. I want that girl and you don't need to be in the way, you get it?"

Ricky just smiled. "Stick your head up your ass, Corbin. She's big enough to decide what she wants. I'm not big on fighting, but if you do anything to hurt her, you'll be the one that needs to watch your back."

"Then why isn't she with you after all this time?"

"Look, I get it. I know she's awesome, but you don't own her. She may not be my girlfriend, but she sure as hell's not yours, either."

"Not yet," Corbin said. "If you think I won't take you down, keep pushing."

Freddy leaned in as Corbin walked towards Ellie, cutting her off on her way back.

"What was all that about?" he asked.

"I don't know. Did you hear everything?"

"Dude, I've been eavesdropping on my older sister for years. Of course I heard it. Was he messing around or really being a douche?"

"I think he was serious. Don't know him well enough to tell if he's just acting big or really means it."

"What are you gonna do?"

"I guess see if he was serious. Let's hang out. Hold on."

Ellie walked up and handed them some water. "Here you go, boys."

Corbin was right behind her, just in case Ricky decided to say something.

Ricky gave him a hard stare and Ellie caught it. She didn't want to ask out loud but gave him a questioning look.

He understood and shook his head. He knew she'd want to talk about it later. He had a lot to talk to her about.

"Ellie, you ready to go home?" Corbin said.

"You know I can't get on your motorcycle. It's okay, Ricky was going to take me and Freddy on an errand."

Corbin sped off and Ricky and Ellie got in his truck. Rather than driving down a few houses to Ellie's, Ricky drove the other way. He knew something was coming.

Ellie turned. "All right. What was going on back there?"

"Nothing, Ellie. Just being guys. Nothing serious."

"It looked like it was getting serious. Come on, he's new."

"Why are you letting him hang out with you all the time?"

"Not like you guys are inviting him over. He's nice to me."

Freddy moved his head up from the back seat. "What do you mean by nice?"

She slapped him gently on the forehead. "It's none of your business but nothing."

"Well, I think he likes you," Freddy said.

"And so what if he does? Not like I have a boyfriend right now," Ellie said, the air getting thick with silence.

Ricky didn't look at her. "He's kind of a jack, but I guess he just wants attention."

"You're just mad because of the whole Pre-K thing. You have to admit if Freddy had said that it would be fine."

"Yeah, but he's not Freddy or any of the guys. We don't even know him. You don't even know him."

"Yeah, he's not me," Freddy threw in.

"Lucky him," she said. "He's new and I'm just trying to be nice to him like when you first moved here, Freddy. I know he can be a little too much, but come on. He's not that bad."

"Not yet," Freddy mumbled. "I don't trust him."

Ellie stared at Ricky, but he kept his eyes on the road.

"I'm getting that outdated macho protective feeling all over this vehicle," Ellie said. "I'm a big girl and can handle myself."

Ricky took a quick turn. "I know you are, Ellie, which is why I'm going to keep my big mouth shut."

She half smiled. "We need to talk when we have more time and Freddy isn't around."

"I'm right here," Freddy said.

"We know," Ricky and Ellie said at the same time.

CHAPTER TWENTY-SEVEN

FREDDY WENT HOME THAT NIGHT AND MYRA WAS STAYING OVER at Karen's again. Lori had returned a few hours before but just told him goodnight before going to her room. He hadn't heard from her since. He was alone in the living room and still sore and stewing from the football game. The TV was on a cartoon channel Myra had been watching earlier, but he was lost in thought and not paying attention. Then he heard the doorknob turn.

After hearing it move a few times, he wondered if Lori had invited someone over or if Freddy was coming by unannounced. He got up to check.

He opened the door, but no one was there. It was a little windy, so he just brushed it off and went back to the couch.

He looked up at the TV and wanted to change the station. He looked around for the remote but didn't see it. He sighed. Myra never put it back on the coffee table where it belonged. He started feeling between the couch cushions, then moved to the loveseat. He stuck his hand on the far end where Myra typically sat and felt a sticky goo between his fingers.

"Marshmallows again, Myra?" He loved his sister, but he

was going to ban her from eating marshmallows in the living room the next few weeks.

He pulled his hand out so he could go wash them, but something was dripping from his fingers. He looked down. Whatever was on his hands, it wasn't marshmallows. He held up his fingers and they were dripping with a clear, sticky gel.

"What is this?"

He put his hand back between the cushion and pulled it open.

An eyeball was staring back at him, looking from side to side.

Ricky screamed and tripped on the coffee table as he tried to back away.

He was on his back but leaped up. The TV screen clicked off and as he looked up, the face of the creature he had seen in the mirrors of downtown and on the bus was now filling the screen.

There was a loud moan coming from upstairs. The shadow figure was standing at the top in the reading room, looking down at him.

The doorknobs in what seemed like every door in the house started to rattle. Ricky's room door flew open and he saw a bright blue light glowing from inside. The skull appeared in the doorway, its eyes glowing blue as it hovered in mid-air.

Enemies on three sides. Ricky backed away towards the kitchen. The face on the TV moved off the screen and then he saw it in the refrigerator's reflection and on some framed pictures on the wall, some of the family and others with prints of some of Lori's paintings. Six total reflections were staring back at him. A gravelly snarl came from the stairs as the shadow stepped down slowly.

Ricky's breathing accelerated and he could hear his heart pounding in his chest. Fear overtook him as he started to panic. He glanced and saw some clean dishes in the dish rack next to the sink. Without thinking, he squeezed his hands together. A wooden spoon shot from the rack at the shadow as it took another step down. The spoon flew straight through it and it landed somewhere upstairs.

The reflections snarled in unison, filling the house with an animal growl. "No!" Ricky yelled as dishes started flying towards the refrigerator and picture reflections. Several of the ceramic plates shattered against the refrigerator and plastic cups bounced off it. Two glasses hit a picture, smashing it and making it fall to the floor.

The other dishes hit the walls and made a huge crashing sound. The reflection disappeared.

The shadow kept coming. The rest of the dish rack emptied as Ricky concentrated on the slow-moving darkness coming down the stairs, but every piece went through it and bounced or broke off the rail or a step. Ricky turned to look at the skull, but it was still in its same spot, hovering and glowing.

Ricky moved back toward the front door as the shadow reached the floor. He squeezed. The couch cushions rose and flew at the shadow, but they also went straight through it. The shadow stopped and looked like black smoke quivering in the wind. Ricky was petrified and didn't know what to do. He wanted to throw everything at it, but he knew it was no use.

He heard a loud screech, but as he looked up, he realized it wasn't the shadow, and the reflection creature was still gone. It sounded like Lori.

The shadow then turned and took its time as it headed toward the short hallway leading to Lori's room. Ricky couldn't see it from where he stood.

"Mom!" Ricky yelled.

His fear subsided enough for him to gather himself and

run to Lori's room. As he got to the hallway, he saw the last of the shadow drift through Lori's closed door. Then everything went quiet.

Ricky stood in front of the door and put his hand on the doorknob, but his hands were shaking.

"Mom?" he finally got out. "Mom, are you okay?"

There was no response. He took in a deep breath and turned the knob.

Ricky eased the door open. Lori's small TV was on but muted. She was under the covers and facing him, and her eyes were closed. He looked around but didn't see the shadow.

Lori started giggling like a dreaming baby.

"Mom, are you awake?"

Lori chuckled and her eyes popped open. They were completely black. Ricky stepped back. He thought maybe the darkness and shadows in the room were making her eyes look that way, but that had never happened before.

"Hi, Son," she said in a hoarse voice. "I'm just fine. I'm more than fine."

She smiled as her eyes closed.

Ricky left the room and shut the door, shaking. He took some deep breaths and tried to put what he had just seen out of his mind.

It was just a shadow. Nothing more, he repeated in his head until the chill passed.

He walked back and saw the picture and shattered glass and dishes on the floor. He looked back and the sugar skull was still floating, but its glow dulled and it floated back into his room. He ran towards it and as he looked in. The skull was back at his desk, no longer glowing.

Ricky stared at it and squeezed one more time. He looked back and the shattered glass was floating. He turned his head and guided the debris into the trash can. He walked over and other than the one picture that had fallen, there was nothing else to sweep up.

He picked up the picture. It was one of Lori's paintings of a Paris street using bright blues and reds on surrounding trees with duller streetlights and buildings in the background. Whatever these creatures were, Ricky was now convinced they were connected to Lori somehow. The one thing he knew for certain was that he could definitely move things himself. That wasn't caused by someone or something else. He intended to empty that dish rack, and his mom wasn't in the room. It had to be him. He didn't know or care why at this moment, but he knew it might not be such a bad ability to have in the right situation.

CHAPTER TWENTY-EIGHT

FREDDY CAME BY THE HOUSE THE NEXT DAY AND RICKY WAS sitting in his room, staring into nothing.

"What are you doing?" Freddy asked.

Ricky snapped like he was in a trance.

"Nothing. What? What was I doing?"

"Staring off into space like you were thinking about Ellie," Freddy said.

He shook his head and realized he was spaced out. He was still consumed with the events of the previous night and trying to figure out what it all meant.

"What do you feel like doing? Want to see if Ellie wants to come over?"

Ricky stared at him and asked, "Why do you want Ellie here?"

"I don't know. To hang out. You've been a drag the last few days."

Ricky straightened up. "What's that supposed to mean?"

"Don't get all pissy. I'm just messing around."

"Maybe I'm not in the mood to mess around."

"What is your deal? Did Corbin come around or something?"

He sat there again in a daze. He thought of Corbin with Ellie and felt heat rise in his throat.

"What?" Freddy asked.

"Thinking about Corbin just ticks me off."

"Did he say something to you again?"

"No, haven't heard from him since the football game but he was with Ellie when I called her earlier."

"He was? How do you know?"

"He went out of his way to talk extra loud while we were on the phone. You could tell."

"Man, why don't you just tell Ellie how you feel and get this over with?"

"I know. It's just not easy with everything going on."

"How long's it been?"

"Since I first decided I liked girls and they weren't all gross."

"So why wait any longer? I don't know what else to tell you. You'll regret it the rest of your life if you don't at least try."

Then a noise pinged on the computer. Ricky looked up. "Stud49."

He walked over to the computer, but Freddy beat him to it.

"That's Corbin!"

The message said, "How's it going at home alone? You should see what she's wearing. H-O-T. I'll bet it'll look better on the floor right next to the bed. I'm already sitting on the couch, so maybe I'll just try it right here."

"What? Is he serious?"

"It's not the first time," Ricky said. "He said some stuff like that to me after asking if I was her boyfriend."

"Why didn't you say anything?"

"It'd make me look worse. Petty. I'm trying hard to trust that she won't let him fool her."

Ricky thought for a second and typed back.

"In your dreams."

"The wet ones," came back almost immediately. "I'll be sure she takes care of that. Make my dreams from last night come true. She was in a bikini and couldn't wait to get it off."

Ricky's breath grew heavier.

"Come on, man," Freddy said. "Let him talk shit. Ellie won't give him the time of day."

"You don't know that," Ricky said. "And like she likes to remind me, she doesn't have a boyfriend."

"Numbnuts. What do you think that means? She's throwing hints at you and you're like the dumbest dude alive."

"You don't know that."

"Yes, I do. She flat out told you you needed to talk. Have you?"

Another ping. "Mmm. I'm going to accidentally drop my drink on her so she has to change into something else. Then I'll follow her to her room. Then I'll get her. I'll get her good. You picturing that? Then we'll laugh at how you never even had the balls to try."

Ricky stood up and slammed his hands on his desk.

"Come on, Ricky. Don't let this dude get to you."

"I owe him," Ricky said. He squeezed his fingers and there was a noise behind them. The skull jumped up and landed back down as he flexed, but by the time Freddy looked back it was still.

"Let's go over there now."

"And do what?"

"I'm going to see if he was serious the other day."

"When was the last time you've been in a fight? Freshman year? And that was with me. You punched me once, grazed my face and hit the wall. Your finger hurt for weeks."

"I'm not playing this time," Ricky said as he started out the door. "You coming?"

"You think I'm missing this?"

They got to the truck and he peeled out on his way to Ellie's house.

They parked on the curb by her house and Ricky pinged Corbin back from his phone.

"I'm here big mouth. Come outside. I want to know if you got the balls to back that mouth up. Don't tell Ellie, like you told me."

About a minute later Corbin walked outside. Ellie was right behind him.

"What are you doing, Ricky?"

"You told her?" Ricky said.

"I figure if I was going to humiliate you, I'd want her to see," he said.

"He's been talking smack," Ricky said.

"And?" Ellie said. "When has that ever made you want to fight? Stop this. You came over here, remember!"

"You gonna stop it and listen to her like a puppy, doing whatever she wants?" Corbin taunted.

"Let's go, then," Ricky said. "I think you're full of it."

Corbin moved toward him and pushed him, knocking him on his rear. Ricky got agitated and stood right back up.

He took a swing at Corbin, but he darted back and the punch missed.

"Come on. That's the best you got, Pre-K?"

Ricky rushed forward and tackled him. They fell to the ground.

Corbin threw some punches behind his head as they went down.

Ricky felt his face turn red with each blow.

"I'm gonna take you out."

He flexed his fingers, imagining throwing Corbin back.

Nothing happened.

Ricky looked down at his hands when Corbin hit him across the face with a fast hook.

His face recoiled.

"Oooh," Freddy said from behind.

Corbin pointed at him. "This ain't your fight, stay out of it!"

"Stop it!" Ellie said.

Corbin turned to look at her and Ricky hit him in the chest, knocking the wind out of him. Corbin couldn't breathe for a few seconds and walked back. Ricky could have taken a free shot but was still trying to squeeze and wondering why nothing was happening. It made no sense. He looked at Corbin and tried to concentrate more.

Ellie jumped in front of him.

"Ricky!"

He looked back at her. "What?"

"Why are you being like this?" Her eyes moistened.

"What do you mean? The stuff he told me!"

"Whatever he said, they're just words! I've never known you to be so petty."

"Petty? Me? What about him?"

"You're the one that came over ready to fight. And in front of my house! What if Mom comes out here and sees you? You need to leave RIGHT NOW!"

Ricky stopped caring about Corbin and looked at her, then back at Freddy. For a moment he couldn't believe he had taken it this far.

Ellie placed her hand to the side of his face.

"You're bleeding. Just leave, please. And put some peroxide on that."

He felt a ping of guilt. He looked down. "I'm sorry."

He turned when Corbin looked back up.

"Told you I'd back it up. Remember that when you look in the mirror. I won't stop next time!"

"Shut up, Corbin," Ellie said.

"He came over here!"

"I think you need to go home, too."

She walked in the house and shut the door behind her. Ricky was getting into the truck when Corbin came back up to him and put his face in Ricky's.

"If you messed things up with her, it's gonna get worse. You think this was a beat down, wait 'til next time."

"A beat down?" Freddy said. "Y'all threw like three punches. I've seen cats fight worse."

Neither Ricky nor Corbin looked at him.

"Leave her alone," Corbin told him.

"Go screw yourself," Ricky said.

Corbin walked over to his motorcycle and opened the side bag. He eased something out.

"Check this out, Pre-K," he said, moving his back to block Ellie's window in case she looked out.

He eased out the grip of a handgun. He pulled a little more and flashed it quickly before putting it back in his bag.

"This is who you're messing with, Pre-K. You think you know me? Push me again, and maybe you'll see this instead of my fist."

"Let's go," Freddy said, sounding serious.

Ricky kept staring.

"Let's GO! Not worth messing with a psycho with a gun. Come on."

They left and returned to the house. Ricky didn't say anything as they got to the room.

"He has a gun! A GUN!" Freddy said, still freaking out. "Why would he have a gun and threaten you with it? It was a fight and he won!"

Ricky eyeballed him.

"Well it may not have been by much, but he did."

"I don't understand," Ricky said dryly.

"Understand what? Gun mixed with crazy equals death."

"I don't understand why it didn't work."

"Why what didn't work?"

He raised his hands and the curtains jumped up as the skull flew up in the air and stayed there.

"What the hell?" Freddy said.

He looked at Ricky. Ricky was staring at the skull with his right arm out, squeezing the muscles on his hands and forearm.

"Wait, are you doing that?"

Ricky kept staring. He moved his arm to the side and the skull moved with it. Some pens and pencils jumped off his desk and they spun around the skull, forming an orbit around it.

"How are you doing that?"

"Why didn't it work?" Ricky said out loud. "Why does it work here and not at Ellie's?"

"Wait, you were trying to do that to Corbin? What were you going to do? Spring him up in the air and throw him across the street? Wait, HOW ARE YOU DOING THIS?"

Ricky let go and the skull and pencils fell on the bed.

"I don't know. I thought it was just my mom or those things doing it the other day, but now I know I can control things, too. If I concentrate and kind of squeeze my muscles, I can make a few things move. I just wasn't sure if it was all me. At least until last night."

"What happened last night?"

Ricky gave him the details.

"You know that's not normal, right?" Freddy was freaking out, but then calmed down. "But it is pretty damned cool. What do you think it is? The skull maybe?"

Ricky snapped. The skull.

"Maybe I have to have the skull near me for this to work."

"Can you pick me up?"

"I don't know."

Freddy's voice was shaking. "I can't believe I'm saying this, but try it. Just don't let me smack my head on the ceiling. Or the floor. Or anywhere if you can."

Ricky looked at him and raised his hands. Freddy was standing straight up, and then his feet lifted an inch or two off the floor.

"Wait, wait! Don't drop me!"

He fell right back. Ricky concentrated, but this time nothing happened.

"What do you feel?"

"I don't know! It tingles like when your foot's asleep. Maybe I need to try again."

"No, I think that was a good enough experiment."

Ricky ignored him and raised both hands, concentrating harder this time.

Freddy lifted an additional inch, protesting the entire time.

"No! No more!"

Ricky lost his grasp and Freddy landed back on his feet. Ricky lost his concentration and threw both his hands out with a grunt. Freddy went flying into the back wall, his arm hitting the window. It shattered.

"Hey!" Freddy shouted.

"Freddy?"

Ricky ran to him. He got close and Freddy jumped back.

"Come on, Freddy, you're bleeding!"

Freddy looked at his arm. The part of his elbow and rear forearm that had gone through the window were scraped. They weren't bad, but there was some blood.

"Let me see it."

"Get away from me, man!"

Ricky recoiled. "I'm sorry, I didn't mean to."

"How did you throw me like that?"

"I don't know. I just don't know."

"You're pissed at Corbin and Ellie, but how come I'm the one here bleeding?"

Ricky looked over at the skull, but it was still.

"It had to be the skull," he said. "I couldn't do anything to Corbin and I really wanted to hurt him at the time. I never wanted to hurt you."

Freddy just stared up at him.

He sat up and when Ricky tried to help him, he balked.

"Don't. Let me get up on my own."

Ricky's face flushed. He went to his bathroom and grabbed a hand towel and wet it. He had just hurt his best friend, who had always remained by his side, even though Ricky knew he feared his house and everything that had been going on.

He came back out. Freddy flinched as Ricky reached over to hand it to him.

"Are you scared of me?"

"What do you think?" he shouted, his voice shaking.

"It was an accident."

"It's not just that. I hear you mumbling under your breath all the time. And that look. Have you checked in the mirror at night lately? Your eyes look freaky and sometimes you just sit there looking into nothing. And the other day with your mom? You kept saying she was doing and saying things she wasn't."

Ricky was in shock.

"I still don't understand what happened, Freddy, but I saw and heard everything. She was being a monster."

"No," Freddy said, rubbing his elbow and forearm with the towel. "I got used to seeing your mom look so bad, but that day, that was the best I'd seen her in forever. She looked normal, Ricky. The food was good, Myra was happy, and she never said a bad thing. It's like you want her to stay the same so badly you can't even admit that she might be getting better."

Ricky looked down. "That's not what I saw. I still don't get why."

"You don't? Maybe I do. Something's up with you, and I'm the one that just paid for it. Whatever's been going on, I think it's inside you or controlling you. You're not the same. You're jealous over Ellie and ready to kill Corbin. Yeah, he may deserve it, but it's just not you. And I'm freaking scared of you! Scared! I've never been scared of you. Ever. You've never done anything mean to anyone and tonight you were ready to go fight over some BS that you think Ellie can't see through."

Ricky felt heat rise up his neck. He could feel the anger coming back.

"I don't know."

"Maybe you're finally going through puberty," Freddy said, smiling but not taking his eyes off him.

Ricky looked at him.

"See. See that? You're actually getting pissed. I've talked shit to you my entire life--our entire lives, and we've always laughed. Now you can't even take a joke. Your face is red!"

Ricky took in some quick breaths, trying to calm down. Freddy looked away and pointed. The skull was floating a few inches over the desk.

"That's all you. I'm going home. I can't be near you right now."

Ricky clenched his fists. He wanted to make Freddy understand, but then took a long look at his hands and the floating skull. Of course Freddy was scared. Ricky didn't even know what was going on, but he knew it was getting out of control. His lack of sleep felt like he was losing time and he would find himself just staring into nothing. And lately he wasn't even thinking about Ellie. Sometimes it just felt like an empty daze.

Freddy was gone. He was alone.

He spent the next two hours on his bed, back in a daze, thinking about Corbin. Every time he looked at the computer, he saw the IM session sitting there and seethed even more. He wanted to control it and was so consumed that he never realized the skull had been free floating for over thirty minutes straight.

CHAPTER TWENTY-NINE

It was morning. Ricky wasn't sure when he had fallen asleep, but his phone was buzzing. He saw his notifications and had several missed calls and messages. Before he could check them, his door flew open.

Ellie burst through.

"Ellie? What are you doing here?"

"You're lucky I am. Is something wrong with your phone?"

"No, I just woke up and saw I had a bunch of missed texts and calls."

"Yeah, a few of those are from me. Professor Jackie called me. She's been trying to get a hold of you all morning and wants to see us. Said she has some information but wants to give it to you in person. She wants us there within the hour because she has to leave.

"Okay, let me get changed and we'll go."

Ellie stepped into the living room to give him time to take a quick rinse and get dressed. They were on the road fifteen minutes later.

Ricky couldn't hold it in and before they got out of the block he blurted, "I'm sorry about yesterday."

"Sorry about what exactly? Trying to start a fight in front of my house for nothing? Look, I know Corbin's been a jerk to you, but I get it. He's just trying to fit in. I don't really like him much, to be honest, but he's been fine and hasn't tried anything."

Ricky thought about telling her everything he'd been saying.

"It's just that he's been saying stuff, nothing I want to repeat and I know he's just trying to get under my skin."

"So what? Even if he is talking about me, SO WHAT? Nothing's happened, so he's just moving his mouth."

There was one thing he couldn't keep inside. If something happened, he knew he'd blame himself.

"He threatened me with a gun," Ricky said.

"What? When?"

"When you went inside after the fight. He had it in his motorcycle."

Ellie's frown flattened. "Do you think he was serious?"

"I don't know. He seems harmless, but he got me so mad. It's like I couldn't control it."

"You were being so unlike you, Ricky. Why?"

"Because it's you, Ellie. I don't like the way he is around you."

"You have no right to be jealous."

"I know. I know I don't have a right and I'm being selfish."

"Dang it, Ricky. After the carnival and some of the moments we've had this summer, I was waiting for the next step, but I know things got bad with your mom and you're still dealing with losing Grandma Bea, so I didn't push. I know we said after all this blew over we might see what the future holds, but what if that doesn't happen? And yes, I might have used Corbin to make you a little jealous. I saw how it bothered you at registration."

He shook his head. "Why?"

"Like Freddy and your mom said, so maybe you'd pull that finger out of your butt! We're going to be seniors, Ricky. We've been best friends since we were tiny! You know I don't just like you. I love you to pieces, and I think you love me, too, you idiot."

"You know I do," he mumbled.

"What? I'm sorry, I couldn't hear you?"

"You know I do! I've just been so scared that you didn't feel the same and would end up hating me and never speak to me again."

"Is that part of the reason we've hardly spoken at school since freshman year? I know it was a clique thing and we were in different groups with different friends, but it was more. I felt you pulling away."

"And I felt you pulling away."

"It's not like you didn't have girlfriends."

"It's not like you didn't have boyfriends, either."

"Yeah, and how long did any of your relationships actually last?"

"I don't know. A couple of months. Maybe weeks sometimes."

"I know you were with Angela for like 48 hours."

"Yeah, she was talking about getting married by the end of the first day. Big scare. I mean, we're in high school."

She smiled. "Maybe we were both just waiting to see what the other would do. I was scared, too. We both were so scared we may have blown a chance to be happy together. How stupid is that?"

"Maybe," Ricky said, knowing she had hit it on the head. "I just never really knew how you felt."

"I guess I should carry a big sign since I don't think you'll ever get it. We hugged, we kissed. I basically told you I was ready the other day."

"I thought you were just feeling sorry for me because of

Grandma and with what happened with my mom, I'm not sure what's real anymore."

"There's another reason you're an idiot. The signs were there before any of this happened."

"So what do we do now?"

"I don't know. The fact that we have to talk about it just kind of kills it."

"Yeah," Ricky said.

"Maybe you need an incentive."

"Incentive? What do you mean?"

Ellie unhooked her seat belt, then leaned over and put her mouth near his ear. "If we can get past this, maybe by the time Homecoming rolls around, we can roll around."

The truck jerked to the left, pressing Ellie closer to him. "Are you serious?"

"Maybe that's why nothing ever worked out with my other boyfriends. I can't believe I'm saying this, but I'm still a virgin, contrary to what some may think. Maybe I knew I was waiting for you. The time and the person just has to be right. I've got a good feeling, but let's see how things go."

Ricky didn't know what to say. "I'm, uh. Me, too."

"You too what?"

"I'm still a virgin, too. Contrary to what some may think."

"Ricky, I know. And I'm not sure who thinks that."

"What? How?"

"I don't need a supernatural skull to tell me. Some things a girl just knows."

Ricky smiled as Ellie put her seatbelt back on.

"Like I said, incentive. No promises, just possibilities, but I meant what I said. I'm trying to be as clear as I can so there's no confusion or excuses. It's in your court."

"I understand."

"I hope you do. Your track record says otherwise."

"I do. Homecoming."

"Maybe whatever Professor Jackie knows will help us sort this out faster. Once we figure out what's going on with you and this skull thing, maybe you won't feel the need to wait that long."

They reached the University. Ricky took in a breath and tried to clear his mind since all he could think about was Homecoming.

"Let's go, Loverboy," Ellie said. "The sooner, the better."

They rushed into the building and up to the office. The professor's assistant Kayla wasn't there.

"Come on in," they heard Professor Jackie's voice say from her office.

They walked in and the professor was at her desk with her hands on a few books.

"What did you find?" Ricky asked.

She took a long look at him as he sat down. "You doing okay, Ricky?"

He nodded.

"You don't look so good, kid. Things a little rough lately?"

He touched his face. "Oh, I kind of got in a fight."

"Really? Who won?"

Ellie smirked. "Not him."

Ricky felt anger and embarrassment, but let it go.

"Did more happen since we spoke? Tell me everything. The smallest detail might be critical."

Ricky looked down.

Ellie nudged him. "Tell her. I'm sure you haven't given me all the details and I understand. But it's time. Tell her everything. I'll leave the room if it makes it easier. Please."

Ricky told her about the lunch story and what he had heard Lori say and how the food tasted, which Myra and Freddy didn't experience.

"I still can't understand how Myra and Freddy saw Lori in

such a different way than I did. It was so real, but Myra wouldn't lie about that."

"Anything else?"

"Yes," Ricky said after hesitating.

"Do you remember the first time we met and I told you my mom and I had argued?"

"Yes."

"It was worse than what I made it out to be. That night my mom was home alone when I got there. She was just sitting in a daze, by herself in the kitchen."

"What happened?" Professor Jackie asked.

"She said that she wished Myra and I had never been born. That we ruined her life. She cursed at me and was upset Grandma Bea left me in charge of the money."

"And what did you do?"

Ricky kept looking down. "I got upset. I told her stuff back and how it was her own fault she did the things she did. Like I told you before, it got ugly."

"How ugly?"

"It was the worst fight we've ever had. She said some of the vilest things ever."

"What was different about this than in years before?"

"She sounded like she meant every word, and it was just cruel. I wasn't much better, but when she said what she said about Myra, I couldn't take it. If she was mad at me, fine, but the things she said about my sister. They were unforgivable."

"And you said Freddy and Myra think she was being an angel, all cleaned up at a later time?"

He nodded.

"And what about you? Any change in you?"

"I don't think so."

Ellie backhanded him across the arm. "Tell her."

He paused. "I don't know. It's been harder for me to keep

calm. I'm losing my temper more easily, even when I know it doesn't make sense."

Ellie nodded. "He hasn't been himself. Looks like he hasn't slept in days and then picked a fight. I've known him almost my entire life and I don't think I've ever seen him pick a fight."

Professor Jackie looked at her. "Were you the reason for it?"

Ellie also looked down. "Apparently."

"Understandable. I know you have both been close since you were kids."

"This is different," Ricky said. "I'm 17, not 12 and just hitting puberty."

She looked at him. "Something you're still holding back?"

He looked at Ellie and the professor.

"The skull. Lately, I can move things. Seems to be only when the skull is around."

The professor stared at him. "Move things?"

"You can ask Freddy. I hurt him last night. I didn't mean to, but I did. I was still mad about the fight and he wanted me to test what I could do, but I didn't think I was that strong. He flew across the room. I have a taped up window to prove it. There's also the bus."

"Bus?"

Ricky told her about the night of the carnival and the shadow and reflections he had encountered.

"Why would you leave that out, Ricky? It's not just the skull?"

"Because. Up until recently, I was never sure that had happened. I thought it was just a nightmare, but, and not even Ellie knows this yet, they showed up again in my house."

He told the professor and Ellie about what had happened and how he had been able to throw things around.

"I know now the bus wasn't a nightmare. They were there, and that shadow went into my mother's room and her eyes... her eyes were completely blacked out. And there's something else."

"More?" the professor asked.

"Yes, Ellie convinced me to tell you everything."

He looked at Ellie and wanted so badly not to say it.

"It's okay, Ricky," Ellie said as she put her hand on his shoulder.

"My mom started bringing strange men into the house again. She did it one night with me, Freddy and Myra at the house."

"She's done that before, right?" Professor Jackie asked.

"Yes, but not like this. She flaunted it, but that's not the worst part."

The professor and Ellie kept quiet.

"The man tried to pay my mom to mess with Myra. My mom actually encouraged it for the money and got angry with me for trying to stop him. The man was big and could have killed me, but I got so mad I almost killed him. I made knives fly at him and one stabbed him in the leg, but then my mom kind of turned everything against me afterward. She made things fly in the air and stopped what I tried to throw at her. I thought maybe she had been the one who had actually done it all, but I guess we both have that power."

"My God," Dr. Jackie said. "He could have killed her. Have you left her with your mom alone since?"

"No, Professor. I made sure she was at her friend's house or that mom was out. Even when mom started acting almost normal again, I haven't left them alone together in the house."

"If that ever happens again, don't let it get that far. You do whatever you have to do to protect your sister, including calling the police."

"I will. I promise."

"Thank you," Professor Jackie said. "Every little thing is important, remember? And that wasn't so little."

Ricky couldn't raise his gaze.

"So what do you think this is?" Ellie asked.

She pulled up some books.

"I think, whatever got into your house came in that night your Grandma Bea died, or maybe was already there. That little girl you saw that late night?"

Ricky looked up and nodded.

"I think she was some kind of evil spirit or demon. Your grandmother said others in the neighborhood saw her?"

"Yes, that's right."

"I think whatever she or it was, it was scouting. Looking for something it could use as a doorway."

"A doorway to what?" Ellie asked.

"If it was an evil spirit of some kind, it needs to find someone who is weak or vulnerable to either communicate with or come into this world. If it was in the spirit of that little girl, then it wasn't fully here. It needed a corporeal body to invade."

"As in a human, right?" Ricky remembered his grandmother telling a story about something similar.

He thought for a minute.

"My mom. She was out of it that night. I remember the girl looking past us and noticing her."

"That's what I'm thinking," Professor Jackie said. "How long after that night did Lori start acting differently?"

"It's hard to tell, to be honest. She's been so unpredictable all these years, it may have been going on for days or weeks and we wouldn't have really noticed. She's so up and down."

"So assume the spirit or demon or whatever took her over. It gets stronger the longer it's there, and it seems it wanted to antagonize you, then you bring in the skull. So maybe it's using the skull, or it's in the skull, too. That I haven't figured out yet."

"The skull is always there," Ricky said. "I've gotten used to it. And I practiced with it, too."

"So you think it's trying to get into Ricky now?" Ellie asked.

"I don't know. Maybe it's trying, maybe it's playing nice and still in mom to help make you weaker, or maybe it's inside you now. The fact that you are here and coherent tells me if it is trying to take you over, it's struggling, but you may not be too far from breaking."

"So what do we do?"

"That's where a few of these books come in. If we had a way to figure out exactly what might be in your house, it may be easier to destroy it or make it leave."

She reached for a book.

"There is a Guarani tribe in South America that is extremely secretive. No pictures or recordings are allowed, but I did find a reference to their folklore. There is a being they considered a god named Luison, their God of Death. It was an evil god and if anything bad happened in their village, like a poor crop or a death, they blamed it on this deity. This book details the only written observation of a time when their crops were almost ruined. They believed this spirit possessed a villager. The man was one of their elders, and once they determined and believed it was Luison who had taken him over, they gave it what it wanted. This god is supposed to desire the taste of flesh. So they sacrificed different animals. A deer, a goat and a wolf, but nothing worked. They knew they had to give it a bigger sacrifice, so they took a day and let their bravest fight until only one was standing and considered him the strongest of their tribe. This winner was then cut open, alive, and pieces of his body were offered to the elder, who ate each piece raw and consumed so much that the winner died. They repeated this twice until things miraculously got better. Within a day the almost dead crops came to life and flourished that season."

Ricky and Ellie just stared at each other.

"So you're saying that we have to offer either my mom's flesh or maybe mine? An actual body?"

"No, no. What I'm saying is that IF, and that's a big IF, this is any kind of spirit or demon, without knowing, we have to give it whatever it desires to satisfy it. Once it has its fill, it should engorge itself and leave. Every spirit or demon has its purpose or special need."

"But at what cost?" Ellie asked. "What if it wants a sacrifice?"

"When the cost is too high, we have to exorcise it or banish it, depending on how it's manifesting. Even though it seems to be inside Lori, it's still possible it's connected to the house or skull or even to Ricky."

"How are we supposed to find out?"

"No one except your grandmother knows what I'm about to tell you."

"What is it, Professor?" Ricky asked.

"Do you remember the Shaman story I told you about in East Africa?"

"Where you saw the man possessed and exorcised?"

"Yes. Bea and I did more than just take notes. When the Shaman first tried to remove the evil spirit, it didn't work. However, he received a vision that somehow our presence would help. This is why they let us in so close. The Shaman believed that since we were outsiders, but true in spirit and not trying to harm them, that he could use our life force to help since the evil spirit had poisoned their village."

"You weren't just observers, were you?" Ellie asked.

"No. In order for us to help, we became part of the ceremony. The Shaman gave us a crash course in what we had to do to isolate the spirit. He used our life force to join in his ritual. He said what had happened would give us the ability to draw out darkness if we chose to."

"Are you saying you can help us figure out what's going on?" Ricky asked.

"I'm saying I might."

"Have you done this before?"

"Yes. A few years after our East Africa trip, we encountered another tribe in the Amazon. They were going extinct and there were less than twenty in their entire tribe with no children. Their healer had died long before, but while we were studying them, they had a similar issue where they believed a woman in their tribe was possessed. Bea and I used what we had learned, only after they begged us to help, and we did a modified version of that ritual. It lasted seventeen straight hours, and whether we actually removed a dark spirit or just dumb luck, the woman got better. Can I say she was possessed? Not with 100% certainty, but her eyes were white. She spoke in different languages and she did perform some mid-air flips before the villagers tied her down. Do I *believe* she was possessed? Yes. Yes, I do."

"So are you willing to come to the house to see what you can do?" Ricky asked.

"Yes. I only plan to try and determine what's happening and if I think there is a possession, I'll stop and call for help. Even with my experience, I wouldn't trust myself to do this alone. I will only try to help determine what might be causing all this to happen. Is that okay?"

"Yes, Professor. It's more than okay."

"Is Lori home?"

"I don't know. Myra's been at her friend's house and I don't know if my mom was in bed or gone this morning. I didn't check."

"Hopefully she will be. Let me gather what I need. I'll

need to stop at an herb shop real quick, but let's go. I think the sooner we know what we're dealing with, the sooner we can figure out how to fix it."

Professor Jackie stood up and Ricky went around her desk and embraced her tightly. "Thank you, Professor Jackie. Thank you for doing this."

"I haven't done anything yet. We did this out of necessity before, but your grandmother was with me."

"In a way she is," Ricky said. "It's because of her I even trusted you. Maybe she helped guide me here since she knew you could help. Still, I really wish she was here."

"So do I, Ricky. Let's hope somehow she'll be around us."

"She will," Ricky said. "I know she will."

CHAPTER THIRTY

RICKY AND ELLIE RUSHED INTO HIS HOUSE. HE CHECKED ON LORI and she was still in bed. He started to say something but decided against it and left her alone.

"Is she here?" Ellie asked.

"Yes, but I think it's better if I don't warn her. Professor Jackie said she'd only be a few minutes behind us, so let me check on Myra. Not sure if he'll show after what happened, but you want to tell Freddy?"

Ellie nodded and started texting.

Ricky called to talk to his little sister. She was returning home later that night, but not for a few hours. Dr. Jackie arrived within ten minutes and entered the house carrying two leather satchels, one on each shoulder.

"Where do you need to be?" Ricky asked.

"The kitchen table should be fine. Can you clear it off?"

Ellie and Ricky moved the glass vase and a few books that were still there from their earlier research onto the kitchen counters.

The professor laid her large satchels on one side of the table and took a few items out. She pulled out a round stone item that looked like it could be an ancient cake pan. The stone was smooth, but it had an open top and then a smaller metal circle in the center. She carried the item to the sink and filled the outer circle with water before placing it on the center of the table.

She then took out a couple of small glass vials and some herbs.

"Do you still have your grandmother's *molcajete*?" Dr. Jackie asked.

"Oh, yeah," Ricky said. "The stone salsa grinder, right?"

"Ricky," Ellie said. "It's used for more than grinding spices for salsa."

"The only thing I remember is that Grandma Bea used that thing for the awesome salsa she used to make."

Ricky opened one of the cabinets and it was still in its spot. No one had used it since Grandma Bea had died. He pulled down the black shaped stone bowl and the grinding stone inside it and handed it to the professor.

She took it and smashed some herbs together. Once they were finely ground and mixed, she took the two vials and poured some of the liquid inside them into the center of the stone pan she had placed on the table. She pushed the herbs from the *molcajete* into the liquid mix.

"What is that?" Ellie asked.

"The liquids are rose oil and a conjuring oil the shaman showed us how to make in Africa. The herbs are Silene Capensis, also known as the African Dream Herb, Devil's Claw, and Althaea leaves. Then there's also this."

The professor reached into the second bag and pulled out a metal flask with a cross on it and a sealed Ziplock of white powder.

"Holy water and salt."

She poured the holy water into the outer pool of sink water she had filled earlier. She then took the salt and threw a few pinches in the center with the oils and herbs and then poured out an almost complete circle around the main stone centerpiece, stopping and leaving a small two-inch gap before completing it.

The professor pulled out one more small red glass vial and a box of matches.

"Okay," she said. "Just about ready."

"What do we need to do?" Ricky asked.

"Just stand around the table and watch. This is just to detect if there is any kind of spirit and maybe what kind it is."

The door opened. It was Freddy. Ricky met him at the door.

"I wasn't sure if you'd come."

Freddy has a few bandages on his arms and elbows.

"Yeah, well Ellie said it was important."

"I'm sorry, Freddy. You know it wasn't me."

"I'll get over it." Freddy looked over at the table. "What's going on?"

"This is Professor Jackie. You remember her?"

"Yes, from the funeral."

"It's good to see you again, Freddy," the professor said.

Freddy nodded.

"Professor Jackie is about to check for any spirits in the house," Ricky said.

"Like she's going to call spirits out? Should have told me this first. I'm leaving."

"I am only going to check if any are present," the professor said. "If it turns out we find something, then I will gather others with more experience on what to do next. I wouldn't feel comfortable doing any more than that."

Freddy looked down at the spirit detecting cake pan and nodded.

"Okay, I'll stay."

"Then let's begin. Go ahead and turn off all the lights, but leave a lamp on in the living room so we aren't totally in the dark."

"Why do we have to do that?" Freddy asked.

"We need to concentrate on the flame."

Ricky flipped on one of the living room lamps and shut off all the rest of the downstairs lights before returning to the table. Ricky, Ellie, and Freddy stood on the opposite side of Dr. Jackie.

The professor opened the red vial and poured some of the liquid into the metal center. "This liquid is flammable and will contain the flame. Try not to lean in too close."

She picked up the matchbox and mouthed some words that they couldn't quite hear, then struck one match and eased it into the mix. A flame jumped from the liquid, burning softly. The room filled with a sweet but strong scent.

Professor Jackie pulled up her journal and moved to a page she had marked.

"I'm going to read an incantation to search for a spirit. It's a direct English translation from Swahili that the village Shaman taught us."

"Go ahead, Dr. Jackie," Ricky said.

Dr. Jackie took in a couple of deep breaths, then pulled the book up closer to her face.

"Spirits of the Earth, please help me welcome the spirits of the dead, the lost and the strong that are not of our living world, but walk among us. I ask that the spirits that are near our spiritual flame accept it as an invitation to our gathering. Please let us know that you are here and accept our humble invitation to seek your presence. May you take no offense and allow us to see that you are with us."

Dr. Jackie set the book down and pulled a small box from a satchel. She reached two fingers inside it and then gently tossed a red powder over the table. As it eased down into the flame, it reacted and sizzled and the red powder rose into a cloud and danced around the table.

"What are we looking for?" Ellie asked.

"Watch the red cloud and the flame for any change in color or behavior. The powder should turn blue or black if it finds anything."

The cloud continued to circle the room but didn't change its pattern. A door creaked.

"What are you doing?"

They turned back and Lori had emerged from her room. It was still dark and hard to see her, but she had an arm against the wall and her hair was down over her face.

"What are you doing? Jackie? Jackie, why are you here?"

"Mom, it's okay," Ricky said. "We're just trying an experiment."

Lori moved closer and in the light she was wearing a long pink nightshirt that had the Eiffel Tower and the word "Paris" underneath it.

"Look!" Ellie said.

The red cloud was spinning in a circle and drifted towards Lori. It spun around her head and then the flame in the center of the table brightened as the cloud of red powder turned a bright blue and crackled as it darkened to black and hovered over Lori's head.

Lori looked up and her eyes were completely dark.

"What is this?" she yelled.

"We are looking for spirits," Professor Jackie said. "Ricky told me what's been going on in the house and I'm trying to help."

Lori raised her head and opened her mouth. The now black cloud shot down her throat.

"We are here," Lori said, her voice lowering a few octaves. "We are stronger."

Lori fell on all fours and her back started to spasm. She grunted and then went still.

The flame made a popping noise and they turned to see the demon face Ricky had seen in the reflections staring back at them.

Freddy moved back toward the living room and reached for the front door. The three small half-moon windows that decorated the top of the door were each filled with the demon face.

Freddy screamed and fell on his back as he tried to step away. As they all turned to look, the shadow appeared in front of the door, only inches from Freddy's feet. Freddy's hands were shaking and his face was bathed in sweat.

"We are stronger," Lori said without moving.

The demon face in the reflection laughed as the shadow reached its hand toward Freddy.

"Get away from him!" Ricky yelled.

"Professor Jackie, what do we do?" Ellie said, feeling the back of her neck start to tingle.

The professor looked at her book and back at the shadow in front of her. She was shaking.

"Can you exorcise them?" Ellie asked.

"I wasn't prepared--"

"Professor Jackie," Ricky said. "You have to try."

The professor pulled up her book and flipped frantically through it.

She spoke in Swahili as she read through her notes. She was speaking fast and sweat trickled down her face as the shadow looked up and took notice of her for the first time.

The professor's voice rose to a higher pitch and she started speaking faster. The shadow stepped over Freddy.

"Your mother," the professor said. "I need to get to your mother."

She ran towards Lori, who was still on all fours, and placed her hand on her head and recited from the book again.

Lori grabbed the professor by the arm and tried to pull her down. Jackie screamed.

Ricky ran over and pulled Lori's hand down and held her. "Keep going, Professor."

Dr. Jackie was panting. "I don't know if I can. This isn't like before. I'm not sure if I can do this alone."

There was a loud thump as Freddy slid across the floor and his back smacked against the living room door and he rose up against it. He tried to scream but his lips were trembling and he could only let out stuttered breaths.

The shadow took another step and Ellie flew against the wall and rose halfway up, shrieking the entire time.

"Ricky!" Ellie yelled, her voice quivering. "Help us!"

"They're in trouble, Professor Jackie! Please try!"

The professor started reciting. The reflection demon went from laughing to grunts that sounded like pain.

"Keep going," Ricky yelled as his room door flew open. He looked over and a familiar blue glow was emanating from his room, but the skull didn't emerge.

Ricky focused on the flame. He raised a hand and gestured toward it. The flame threw out a thick, quick shot at the shadow but passed through it. The dark creature moved closer.

"I can't hurt it," Ricky said. "I tried before."

"Just concentrate on me," Dr. Jackie said. "Concentrate on helping me."

Ricky looked at her and then back to the shadow. He closed his eyes and put a hand on top of the professor's, pressing down gently on Lori's head. He felt an immediate surge.

"Ricky, repeat what I'm saying. It's in Swahili, so just try to listen to the sounds. *Imeanza Roho.* Begone spirit. *Umefukuzwa!*

You are banished! *Imeanza Roho.* Begone spirit. *Dunia inakuamuru!* The Earth commands you. You have to say the Swahili words. Just follow me, okay?"

Ricky nodded and listened as she repeated it. He absorbed each word in his head as she spoke them.

"Imeanza Roho. Umefukuzwa! Imeanza Roho. Dunia inakuamuru!"

"Imeanza Roho. Umefukuzwa! Imeanza Roho. Dunia inakuamuru!"

He repeated them aloud, in unison with Dr. Jackie.

"Imeanza Roho. Umefukuzwa! Imeanza Roho. Dunia inakuamuru!"

The shadow stopped, then took another step forward. Ricky felt something in his head pushing back on him. As they continued to repeat the words, their joined hands on Lori's head heated up and they both pulled away. The shadow took another step.

"Can't stop us," Lori said. "We are stronger."

Ricky felt more pushback, and without thinking, squeezed. The tension towards his hand and his body eased and in his head he pushed on the unseen force. The shadow stepped back.

"I don't know what you're doing, Ricky," Dr. Jackie said, "but I can feel energy through my hands. Keep it up."

"Imeanza Roho. Umefukuzwa! Imeanza Roho. Dunia inakuamuru!"

Ricky squeezed.

"Imeanza Roho. Umefukuzwa! Imeanza Roho. Dunia inakuamuru!"

"Harder," he mumbled to himself. "Squeeze harder."

"No. We are stronger!"

Ricky put both hands on top of his mother's head and tightened his entire body. The window to the front door shattered and the shadow groaned. Ricky felt a rush from Lori, and he and Dr. Jackie were thrown back. Ellie and Freddy fell to the floor from their dangling positions.

Lori shrieked as Ricky sucked in a deep breath, feeling like someone had punched him hard in the chest.

The flame on the table rose, then fell and faded. Lori's mouth opened and the black powder flew out of her mouth, turned into a red cloud and then dissipated. Ellie and Freddy eased their way towards them.

"Is it over?" Freddy asked.

Ricky touched Lori's face. "Mom?"

Lori had fallen flat on her stomach and looked up.

"Ricky? What happened?"

The professor stood up. "The flame's out and the powder left her. That's a good thing."

"Mom? Are you okay?"

Lori tried to stand up and Ricky helped her.

"I think so. I feel. I feel odd. Like something's been lifted. My head. It's been cloudy for as long as I can remember, but it feels clear."

"Mom, I think Professor Jackie might have helped remove whatever was inside you."

"It was you, too, Ricky. I don't understand what happened, but I felt you and Jackie pushing against something dark. It's gone now. It's just gone."

Ricky walked his mom toward the table as Freddy flipped all the lights back on.

"Everybody okay?" Dr. Jackie asked.

"My back's a little sore," Freddy said, "but I'm good."

"Ellie?" Ricky asked.

Her hair was damp with sweat. "I've never been more terrified in my life, but I'll be fine."

Her voice was still quivering as she glanced over at Lori. "More importantly, I think your mom's okay. Maybe this is finally over."

"I'm not ready to say that with a hundred percent certainty," Dr. Jackie said. "However, it's an improvement. We'll have to monitor how everything goes. Lori, I suggest you go to a doctor to get checked out."

Lori smiled at her. "Thank you for your concern, Jackie, but this is the best I've felt in as long as I can remember. If I feel bad, I'll go."

Dr. Jackie gathered her items and washed everything out in the sink.

"Where's Myra?" Lori asked. "I'd like to see her."

"She's with Karen. How about we let you rest and see if you're still good in the morning, okay?"

"You're right. I still feel dirty on the outside. I'll get cleaned up."

Ricky walked Lori to her room so she could shower and returned to Professor Jackie.

"Is it possible this is it?"

The professor shook her head. "I don't know, Ricky. Let's give it a little more time before we say that. Just watch her closely. See what's changed."

The skull.

Ricky ran towards his room. The skull was in the same spot on his desk. He picked it up, took a long look and then threw it down hard on the floor and it broke as expected. He stared at it and waited. He kicked the pieces gently after a few minutes.

Ellie walked in behind him and looked down and the broken skull. "What's happening?"

"Nothing. I don't think it's coming back together."

"So it's really gone?"

"Maybe it is. I guess we'll just have to wait and see."

Ellie put her hand on his shoulder. "And hope."

CHAPTER THIRTY-ONE

THE NEXT FEW DAYS WERE AN ADJUSTMENT PERIOD. LORI WAS keeping up with the house and cooking her children meals and invited Ellie and Freddy over for dinner each night. After a third consecutive dinner, Ellie, Freddy and Ricky retreated to his room.

The first thing Ellie noticed was the skull was still in pieces.

"Why haven't you picked that up?"

"I don't know. I can't bring myself to do it yet. I still keep thinking it might come back."

"At least your mom's back to normal," Freddy said.

"That's just it. Her normal was never this normal. She's almost a completely different person. I don't remember her ever being this engaged. Not even when I was little."

"It wasn't always that bad, Ricky," Ellie said. "Was it?"

"Not always, but even on her best days, she was never this... this nice. She could be kind for short bursts, but she was never this warm. It's just taking some getting used to."

"Myra's happy?"

"Yes, she is. I'm grateful for that."

"Then maybe you need to work on being happy, too," Ellie said. "Are you feeling any different now?"

Ricky shrugged. "I slept a little more the last couple of nights, but can't turn my thoughts off."

"I understand. There's nothing wrong with letting go and letting yourself off the hook."

"I know you're right, but it's hard for me to let my guard down."

"Then don't," Freddy said. "I get it. I think you should keep your guard up because it's always possible this could happen again."

"You're always the paranoid one, Freddy," Ellie said.

"That doesn't mean I'm wrong."

"I agree with him, Ellie. For Myra's sake, I have to stay alert."

"Okay, Ricky. I get it, but don't let this keep you from living. I mean, you don't want to be a shut in and home alone during Homecoming, right?"

Ricky smiled and Freddy looked confused.

Ellie got up and moved toward the skull debris. She hesitated, then reached over to lift one of the larger broken pieces. It had part of an eye on it.

"This skull. I've always thought of how we celebrate the Day of the Dead and how it's never been something I considered scary. Even after witnessing how this thing was unbreakable and its glowing eyes, it's still hard to believe."

She ran her fingers along its shape.

"Have you tried to move things again?"

"I hadn't until earlier today. I was kind of afraid to."

"And?"

"Nothing." He squeezed slightly. "I just tried again."

Freddy looked at the stack of books on Ricky's bed. One was open.

"Why do you still have these books?"

"We're still not exactly sure what the spirits or demons were. Professor Jackie is still looking, so Ellie and I decided to continue to learn as much as we can so this doesn't happen again."

Ellie lifted a book. "Maybe we should read some more. We're coming close to the end of what we've got. We can keep an ear out for Lori and Myra."

She picked up another book and looked at Freddy.

Freddy shook his head. "I'll take watching Myra and Lori duty. I'll check in and go sit with them while you both study. Don't make me read in summer. It's un-American."

"Maybe we can get these done tonight," Ellie said. "You game?"

Ricky nodded and they dove into the books for the next couple of hours. Freddy sat with Lori and Myra in short bursts, and each time he returned to the room, he had another snack.

Ricky read about more folklore and demons and spirits, but most of the stuff sounded similar. Tribes who had their individual superstitions, hauntings in larger areas, but nothing that resonated with what they had experienced. It was still hard to determine if this was a haunting connected to the house, a demon or spirit connected to his mom or him.

Freddy waved his palms in front of Ricky's face.

"What are you doing?"

"Just checking your eyes."

"My eyes?"

"They didn't look normal when you freaked last time and I don't just mean tired like you've looked for weeks. It was your face, too. Did you read anything about that?"

"Can you be more specific?" Ellie asked.

"I don't know. Darker, like a shadow covering his whole face. Like Lori's that night of the ritual, but not quite the same. It was empty, like when you see the computer animated human characters in a video game or a movie. They try to make them look realistic, but there's something that's still off about them."

"So how do I look now?" Ricky asked.

"Fine, I guess. Nothing like the other night. Maybe you're finally going to be normal for the first time in your life."

Ricky punched him gently across the arm. "You find anything new, Ellie?"

"I don't know. So hard to pin this down. I think what the professor said about knowing whatever this thing wanted is key. If we at least knew that, then we'd have something more to search for, but there is something I just read. There were two things. The shadow and whatever was in the reflection of the windows, right? Do we know if it was one spirit with many ways to terrorize you, or was it two distinct creatures? Everything I've read indicates it's almost always a single spirit every time, but you always saw two. Plus the little girl. There are notes on creatures that can appear as multiple beings. Maybe this one could just break itself in two or three things."

Ricky shook his head. "Even if there were multiple spirits or demons or whatever they are, what does that mean?"

"I don't know. Seems like it would be good to know whatever was inside your mom."

Ricky looked back at Freddy for a second.

Freddy was already smiling, "Yeah, that's the perfect mom burn setup. For once, I'm going to keep it to myself."

"Really?" Ellie said. "With all that's going on you both still thought of a mom joke? I swear we could be under a zombie attack and you would both find something stupid to say."

They both laughed. It had been the first time they'd had a normal laugh together since the ritual, but it didn't last.

Ellie's phone rang. "Mom?"

They heard her mother's frantic voice.

"I gotta go. Dad fell off the roof. He was trying to fix the stupid satellite. She thinks he broke his arm. We're taking him to the hospital. She's pulling out of the driveway now to come get me."

"Do you want us to go with you?"

"No, you need to stay here. Freddy, stay with him, please. Keep him reading and keep an eye on Myra."

"Let us know how he's doing, okay?" Ricky said.

"I will."

A car honked. Ellie rushed out, but before she did, she looked at Ricky and then back at Freddy and just shook her head. She rushed to Ricky and gave him a quick kiss on the lips.

"Homecoming," she whispered as she turned and ran out the door.

Freddy's mouth was open. "What just happened? You went from almost killing me a few days ago, to exorcising a demon, and now you're getting goodbye kisses? What the hell did I miss and when did you find time to get to wherever this is with her?"

"We talked a little before we met with Professor Jackie that day. We still need to talk more, but even with all this craziness, there might be some hope for us after all."

Freddy grabbed Ricky's hand and started sniffing it.

Ricky pulled back. "What the heck are you doing?"

"Just wondering if you finally smell better now that your finger's no longer stuck up your ass."

"Eat shit. You hungry? You keep coming back with snacks, but I just realized I haven't eaten anything for hours. I didn't even offer something to Ellie."

"You know I'm always up for food," Freddy said.

Ricky went to the kitchen and opened the refrigerator.

"Whatcha doing?" his mom asked from the couch.

"Looking for something to eat."

"We had pancakes for lunch. You want me to make you something?"

"It's okay."

"No, I want to."

Lori stood up and Myra continued watching the movie. She walked past Ricky and went into the pantry.

"Just something quick, Mom. Don't want you to take too much time."

He was having flashbacks of her last cooking session.

"I'll make you some BLT's. I've got avocado, too. How's that?"

One of his favorite quick sandwiches. "Sounds good, Mom."

She had the bacon on the frying pan and got the toast ready. Ricky stood and smiled, then felt an invisible punch in his chest.

"You think I forgot?" she whispered, putting her face into his.

Her entire expression had changed.

"I remember all that bullshit you told me, and now you want me to make you a sandwich?"

He caught his breath and only mumbled. "No. Please no."

"Don't change the subject. You know what you said and I think you want to say it again. You ruin everything."

"I'm sorry. I told you I was sorry. You said some pretty awful things about me and Myra, too."

Her nose was curled and her face was dark. "I don't regret a thing I said. It was all true."

Ricky closed his eyes and shook his head. He was seeing what wasn't there. Just like before. Things were better, and he just couldn't accept it.

"Maybe I should just kill you both right here, right now. It'll be like you both never existed and I can start fresh. Anything would be a better life than this."

Her whispers were getting louder.

He looked over at Myra.

"What are you looking at? I'm talking to you. You afraid that horrible little sister of yours will hear?"

"Mom, please."

She turned. "Myra, come here!"

Myra turned and ran up with a big smile on her face.

"What do you need, Mom?"

She looked at Ricky and then back at her.

"I need to move on. I need you and Ricky to get out of my life so I can be happy."

Ricky started to reply but then thought his mind was playing tricks on him again and he was hearing something different than Myra.

"Mommy?"

Ricky looked at his little sister's face. It went white.

"Myra, did you hear what I just heard her say?"

Myra looked at him and her eyes started to tear up. "Mommy, that's not funny. Why are you saying that?"

"Because it's true. I told your brother how much he disappointed me and how you're going to end up being the same way. Everything bad that's ever happened is both your faults. If you hadn't been born, I would be happy, living all over the world. Instead, I have to sit down and watch these stupid movies with a daughter I can't stand to be around. While we were sitting there, all I could think about was throwing your head through the TV."

Myra started crying full on now.

"Don't listen to her, Myra. She doesn't mean it. She's not herself."

He could feel the rage building inside him.

"Go to your room, Myra," Ricky said.

"No! You stay here. I AM your mother and you will listen to me. I'm not your damned grandmother who thought she knew everything. And this insignificant little bastard here does not get to tell you what to do."

"But Mom!"

Lori reached back and slapped Myra hard across the face. Myra fell on the floor and just stared at her as she started bawling.

She raised her hand again, but Ricky grabbed it before she could strike.

The door to Ricky's room flew open and Freddy ran out.

"What's happening?"

"Mind your business!" Lori yelled.

"Freddy, get Myra to her room now!"

Freddy hesitated a moment, then saw Myra crying on the floor. He moved towards her and she jumped up and ran to him. He rushed her to her room as Lori pulled her arm away from Ricky's grip. She tried to swing at him, but he caught her fist before it landed.

Ricky was in full rage mode. His face was turning deep red.

"You will never hit her again, do you understand? She's never done anything to you. She didn't deserve that and you don't deserve her, you fucking worthless excuse of a human."

She rushed at him, slamming his back into the marble counter. A corner grazed him and it hurt. He shoved her back and she moved against the refrigerator.

"Maybe today I'll send you and Myra into Hell with your whore grandmother," she hissed. "The world would be a better place."

Ricky threw his arms up and Lori floated up against the refrigerator door, like she was being pulled up with an invisible rope.

She growled like an animal and Ricky felt himself fly backward. He flipped over the island and Lori landed on her feet. She picked up the black pan that was still sizzling with bacon in it and ran at him. She swung at his head, but he ducked and the pan cut into the wall.

Ricky wrapped his hands around her and ran forward, taking her with him. She pounded on him with every step.

He gained some momentum then let her go. Lori flew back and slid into the hallway. He took three big steps towards her.

"Never! Never again! We're better off without you! I wish you were the one that was dead! Grandma Bea deserved to live. You're nothing. You're no one! I WISH IT HAD BEEN YOU!"

He threw his hands out and her body rose, smashing into the ceiling and then hovering mid-air. The door to Myra's room opened and Freddy appeared. He stood there trying to figure out what was happening when he saw Lori floating in the air.

"Ricky, stop!"

Ricky kept his gaze on his mom. He slammed her against the sides of the hallway, bouncing her back and forth, then pulled her toward him. She fell on the floor and slid on the floor to him like she was slipping down a mopped floor and stopped a few inches from his feet. The pan that had stuck in the wall came flying off. It was red and sizzling hot. It eased towards her face.

"This is what you wanted to hit me with? Trying to kill me? Let's see what happens when it's the other way around."

The pan spun. The bacon burned as it headed up, and he tossed his arms down. The pan flew straight for her face, but then flew across the house into the living room as Freddy tackled his best friend to stop him.

"Stop, Ricky! You're going to kill her!"

"I want to kill her! You know what she did to Myra?"

Lori picked up another pan from the sink and swung it at

Ricky's head, banging him on the temple. Freddy jumped, not expecting it.

Ricky fell to the side, his head spinning. He was dizzy and could barely focus, but he saw the dark swish of the pan coming back for a second shot and raised his arm to block it.

He yanked the pan out of her hand and swung back, hard, connecting with her forehead.

Lori fell in a slump. He pulled back to strike her again, but Freddy grabbed his arm.

"Stop, Ricky. She's not moving. Stop!"

His rage subsided and his mom came into focus. She was in a heap on the floor. She wasn't bleeding but looked like she was knocked out cold. He wanted to hit her again. Her chest heaved up and down. She was still breathing, but unconscious.

He got up on his knees and looked down at her. He raised the pan again, but Freddy pulled his arms down.

"Let me!" Ricky yelled.

"Stop, man. Just stop. She's down."

"Did you hear all the things she said?"

Freddy nodded. "Yes, I heard most of it once things got louder. Is that the kind of stuff you heard her tell you that day?"

Ricky nodded, gathering himself long enough to ease the pan down.

"I thought for sure I was the only one that heard what she was saying. At least until she hit Myra."

Ricky felt no relief. He still wanted to slam Lori's head with the pan.

"Think about Myra," Freddy said.

Ricky looked up. "I'm sure she heard everything and she's probably terrified. Make sure she's okay."

"I think you need to go talk to her."

"She got scared of both of us. I don't think she should see me like this."

Freddy looked at Ricky's face, which was facing down. "Your eyes, man."

Ricky didn't move.

"What do you see?"

"Your eyes are dark and shady all around. Like before. I can barely see the white part. You look like you have Halloween makeup around your eyes. Those things are back, aren't they? What happened?"

"Go talk to her."

"What about your mom?" Freddy asked.

"I don't care. Just make sure Myra's okay."

Freddy pulled back reluctantly, easing the pan out of Ricky's hands, which were still locked tight on the handle.

"Okay, I'll check on Myra, but just promise you'll stay calm for a few minutes and won't touch your mom. Promise?"

"As long as she stays down, I promise."

Ricky didn't react as Freddy took off and knocked on Myra's door.

"Myra, it's Freddy. Are you okay?"

He could hear her crying.

"What happened?" Myra said. "Is it safe to come out?"

"Yea, Myra. Your mom and Ricky stopped fighting. She's... sleeping in the living room and Ricky's calming down."

The door opened slowly. She grabbed Freddy and hugged him.

"Did you hear the ugly things she said to me and Ricky?" she asked as she continued to cry. "She never wanted me. She never wanted us."

"She's not herself, Myra. Something's wrong with her, but hopefully she'll be better soon. She didn't mean anything she said."

"Then why would she say it? How could a mommy say that to her own kids?"

"She didn't mean it. I swear she didn't."

Ricky was still standing over his mother, thinking of how he could smash her face in and never have to worry about her again.

Then his pocket vibrated. He tried to ignore it, but it didn't stop and vibrated a few more times.

He pulled out the phone and looked at the screen. It was a message from Corbin.

"Guess where I am and who I'm with, Pre-K? Just having a great time downtown with Ellie."

Couldn't be. Ellie was with her dad at the hospital. Or was she? Maybe she just said that to go see Corbin. Maybe everything had just been a show.

He shoved his phone back in his pocket and stood up.

Myra moved down the hall and saw Lori on the floor. Ricky was standing, staring into space. She took a few more steps and Freddy was right beside her, holding her hand.

"Ricky?"

Ricky looked at her but didn't reply.

"Is Mom okay?"

"I don't know. She's breathing, but I don't really care. I just want to make sure you're safe."

"Don't blame her," Myra said. "Freddy said she's not herself."

"No," Ricky said. "No one seems to be themselves lately. Or who they say they are."

He started walking towards his room.

"Where are you going?" Freddy yelled after him.

"Take care of her," Ricky asked. "Stay here or take her home with you. I have somewhere to be."

Freddy didn't know what to say.

Ricky went into his room and wasn't surprised to see the

sugar skull back on his desk, fully formed. Waiting. He squeezed. The skull rose and floated gently into his open palm. Ricky eased it into his backpack and zipped it up.

This is all I need, he thought to himself.

He walked out and Freddy and Myra were crouching by his mother, who had her head up and was mumbling.

She looked up at Ricky.

"Son, are you okay?"

"You're not my mother. The only mother I've ever known is dead."

"Please don't say that."

"Don't play stupid. You know what you said and did."

She looked back at Myra and Freddy, confused. "I don't know..."

"Save it," Ricky said. "Don't leave them alone, Freddy. Promise me. And if she tries to hurt Myra, do whatever you have to to get her somewhere safe. Okay?"

He nodded awkwardly.

Ricky started for the door.

"Where are you going?"

"To finish what I started with Corbin."

CHAPTER THIRTY-TWO

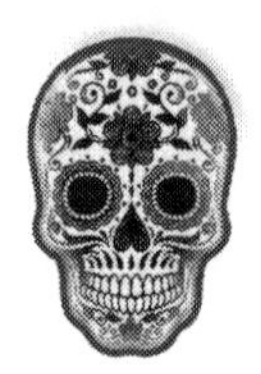

As Ricky walked out of the house, Lori tried to get up, making it on to her knees, but she was so dizzy that was as far as she got.

"Mom, it's okay," Myra said. "Don't try to stand up yet."

Lori turned back to Freddy.

"We need to stop him," she said.

"Why?"

"It's got him."

Freddy looked at her. "What do you mean?"

She tried to talk but started to hyperventilate. Freddy started to freak out, but then looked at Myra's eyes bulging. She was scared, so Freddy forced himself to calm down.

"Come on, let's get you to the couch."

He eased Lori's arm around his shoulder and raised her up. She was already bone thin and wasn't too hard to lift. Freddy led her to the living room and set her on the couch.

Myra came up with a beer, her mom's normal request.

Lori looked at her and shook her head. "No, baby. I don't want that right now. Can you just get me some water?"

Myra hesitated. She couldn't remember her mother ever

turning down a drink before. She rushed to make the exchange.

"Tell me everything you know," Freddy said. "It's important."

She took in a breath and then took a drink from the cup Myra had returned with.

"It had me. I think it was that night when Grandma Bea died. I was high, but something felt different. It was gradual, but I felt a change over the next few days and weeks, and I haven't felt much inside for a long time since then."

She handed the cup back to Myra, but her daughter flinched.

"Myra, my baby. I'm so sorry I hit you. Freddy was right. It wasn't really me. I'm not even sure what the real me is anymore. All this time, all these years before, that's who I was. I couldn't beat this crutch no matter how much I wanted to, but I want you to know it's because of you and Ricky that I even tried. I still couldn't defeat it, though. Not ever."

"Miss Luna, please," Freddy said. "For Ricky."

"I didn't sense much once it took over. My strongest desire was just needing another fix, you know? But then I started getting overcome with anger. Every little thing piled up. I kept seeing my life in Paris and traveling, but being pulled back by my kids. I can't entirely explain it, but it's like every old negative thought I ever had just kept shooting up to the surface. It was horrible, but that's what happened."

Myra nodded and grabbed her hand. "It's okay, Mom. Keep going."

She took another drink of water.

"It uses your worst thoughts against you. It got to the point where that's all I could think about. I felt so much resentment towards my children, especially Ricky. I'd see him with friends like you, Freddy, and taking care of Myra, so I figured he could just take care of her forever and I could just leave, but I couldn't do it. I kept bringing in these strange men and kept on drinking and taking whatever I could get them to buy me. When I was really gone, those feelings subsided. They never went away. I know Ricky and I had a horrible fight and I don't remember half of what I said to him, but I remember everything he said to me. I'd black out sometimes and then see how he was looking at me, but tonight--tonight I just wanted to kill him. Just like the other night. When I got close to it, though, it stopped me. It wanted me to get enraged, but not actually kill Ricky. It just wanted to break him down."

"Why, though?" Freddy asked. "Why Ricky?" Freddy asked. "The ritual? We thought everything was fine."

"It couldn't control me. My own demons. My need to stay drunk and..."

She looked at Myra. "I'm sorry, baby, but my need to get high. It dulled its control over me. So when I was coming down is when it would take advantage. That's when I'd feel like I was most lost, but I knew it was there."

"But why Ricky?"

"It knew if it could get into Ricky, it could take over. I would feel jealousy and guilt when I saw how Myra was with him and how much they loved their grandmother and looked at me like I was a pathetic burden. And I felt even worse because I knew it was true."

"No, Mom, that's not..."

"No, Myra. It was right. It knew what I was and amplified those negative feelings. I was a terrible daughter and made Grandma give up a job she loved and her life because of it. Because she loved you both. She loved you more than I ever could."

She started to tear up and Myra hugged her.

"It's hard to admit, but it's true. I couldn't give up my needs for either of you. I know I'm sick, but I had plenty of chances to choose you both before I crossed a line I couldn't come back from and I didn't."

"Miss Luna, please continue."

"I was jealous of you, too, Freddy. That you had each other to lean on with your parent's divorce and Ricky having to deal with me. He had a best friend who knew what he was going through, and you hardly left his side. I know you were scared. I could feel your fear growing and I know you're scared now, but you're here. I felt worse for that. And then there's Ellie."

"What about her?"

"They love each other. I sensed that more than anything. And it hated that. It made me hate it. That love is strong and a type of bond that this thing fears, because it's a bond it can't break. That was a jealous, angry rage and I envied that, but then it made me feel worse that we couldn't have the kind of love a mother and child should have. Instead Ricky felt it for his grandmother, and for his friends like you and Ellie, but his love for Myra was strongest."

"Then why is he so mean to me, sometimes?" Myra asked.

Lori smiled. "He's still a big brother. But you know he never meant any of that and was always laughing when he messed with you."

She smiled back.

"So are you saying it's gone now? What about the night of the ritual? Was that all fake?" Freddy asked.

"What was in me, it's stronger than you think. The ceremony weakened it a little, but it decided to play dead for a few days so everyone, especially Ricky, would think it was over. It buried deep inside me and let its grip go. I've only had a few beers the last couple of days and I'm out of my normal drug supply. I had someone coming later tonight to give me some, but I was about as clean as I could be. I was fine here with you and Myra, but in the last few hours, I started loathing every scene in the movie we were watching. I wanted the dragon to burn that Princess before she could be rescued. My Disney movie was way different than the real one. But when Ricky walked in, I was gone. I lost my senses and just wanted to attack him. He looked vulnerable."

"Ricky was afraid this was only temporary," Freddy said. "But I could tell he wanted so badly to believe everything was fine."

"That's how it played him. It had already been trying to get to him, like an infection. It couldn't completely leave me until Ricky was vulnerable, but it couldn't escape me either. It had to build over time with Ricky and test him when it could, but today was the day. Ricky was vulnerable, I was sober, and it didn't take much to get him angry again. That fight broke us both open and this thing took advantage. Ricky was dark and his soul was the angriest it had ever been, plus I wasn't holding it back. It needed one big push and that fight did it. These last few days of letting me heal gave it the doorway out. Ricky wanted to kill me, but it was the parts of whatever was inside me that drove that. It makes you see and hear things that aren't there when it's at its most potent."

"So what do you think's going to happen now?"

"Whoever Corbin is, Ricky is super jealous of him. It's what's inside him now. Ellie doesn't have any feelings for that boy, but Ellie is just too nice to tell him to leave."

"Yeah, that sounds like Ellie," Freddy said.

"That rage he felt when we almost killed each other. It broke him. I didn't know it until I came to just now, but I don't feel anything dark inside me anymore. I think it took my craving away, too. I feel like my soul was pulled out, run through a car wash and put back in. Even the air smells different."

"Do you think he's in danger?"

"Yes, but I think he's more dangerous to others than to

himself. You need to find him before he does something. He's stronger than I am, but this spirit or demon or whatever it is that has him is even stronger. I don't know if Ricky has a way to stop himself if he's pushed too hard."

Freddy grabbed his phone and dialed.

Ellie answered on the second ring.

"Ellie, something's happened. How is your dad?"

"He's better," she said. "Minor fracture. What's going on?"

"It's Ricky. His mom was being possessed by something, but it got out. She's fine now, but now we think it's inside Ricky and he just left here. He took the skull and he said he had unfinished business with Corbin. Whatever it is, we think it's fully taken him now."

"Did you find out any more about it? Did you talk to her?"

"Yes, that's why I'm calling. She said it kept making her feel jealous, but mostly guilty. Guilt with everyone and everything around her, and now it's doing the same thing to Ricky."

Ellie muted the phone for a few seconds.

"I just talked to my mom. I'll come get you. Try to find out where Corbin is."

"How do I do that?"

"Check social media. He posts more than my cheerleader friends."

"Okay, I'll check. Ellie, I'm worried."

"So am I. I'm going to call Professor Jackie and tell her what we know."

"Okay, hurry."

Freddy jumped online to check what might be going on. He looked for Corbin's name and saw a few posts. He also had a bunch of text messages on his phone he hadn't had time to read with everything going on, but some of the neighborhood guys were getting together at Miss Pepperoni's. He scanned through the numbers. There were two he didn't recognize, but one had a different area code. He did a quick search and found it was a California number. He figured that had to be Corbin.

He started dialing.

"Hello, Mom? Can you come over to Ricky's house? I need you to watch Myra and Miss Luna."

"Freddy, I can watch Myra!" Lori protested. "It's okay."

He covered the phone speaker.

"I'm sorry, Miss Luna, I believe you might be fine, but I told Ricky I would watch over you and can't leave you alone with Myra. There's no way I can tell if you're 100% cured. I mean, you just tried to kill your son less than ten minutes ago. I'm really sorry."

She looked down and nodded. "No, you're right."

Freddy got back on the phone. "Mom, can you hurry? I'll tell you what I can, but Myra and Miss Luna can fill in the rest."

He hung up and returned to the couch, still scanning for more information. He texted some of the guys to see if Corbin might be there and then sat and fidgeted, waiting for Ellie to arrive.

Freddy knew Ricky was in serious danger. Maybe they all were.

CHAPTER THIRTY-THREE

THE MOMENT RICKY SLAMMED THE FRONT DOOR BEHIND HIM, HIS mind started racing.

Ellie. You lied to me about that phone call. You used your Dad. How could you?

He didn't want to believe she was with Corbin, but deep inside, he felt it was true. It was eating away at his mind and he felt empty in his chest.

He pictured Ellie and Corbin downtown at Miss Pepperoni's Pizza House, eating and sharing a drink, talking about him. Ellie was saying how she felt sorry for him because his Grandma Bea had died, and how she had to make an excuse about her Dad getting hurt just to get away since Ricky was having a mental breakdown and she couldn't take it anymore.

He could smell the pizza and Ellie's perfume.

You're telling him about how you lured me with Homecoming. You're laughing at me, aren't you? You both are.

Ricky got in the truck and headed downtown. He ran a few stop signs without even realizing it.

He was tired of this new guy.

Everything would have been fine if you had never shown up, Corbin.

He reached downtown within minutes. The parking spots were almost all filled on both sides of the street, but someone pulled out near Miss Pepperoni's and he was able to take it. He was near the same spot where he walked from the bus that night.

You'll never embarrass me again. Never again. I am stronger. We are stronger.

It was time for Cali-boy's reckoning.

CHAPTER THIRTY-FOUR

RICKY SAT IN HIS TRUCK AS IT GOT DARKER OUTSIDE AND THE streetlights came to life.

It was a busy Saturday and although most of the older downtown businesses would close by seven, Miss Pepperoni's Pizza House, the two clothing stores and the candy store would still be open late. The two bars that were a block over would be open even later.

Ricky was staring at the window to Miss Pepperoni's Pizza House, still imagining Corbin inside with Ellie.

He picked up the small backpack with the skull in it. He unzipped it and held the *calavera* in his hand. The eyes were already glowing.

He looked up and saw a family walk by. A toddler was carrying an ice cream bar and dropped it. She reached down to pick it up, and Ricky tilted his head. The bar stopped and floated in the air for a brief second, and she picked it up without noticing. She was just happy she got her ice cream back and Ricky was satisfied that he finally found success controlling something outside of his house.

He looked back at the skull. This is what was missing. It's what he needed all along.

He opened the truck door, strapped the backpack on, and walked into the Pizza House. The cash registers were up front and there was a large dining area in the back, along with an adjoining game room with an arcade, pool tables and foosball tables to the left. He walked in and saw a few of his friends in the back shuffling around. The place was full of families. There was a birthday party of about thirty people in the back right corner of the dining area, taking up three tables decorated with balloons. The birthday girl looked like she was about seven or eight. She had an enormous smile on her face as the rest of the party sang "Happy Birthday." Ricky looked around and didn't see anything that interested him. One of his friends popped out from the arcade, saw Ricky and waved. Ricky just stared at him and then moved towards the game room. There was a smaller dining area there with only four booths and two smaller tables. Ricky stuck his head in and found them. Corbin was sitting in a booth with a slice of pizza in his mouth and his free hand on the table. His hand connected to another one. A hand he recognized immediately. Sitting there, smiling at Corbin as he devoured his pepperoni slice, was Ellie. She didn't notice Ricky or seem to notice anything around her. She looked blissful. It was the way she had looked at him on the Ferris wheel. The same way she had looked at him just earlier today, when she had lied to his face.

He pictured her father at home watching TV, his arm perfectly fine, while Ellie was here because she couldn't take being around her pathetic, crazy friend any more.

He walked to their table and Corbin nodded at him.

"Hey, bro!" Corbin said. "What's up?"

He looked at Ellie. "What's up is that you're here with my girl. And we have unfinished business."

Corbin put his slice down and looked at him. "What are you talking about? You like this girl, too?"

He pointed at Ellie, who was looking back at Ricky strangely.

"Man, Ellie already made it clear she had no interest. I'm moving on."

Ricky looked back at him. "You're sitting here with her and trying to tell me you moved on?"

Corbin looked at him and back to Ellie. A few of the guys heard them getting loud and came up to the table.

Joey was up first and slapped Ricky on the shoulder.

"What's going on guys? Glad you made it, Ricky. You never replied to our messages earlier."

Ricky stared back at him.

"I'm not sure," Corbin said. "He seems to think I'm with Ellie even though I'm sitting here with Janie."

"Jamie," the girl mumbled.

Ricky looked back at him. Jamie was sitting there, still looking at him with a confused look on her face.

"She was just here," Ricky said. "Where did she go?"

"I haven't seen Ellie since we've been here," Joey said. "Ricky, you okay?"

"I guess she doesn't want Pre-K either and he's losing it," Corbin said.

Joey smiled, but that's not what Ricky saw.

He saw Joey bent over and laughing so hard he could barely breathe. The rest of the neighborhood friends, some he'd known his entire life, walked over from the arcade area and started laughing, too.

"Pre-K!"

They were pointing at him.

Corbin smiled and was eating it up.

"I think you need to get some sleep, Pre-K."

Ricky pushed Joey away from him and grabbed Corbin by

the shirt.

"I said you and I have some unfinished business."

"Oh, you want me to kick your ass again?"

The guys "Ooohed" a few times.

"Calm down, Ricky," Joey said. "Seriously, are you okay? You don't look so hot."

"I'll be okay when I get rid of this California pussy."

Then it got quiet. A dad's voice from another table said, "Hey, watch the language."

Ricky didn't bother to reply.

Corbin looked at him. "All right, Pre-K. Let's take it outside."

Ricky started heading out before anyone could move.

Joey stepped in front of him. "What are you doing, Ricky? Calm down. I got here before Corbin did. Ellie hasn't been here."

Ricky turned to him with his eyes blazing with rage. "If you keep defending him, you're next."

Joey stepped back and felt a twinge of fear. Ricky's eyes weren't all there. They seemed to be completely black.

Maybe he got a hold of his mom's stash, Joey thought to himself. He felt pity for his friend.

Ricky walked out of Miss Pepperoni's Pizza House, followed by Corbin and about ten of the neighborhood boys. A few others had seen the situation and followed out just in case there was a fight.

Corbin stopped on the sidewalk, wearing his Angels cap and a black t-shirt and jeans. Ricky turned around. They were standing on the sidewalk. Traffic was low, with an occasional car or truck passing by.

"So, are you going to do anything Pre-K? You were trying to sound all big shit and brave in there, but are you gonna back that up?"

The door to Miss P's opened and Jamie walked out, but it

was Ellie that Ricky saw as she stood against the entrance window.

"Just kick his ass once and for all, Corbin. He deserves it, as pathetic as he is. I waited for years for him to make a move and he wasn't man enough to even try."

Corbin didn't react or turn back. Ricky felt his hands clench and his body shaking.

"You going to puke like a scared little bitch, Ricky? You look like you might cry."

Ricky didn't cry. Instead, he let loose.

He threw his arms back and thrust them forward. Corbin jolted backward and hit the front door handle of Miss Pepperoni's. He fell down and grimaced, reaching for his back as the pain shot up.

"What the hell? How did you do that?"

"I'm just fast," Ricky said. "Faster than you can see."

Corbin rushed and tackled him to the ground. They went back between two parked cars and fell into the street. A car was passing by and had to swerve not to run into them.

"Get out of the road!" the driver yelled.

The crowd got bigger and moved into the street as Ricky got to his feet, standing about ten feet from Corbin.

Corbin rushed up and threw a punch. He hit Ricky across the jaw, but Ricky never felt it. His head turned, but the rage took over any feeling of pain he might have had. Ricky's right hand came up and landed, even though he was still nowhere near enough for contact. Corbin fell, looking like he was a stunt man filming a fight where the punch missed him by inches. In this case, it was more like three feet.

Corbin stood up. The crowd was quiet as Joey said, "Is he faking it? Ricky never even touched him."

Corbin ran at Ricky, who lifted his hands, causing Corbin's feet to go out from under him and he skidded on his rear against the street. Ricky kept his hands up, then turned his head to the side and Corbin's sliding path shifted and he slammed into a parked car.

Corbin got up quickly, but Ricky squeezed his fists together. Corbin's baseball cap flew off and his hair stood up. He reached up and tried to grab the Angels cap, but it was floating over his head, just out of his reach.

Someone in the growing crowd screamed, "How is he doing that?"

As Corbin felt his hair standing up, Ricky pulled his arms towards himself and Corbin slid across the street gravel until he was a foot in front of Ricky.

Ricky cocked his arm back and low and hit him with a single uppercut and then followed up with a punch straight to the nose. Corbin flew back as blood splattered off of Ricky's fist, sliding right into his motorcycle.

Corbin used the motorcycle to keep his balance and remain standing. He reached into the side bag and pulled out his gun.

He straightened up and held it to his side.

"I don't know how you're doing this," Corbin said as he spat out blood and wiped his now broken nose with his sleeve, "but no more."

The crowd moved back as Corbin raised the gun and pointed it at Ricky.

A car flew into the middle of the street. It was Ellie. Freddy was with her, and they jumped out of the vehicle.

"Ricky, stop!" Ellie screamed.

Ricky didn't turn. He was looking at the gun Corbin had pointed towards him.

"Corbin, get back! Put the gun down!"

Corbin was breathing hard and still spitting blood. He took a slow step forward with the gun still pointed.

"You can't stop this, can you? Get on your knees!"

Ricky didn't move.

Ellie ran towards them. "Stop, Corbin! You don't know what he's capable of! Please stop!"

"You're not so brave now, are you? Whatever the hell you're doing won't beat a bullet, will it, Pre-K?"

Corbin raised his arms higher and his hand was shaking.

Ricky never flinched. He stared right at him.

"Shoot me, then, Mr. California Tough Guy. I'd rather take a bullet than hear your whiny Cali mouth say another word."

Corbin was shaking, but his face was serious.

"NO!" Ellie screamed as Corbin pulled the trigger.

No one breathed the next half second. Ricky hands were still out and the bullet stopped in mid-air, two inches from the center of Ricky's forehead. Some of the crowd ran, but others stood there in disbelief.

The bullet fell straight to the ground and landed between Ricky's feet.

Ellie jumped in front of Corbin.

"Ricky, don't!"

He looked at her face. Fear. He could sense it. He could almost smell it.

"He just tried to shoot me and you're defending him? Even after lying to me and being in there with him?"

"What?" she said. "You saw me just get here with Freddy. I wasn't with him."

Freddy ran up. "Ricky, she's right. We just got here. Come on, man. You need to stop."

"He just tried to kill me," Ricky said in a lower, grumbling voice.

"Come on, Ricky. You drove here on purpose to fight him. Tell me you didn't want to kill him first," Freddy said.

"He has a gun. I wasn't trying to kill him. I just wanted vengeance. He tried to kill me. I'm just defending myself now."

He raised his hands and squeezed a few times.

"Please, Ricky," Ellie said. "Whatever you think he did. Whatever you think I did, it's in your head! Your mom is better. She says this thing that was inside her, the shadow we saw, it's in you now. It makes you see things that aren't there. Please stop!"

"Did I imagine he just tried to shoot me?"

Corbin pushed Ellie aside and she fell.

"No, and you're not imagining this, either."

His hands weren't shaking as he pulled the trigger twice.

Ricky reached out and stopped the first bullet and caught it in his palm, but wasn't expecting the second one. He felt a slight sting of pain on his arm. The bullet grazed him. As he checked the wound, there was a groan from behind.

He turned. Freddy was on the ground, holding his side.

"Freddy?" Ricky said, his voice returning to normal.

Freddy took a second to catch his breath. "I... I think I'm okay. Man, this hurts."

He got up to his knees, still holding his side as blood dripped to the street.

Ricky turned back and Ellie was on the ground where Corbin had pushed her.

Ricky's face was red and the veins in his neck were throbbing. Some of the people in the crowd were close enough to see his eyes turn completely black.

Ricky shot out his hands and Corbin flew straight up in the air almost twenty feet. Ricky arced his arms like he was spiking a football and Corbin came crashing down on his motorcycle and it crumpled like an aluminum can as he slammed into it. Corbin didn't move. One end of the flattened handlebars was sticking through the center of his torso.

The crowd scattered and people screamed.

Ellie moved towards him.

"Oh, my God! Ricky, what did you do?"

"He just shot Freddy and tried to shoot me and you're still

worried about him?"

Ellie saw Corbin's pale face and knew he was dead.

"You killed him!"

"He was going to kill me! And what about Freddy? He's bleeding out over here and you don't even care about him, either? Is that how much he meant to you?"

A truck pulled up and braked hard between Ricky and Ellie.

Professor Jackie rushed out of the truck with one of her leather satchels.

"Ricky, you need to stop."

"Go away."

"Ricky," Ellie cried. "I called her. Listen to her. She can help you!"

Dr. Jackie pulled a jar out of her satchel, placed it on the hood of her truck and pulled out more items and set them next to the jar.

"There's something evil in you, Ricky. Something strong. The spirits we saw, they have to be demons of some kind. I think the shadow demon is what possessed Lori and now you and it's what's feeding on your negative energy. Guilt and jealousy, whatever it can use. I'm sorry that what we tried didn't work, but I wasn't prepared before. I think I know how to get it out, but I need you to take a breath and control yourself for just a few minutes to let me try this."

Ricky looked at her and smiled menacingly. "I don't think so. The dark spirit. The shadow demon. It's right here. I can feel it in my throat."

"Ricky, you got to fight with all that you can, young man. I know you're stronger than this."

A voice filled Ricky's head.

We are stronger.

The professor's truck flew back as Ricky turned. He was staring at Ellie, still tending to Corbin's body.

"He killed him, Professor Jackie," Ellie said, crying. "It was self-defense. Corbin had a gun and shot Freddy, but Ricky killed him. Please don't let him kill anyone else."

The sound of sirens approaching filled the air.

"Look, Ricky," Professor Jackie said. "The police are coming. If it was self-defense, you'll be fine. Just please stop before things get worse."

"He shot Freddy," Ricky said. "It's my fault."

Freddy was still on his knees. "I'm okay, Ricky. Really. I'm okay."

A few of the neighborhood boys led by Joey went by to check on Freddy. Most of the crowd had moved further away, but were still fascinated and scared and couldn't bring themselves to leave. Some had their cell phones out. Even the family with the toddler and the ice cream was standing halfway down the block. More people from the adjoining stores had come out or were staring from the windows.

"There's a lot of people out here that could get hurt, Ricky," the professor said. "Just give me a few minutes. Do it for Ellie. For your grandmother. Please."

The professor opened the jar that was filled with herbs and plants. She poured some liquid in it and it started smoking. The smoke turned green and had a potent odor.

Ricky ignored her and stared back at Ellie. He saw Corbin sitting up and Ellie was kissing him on the mouth.

"Lying to me again?" Ricky screamed. "You said he was dead and now you're kissing him?"

Ellie looked up at him. "What are you talking about? He's DEAD, Ricky! You're seeing things that aren't there! Just like with your mom and her food. How do you not know that!"

Now Ricky was the one shaking. The heat rose to his face and then he started choking. He looked back at the music store windows behind him. The image of the window creature he had seen on the bus and stores had returned. Its reflection looked straight at him and it looked panicked. The image moved quickly, then stopped and pointed.

Ricky turned to see what its bony, fleshy finger was pointing towards.

It was Professor Jackie.

The smoke from her jar was rising near Ricky's face and easing down his throat, making him choke even more. He could feel the demon inside him trying to fight back. Ricky felt it and everything cleared in his head for a second. He saw Corbin dead and knew whatever he thought he had seen with Ellie and Corbin tonight was a lie. He had killed Corbin in self-defense, but he had instigated this. If he hurt anyone else, it wouldn't be self-defense anymore. He would just be a murderer. He needed to get this thing out of him. It wanted him to kill. To kill everything and everyone around him.

He gasped for breath. He couldn't breathe. He felt himself rise over the street. It was fighting back. It wanted to kill the professor. He had to stop it. Ricky fought with everything he had. The reflection demon then shrieked so loud the window it was on cracked.

We are stronger!

The jar shook. Dr. Jackie's concoction was working, and the demon had to stop it. The crack on the music store glass spread across to an adjacent store window and grew bigger with every second.

The jar. Destroy the jar. We are stronger.

The jar cracked in half. Professor Jackie tried to hold it back together, but the jar was so hot it scalded her hands as she tried to keep the smoke going.

The stuff that was burning blew away like a flaming tumbleweed and dissipated into the air.

Ricky was losing all control. He wanted to attack Professor Jackie, but the need to look back at Ellie was too strong.

He looked at her. She was straddling Corbin now, kissing him hard. Corbin raised his head, looking at him upside down from his back.

"I told you she wanted me. She never wanted a little pre-K prick like you."

Ricky yelled and felt a distant grip around both of them. Ellie was up on her feet.

"Ricky, what are you doing?" Ellie yelled.

"I can't stop," Ricky yelled. "I still picture you with him. I know it's not real, but my head won't let it go!"

"Ricky, please!"

She walked towards him, feeling an invisible grip holding her arms against her torso.

"You're hurting me!"

"I'm sorry, Ellie. It's not me. I'm trying. I can't stop!"

His breathing was rapid.

"Fight it, Ricky," the professor screamed. "You have to fight!"

He was squeezing his face as tightly as he could and shaking his head from side to side to try and will it away. He couldn't hurt Ellie. He had to stop, but felt the thirst for vengeance. A need to rip her apart.

"Ricky," Ellie said, tears falling now. "It's always been you and me. It's always been us, and after all this time, we're almost there. We belong together. You know it and so do I. We have time to build something. Please, you need to let me go!"

Ricky was struggling as hard as he could, but he was weak.

We are stronger!

His mind raced with his mother's words, telling him how she wished he never existed. How he and Myra would have been better off as abortions so she could have enjoyed her life. He knew somewhere it wasn't true. He saw Ellie with Corbin, kissing him. She was kissing him! How could she do that?

After the Ferris wheel. After their time at the house. After the kiss. That kiss... was all a lie. Homecoming was a lie. She had played him. All for Corbin. His mom didn't want him. Ellie didn't want him. No, that wasn't all true. Something wasn't true...

His hands squeezed harder and Ellie squealed in pain.

"You're hurting me, Ricky, you're hurting me!"

"You hurt me. You lied to me. I thought we had something."

"Ricky, this isn't you, please fight. Fight for me. Fight for us."

He let her go for a moment and she stood there on her own free will.

"Don't hurt her," Freddy said from behind him. "I know you're not doing this but you can stop it. Whatever you're seeing, it isn't real."

Ricky looked back at Freddy as he rose a foot in the air and floated. The crowd was gasping and screaming even more.

"Stop me, Freddy. Whatever you have to do. Kill me if you have to. Stop..."

He turned back to Ellie. Just as he started to lose himself, something struck him from behind.

Freddy. Freddy coming through.

Ricky's body flipped completely around in mid-air.

Freddy was wobbling, barely able to stand, but he had hit Ricky across the back as hard as he could.

"Freddy. Don't stop. No matter what."

Freddy raised his good arm and threw another blow on his floating friend. His fist landed on Ricky's stomach since he couldn't reach his face.

Ricky pictured Freddy being ripped in half, but fought. He kept fighting. "No, no, no. Not Freddy."

Ricky's body jerked forward and his knee smacked

Freddy across the temple. Freddy spun into a backflip and landed on his head. He groaned as he tried to get up, but was too dizzy.

"You can't make me," Ricky said. "You can't have Freddy and you can't have Ellie."

The effort to fight back had drained him. His body twisted back to face the girl he loved.

Ellie was looking at him with tears in her eyes.

"I love you, Ricky. I always have and I always will, no matter what happens."

His chest felt empty. His heart was beating so hard he felt it in his throat. He loved her. He knew that without question. Even if he never spoke to her again, he would love her until his last day.

"If it means saving her, today will be my last day," he whispered to the demon inside him.

He felt the darkness dim briefly, then it surged. The shadow demon stood before him and the reflection in the window had returned, appearing in all the windows on the block surrounding him. The shadow stared at him with red eyes, and all the reflections in the windows screamed.

Ricky's hands went up without him thinking. He fought. He fought as hard as he could. He loved her. He filled his head with one single thought.

I love her.

He felt the demon subside and he escaped the grip again.

"Ellie, I love you. More than you'll ever know, but I'm not sure if I can fight anymore. I just need you to know that."

Ellie was crying. "I know, Ricky. I've always known. You can do this. For us."

"I'll give my life for yours. It's the only way."

The screeching demon in the windows laughed. A deep bellow that echoed with each reflection. The shadow that still stood before him spoke.

"You truly believe you have a say in your life? You are ours."

"No. My love is stronger."

The shadow disappeared and Ricky felt something fill his insides.

No. We are stronger.

Ricky closed his mind and was thinking only of Ellie's love when her heart exploded.

It rushed out of her chest with a wet pop, splattering all over him. It seemed to happen in slow motion as he saw every detail of her face turn from fear and love to shock, her eyes bulging as her chest split open.

He fell to the ground as the shadow demon let go.

"Ellie!" he screamed. "No! Ellie!"

Three police cars arrived as Ellie fell face first to the ground. People were screaming and running away.

"Step away from her!" an officer yelled as he opened his door and drew his gun.

"No, no NO!"

That's when Ricky lost his entire sense of reality.

He raised his arms and they flailed in all directions.

Many of his neighborhood friends hadn't left. They were still standing around, some helping Freddy and others just watching. They had been yelling for him to stop, but Ricky never heard them. As the bulbs of the streetlights exploded, the bodies of his lifelong friends moved in unison to the left and then to the right, as if an invisible puppet master was throwing them around. One boy ran into the light pole head first and was dead before he hit the ground.

Other boys slammed into parked car windows. Ricky turned to the crowd that was fleeing the street and the stores and heard more gunshots as the police opened fire. There were at least ten shots fired, but not one bullet hit him. He just thought of the bullets and they flipped around, going straight back and striking several officers. Their vests took the brunt of every bullet but one, which pierced the temple of a seven-year veteran.

Ricky stood up and crept to the rest of the crowd. One of the police officers was in his cruiser calling for backup when Ricky lifted the vehicle into the air and shot it towards a large gathering of frightened spectators, killing the policeman and two crowd members on impact. The cruiser hit a light pole that fell and then whipped forward like a javelin, the broken metal piercing through several bodies like a shish kebab, skewering three of them together as the pole struck even more victims.

Ricky was in a rage. He couldn't stop.

Two fire hydrants on the block burst open and the water that screamed out was steaming hot as it tore into the crowd.

"Ricky," Freddy screamed. "Stop, Ricky, Stop!"

He turned back to Freddy and the two friends that had been tending to him.

Freddy was still holding his side but trying to get to him.

"Ricky, please," he said. "These people are your friends. Stop!"

Ricky held his gaze. He split his hands and Joey and the other boy went flying. He and Freddy were alone in the street as more sirens wailed in the distance.

The mirror demon was there in the windows, smiling and laughing.

Freddy turned.

"Can you see them?" Ricky asked.

"I see something. Is that what you see? Is that the demon?"

"No, I am here," Ricky said in a voice that wasn't his, pointing to his chest. "And your friend has granted me more than I could have ever desired. His guilt is overwhelming. We knew he would be worth the effort. That he would be worth our patience."

"Leave him alone!"

Ricky floated up.

"Do you still seek his salvation? You think he wishes to be saved, after everything he has done? He would rather die than face the truth."

"Freddy!" a voice yelled.

Professor Jackie was protecting herself between two cars. "What do you see?"

"The windows. A demon looking thing. Ricky described it before."

The professor tried to process it.

Ricky looked in her direction and Professor Jackie grabbed at her throat. Ricky smiled.

Freddy struggled to get to him and grabbed his arm.

"Don't hurt her, Ricky!"

Ricky knocked him aside.

As Ricky turned back to him, the professor let out a big breath.

"Break the windows, Freddy! Break them all!" the professor yelled.

Freddy heard her, but was still transfixed on Ricky.

"Kill her," is what Freddy heard Ricky say next.

Ricky smirked as he returned to Professor Jackie, who reached for her throat again.

A car came screeching towards them. It was Freddy's mom's car. The doors opened and Lori and Myra came running out. When Lori saw her son floating in the air, looking crazed, she stopped and pulled Myra back. Myra shook herself loose and ran towards her big brother.

"Ricky," Myra yelled, fighting back tears. "Please, Ricky. Stop."

She looked around and saw Ellie's body and Freddy on the ground.

"Please, Ricky. Mom said the evil that was inside her

wanted you because you were stronger than she was. Be strong, Ricky."

Ricky looked at his sister and his black eyes diminished a little.

Freddy took advantage of the distraction and picked up a shattered piece of the streetlight and hurled it at the nearest window.

It shattered and Ricky fell to the ground on one knee. The professor didn't hesitate and ran. She lifted a piece of the crushed motorcycle and shattered the window near her.

"Freddy," Ricky's voice said. "Keep going. It's helping. Trying to get free, but I deserve to die. Ellie. I let it kill her. I killed her."

"No!" Myra yelled. "Don't give up. I need you, Ricky! Please keep fighting."

Freddy picked up some loose car parts from the damaged vehicles and hurled heavy pieces at another window. It bounced back. They both saw the demon in the windows with its palms against its reflection. It was expecting it. It appeared in the remaining windows on both sides of the block, and it was smiling.

Ricky felt like he was drowning, gasping for air. He took in quick breaths, then felt himself being taken over as he started to rise in the air again.

He felt a burning sensation on his back. It was coming from his backpack. He let if fall and tossed it to his side. A blue glow was permeating from it.

He reached down, still fighting.

"Ricky, be strong! Be strong for me!" Myra screamed.

The mirror image was smiling and laughing.

Ricky looked at Myra. She was crying. She was scared. Scared of him.

We are stronger.

"Please, Ricky," Myra said, barely able to get the words out as her sobs grew deeper.

He wanted to turn around and stop Freddy, but he couldn't turn away from Myra. Myra. His hands raised and covered his face as he continued to float as he fought back.

For Myra. I will be stronger.

Ricky reached in and pulled out the sugar skull as his hands shook. Its eye sockets were filled with the blue glow and were the brightest he had ever seen them.

Throw it, a familiar voice echoed in his mind.

He fought with the demon inside him as he raised the skull.

He couldn't breathe anymore. He arched his arm back, but it fell before he could move it across.

The skull, still fully intact, spoke to him.

"Throw it. Now!"

I am stronger.

Ricky fired the skull across the street and into one of the store windows. The skull hit the window and every glass along the block on both sides of the street shattered at the same time. The windows were all gone.

Ricky gasped as he fell to the ground, landing on his feet. He was still choking but could breathe.

"Is it gone?" Freddy asked.

Ricky shook his head, then the familiar voice he had just heard in his head returned.

"Ricky."

He looked up. Grandma Bea was standing there, wearing the same clothes she had on the night she died. Freddy's mouth dropped. He could see her, too.

"Fight, Grandson. You didn't hurt anyone. It was the demons."

"I'm too weak. That's why it chose me. I was weak enough to let it control me."

"No, that's where you're wrong. There were always two

distinct creatures. It wasn't just one creature doing everything. This shadow demon inside you overtook your mother easily, but it needed you to get what it wanted. It couldn't take you by itself so it needed its brother, this demon that lives off reflections, to help weaken and frighten you. They've been working together but now the Reflection Demon is weak. This is your best chance at escaping."

Ricky squeezed and gyrated. The grip wasn't as tight as before, but the guilt he felt for Ellie was still there.

"Let it go, Ricky. Think about Myra. She needs you."

His head filled with thoughts of Myra as he looked over at her, now crying in Lori's arms. He thought of all that she'd been through and realized he could help her deal with it. He needed to be there. He needed to help her.

He felt like his insides were coming out of his throat. He gagged and looked up. The Shadow Demon was before them all, enraged. It reached for his Grandma Bea, when a green mist and foul smell enveloped them.

The shadow stepped back. Professor Jackie emerged with another burning jar. The shadow screamed as its shape thinned out and broke apart, and its remaining pieces flew in the air and into the jar. The reflection demon's face filled the jar's outer glass.

Professor Jackie sealed it. She breathed a sigh of relief as the jar exploded. A fast flash of shadow then flew off into the night sky.

"No!" Professor Jackie yelled. "It's gone."

Five police cars screeched to a stop and the officers came out with guns.

Freddy and Professor Jackie moved in front of Ricky.

"No, don't shoot!"

The officers saw their fellow brothers in blue scattered and dead. They wanted to avenge them and one officer on the far left had a clear line of sight on Ricky's head. He fired.

Grandma Bea stared at them and the gun jammed. The remaining officers' guns glowed orange as the heat they emanated burned enough to make them drop their weapons.

"That's all I can do for you, Ricky."

"Grandma, it was you in the skull all this time?"

"Yes, I had sensed something was wrong in the house and was trying to find out what it was when they caught me unexpected. They wanted me out of the way. Earlier that night I started a spiritual ritual that I hoped would help me figure out what was going on, but the demons realized what I was doing and they attacked me. It was too much and my body couldn't take it. I remembered the skull and was able to lock my spirit into it. That's why I was always there. I was trying to protect you."

"You gave me the powers?"

"No. That was all you and the demons. They helped generate the power. As the power fed you, it fed them. I tried to put it in your head that you needed me so that you would keep me with you if they ever took you over."

"But..."

"I'm sorry, Grandson. I have to go. Remember, you didn't kill anyone. The demons did it. I accomplished what I hoped to do. To free you from the evil that took you and your mother over. I'm just sorry I wasn't strong enough to save Ellie or any of the others. Take care of your sister. Your mom may be free now, but there's no guarantee she won't go back to her old life or that this could happen again. I love you, Ricky."

"I love you, too, Grandma Bea."

She disappeared.

Ricky fell to his knees as Freddy and Professor Jackie moved to put their arms around him.

The officers lifted their guns again as their weapons cooled down.

"Step away from him!"

Ricky raised his arms and stayed on his knees.

The professor shouted at the officers, "This wasn't his fault. You arrest him, but do not hurt him. He didn't do this and he is unarmed."

One officer stepped forward. "He killed cops! He killed our friends!"

She pointed. "All these folks are taking video on their phones. Do you want to be on national TV so your families can see you shoot a teenager without a weapon? Watch what you do next, but I guarantee you he wasn't the one who did this. He won't resist."

The officers approached carefully and they arrested Ricky without incident. The officers were rough, but were aware of the multiple phones pointed in their direction.

As the police car that held him sped away, Ricky looked around. There were bodies everywhere. Cars were on fire, with shattered glass and debris spread all over downtown. The people still standing were staring at him with fear. He had done this. Demon or not, he was the one they saw. He was the one to blame.

He thought of Myra.

He thought of Ellie.

If these demons wanted him to fill their guilt quota, it was overflowing. He knew it wasn't something he had control over, but it didn't matter. He saw everything, even though he couldn't stop it. They were staring through his eyes. Just as Ellie had stared into his eyes. He loved her and now she was gone by his hand. She was never coming back. So many dead. No matter how much he wanted to justify it, he knew he couldn't. His life was over.

The crowd looked on as the police car drifted through the crowd and more ambulances and fire trucks arrived.

Stone Creek would never be the same.

CHAPTER THIRTY-FIVE

RICKY SPENT THE NEXT FEW DAYS IN JAIL AND WASN'T ALLOWED any visitors. Psychiatrists came in to talk to him and lawyers wasted no time offering to take his case pro bono, knowing the media attention the case could generate. Lori and Professor Jackie chose one of the top law firms and defense attorneys in the state that loved the limelight.

Once videos of the events of that day started circulating on social media, the case became so sensationalized that Ricky's lawyers requested a change of venue outside of Stone Creek. The motion was denied.

Ricky spent his time in a single holding cell, alone. The other inmates were terrified of him. One tried to threaten him and Ricky just gave him a sharp look and the 6-foot-2 man built like a linebacker with pure muscle yelled as he retreated in fear.

The story had gotten so widespread the guards showed the inmates some of the videos to keep them in line.

Ricky was uncooperative the first few days. When the lawyers first came to see him, they asked for his thoughts on what had transpired.

"It doesn't matter," Ricky answered. "It was my fault. The videos, the witnesses. There are so many people dead because of me."

The lawyers grew desperate. The longer they could drag this case out, the more publicity they'd receive, but they needed a case they could take to court.

On the fourth day with no progress, Professor Jackie showed up.

They met alone in a room and Ricky wouldn't meet her gaze.

"Ricky, I'm sorry it's taken so long to come see you. It's been crazy, as you can imagine. I've been doing everything I can to help with my research."

Ricky turned to look at her. His eyes were no longer dark, but he hadn't slept and looked beaten. The professor tried not to gasp when she saw him.

"The lawyers told your mom that you didn't want to see her or Myra. She still wants to come."

"I don't want them to see me like this."

"Your mother and I have also been busy securing these lawyers. The firm is one of the best in the state."

"Why bother? They should lock me away."

"No, Ricky. This wasn't your fault. None of it. I don't know how we'll prove it, but I'm willing to do whatever I have to."

"No, Professor. You risk losing your reputation. You'll sound like a crazy lady if you go out there and tell them I was possessed by demons."

"Stop talking nonsense. You and I both know it wasn't you. Are you safe? You look like you haven't slept a wink."

"Every time I try, I see Corbin being impaled on his motorcycle. I see all the bodies. Then I see Ellie."

His voice cracked as he spoke her name out loud for the first time since being locked away.

"Her face. I can't get it out of my head. I'll never see her again."

"Ricky, I need to know what you're thinking. Your lawyers tell me you just want to plead guilty."

"I did this. I'm safer in jail. There's no guarantee those demons won't come back."

The professor listened and took a few moments before replying.

"I saw your Grandma Bea there, too, Ricky. While she was standing in front of you, her voice filled my head and she gave me directions. I had an extra jar in the car and she told me to start it while she was talking to you and to put in enough power for two powerful demons. I hadn't expected them to be that strong and thought it was just the shadow demon and the reflection was a part of it. You had to fight off two strong evil creatures, Ricky! You know how rare that is? I've never even heard of that. Only thing I know is that you did not intentionally kill anyone. They used your body to get what they wanted. They filled you with guilt and jealousy about things that weren't real. Once we broke those windows and your grandmother was released, it was all you fighting them off. You had those demons intoxicated with what they needed and you were still able to escape their grasp."

"I would have never been able to without you, Freddy and my grandmother. I'm too dangerous. I'm too vulnerable."

"No you are not! This all started with that shadow thing attacking your mother. She's been fine since it left her. It's like it took the poison and addiction straight out of her soul. It hasn't returned, but now you'll know what to look for if this ever happens again. You'll have plenty of notice."

"Why? Why did those things choose us?"

"My best guess is you were a way out. They were able to exercise their need to feed off chaos and darkness, and I guess that a mass death was their ultimate plan. But we may never know. Most evil spirits want to escape and crave the life of the living. They are held down in their plane where they are limited. By possessing another person, they can continue to feed their desires. Guilt, pain, lust, suffering. Whatever it may be. They found a way in through your family. Lori was the doorway, but you were the key."

He shook his head but didn't reply.

"What about your sister?"

"Myra is better off without me there. She'll be scared of me the rest of her life."

"How can you say that? I know she was the main reason you were able to fight back."

"It doesn't matter. I won't change my mind."

"Give yourself time, Ricky. Myra needs you more than you know. Your mother has been an addict for most of her adult life. There's a real chance she could go back to that life, even with her fresh slate. It's all she's known for years. You might spend the rest of your life in jail or be put to..."

She hesitated.

"Texas has the death penalty, Professor Jackie. I know this. There's no way they won't kill me."

The professor sighed.

"Okay, Ricky. I hope that doesn't happen. I'll leave you for now but will come back tomorrow. And then the day after that. Just think of your mom and your sister. They need you as much as you need them right now."

The next day Freddy showed up. He was on a single crutch.

"Sorry I couldn't come sooner," he said. "Doctor told me to rest. Got a broken rib, but it caught the brunt of the bullet, so it didn't hit any major organs."

"I'm sorry, Freddy," Ricky said. "I'm glad you're okay. I'm sorry I let you down. I let everybody down."

"It wasn't your fault, man. How many times does everyone need to say it?"

"It was. You know I was ready to kill you, right?"

He gulped. "Kill me? I thought you didn't want to."

"I didn't want to, but if I killed Ellie, what makes you think I wouldn't hesitate with you?"

Freddy looked down. "Because we're brothers. Because you weren't seeing visions of me."

"That's where you're wrong. When you first got there with Ellie, I got visions in my head of you and her making out in the car. I just wanted to take everyone out. At moments that was all I could think about."

"You were seeing all kinds of things that weren't there, right?"

"Yes. I couldn't tell what was real or not sometimes. But the demons and my grandmother? You saw it all?"

"Yeah, I saw everything. It seems like a few people saw the reflections in the mirror, but it doesn't look like anything showed up on any cell phone videos. I don't think anyone else saw the shadow demon in front of you. Some pics show blurry motion, but nothing clear enough to match what we could all see with our own eyes. Some say they saw something, others are saying they just saw things and people flying with an invisible force. I think just you, me, Myra and the professor saw your Grandma Bea. I guess there are some people that are better at seeing things like that, but no one's come forward yet. I still don't understand why I saw everything clear as day at the end. Maybe because I was so close to you."

"Maybe."

"Professor Jackie said you want to plead guilty."

He nodded. "It's for the best."

"What about Myra and your Mom? You know what this will do to them."

"Like I told the professor, I don't want them to see me this way. Not even sure my mom wants to see me. I almost killed her, too."

"Come on, man. You know they've been staying with us and with Professor Jackie the last few days. Your house is surrounded. The cops have had to stay there because they're afraid there'll be a riot if they leave."

"Riots? Who's been showing up to the house?"

"They told me not to say anything to you but you need to know. Families that had someone get hurt or killed that day. They're afraid the house was the problem, especially with your grandma dying and your mom's problems over the years. They don't understand what happened. People are saying the devil is in that house. That it's cursed."

"So you trying to make me feel better?"

"No, I'm trying to make you see they need you. You need to get them out of that house and move on. Everything depends on you. Myra needs you more than you think and you're no good to her locked up. Even though you want them to stay away, they have tried to come see you, but the lawyers and police are telling them it's better if they stay out of sight for now. For their own safety."

Ricky looked down.

"Think about it, Ricky. It's not just about you. You beat those things and I don't think they're coming back. You were stronger, man. You were so strong they couldn't hold on."

Ricky stared at Freddy's crutch.

"Strong? That thing had me do whatever it wanted. Look what I did to you and all those people. Look what I did to Ellie." He paused for a moment. "How many?"

Freddy looked back at him. "How many what?"

"You know what I'm asking."

Freddy looked at his feet. "12 dead so far, 27 injured."

Ricky got quiet and didn't respond. 12 dead. He only

cared about one, but couldn't register that a dozen people were dead and he was the one that killed them. Whether he was possessed or not, it was his thoughts and actions that led to it.

"Ricky?"

He stopped replying.

After a few minutes more of trying, Freddy left, but came back almost every day, alternating with Professor Jackie.

A few more days passed, but Ricky refused to change his mind.

The lawyers also visited him daily and were talking about an insanity plea.

Two days before the trial was to begin, a group of officers escorted Lori and Myra to the jail to meet with Ricky.

"Mom, why are you here? Freddy told me it was dangerous for you to come see me."

Myra looked scared. "People are being mean. They don't know you. They don't know what happened."

"Do you know what happened, Myra?"

"Yes. Grandma told me."

"You saw Grandma?"

"Yes. I heard everything she said to you. She even told me she loved me before she disappeared. Freddy and Professor Jackie told us everything else that happened before we got there."

Lori smiled. "Professor Jackie and Freddy are worried. So are we. You can't take the blame for this."

"Mom, think about it. There is video of me floating around with bodies flying all around me, like I'm in full control."

"But you can't just give up without a fight! You know as well as I do it wasn't your fault."

"That's what everybody keeps telling me, but it sure seems like it is. Can't blame it on a couple of demons, can I? Maybe they'll commit me instead. Some great choices. You're both better off without me."

It got quiet for a few seconds.

Lori looked down at her daughter and then back at Ricky. "There's something I have to tell you. Something you need to understand."

Lori turned to Myra. "Honey, I was going to tell you to cover your ears or leave the room, but you know what? You need to hear this, too."

Myra moved toward her brother and sat next to him. He put his arm around her. Ricky felt some sense of relief as Myra buried her head against him, and he let his guard down for a moment.

The guard watching over them in the room walked over.

"You can't have contact," he said.

"Please," Myra said, her eyes filling with tears. "Just for a few minutes."

She hugged Ricky harder.

The guard moved closer and raised a hand to grab Myra, but Ricky gave him an angry stare and the guard stepped back and didn't say another word, almost tripping as he returned to his post.

Lori resumed.

"If anything, Son, this is my fault."

"How do you figure?"

"I'm the weak one. My addiction gave them the way in. You keep hearing all of us tell you it's not your fault over and over, but look at me. My addictions, my selfishness. When that little girl came to our door that night, you were all so scared. And you know what? I didn't know or care what was going on. She looked in there and saw me as an easy target. I was so high that night she could have come in and killed you all and I would have gone to sleep after taking a drink or snorting whatever I could get my hands on without realizing a thing for hours. Maybe even days. This demon skipped the houses next door, the houses across the street and all the other houses that little girl visited that night. They chose me. Chose me because I was weak. All my sins, all the things I put your Grandmother Bea and both of you through came back on me. If I had just gotten my life together and put you all first, there would have never been a doorway. They would have skipped us, too. The darkness was in me for weeks, and I was so messed up I practically trapped the shadow demon inside me. The other one kept appearing in my bedroom mirror and tried to influence me, but I was so far gone it was like they were high along with me and couldn't control or escape my hold. They needed something else, and they were able to feed off of the resentment I had towards you. Resentment of your relationship with Grandma and Myra. That's how messed up I am. That's how pathetic I am."

"Mom..." Myra said, but Lori raised her hand.

Her eyes moistened. "I allowed that evil to come into our house. Not even two powerful demons could beat my addiction and had to wait until my buzz or high was wearing off before they could even try to use me to get to you. I knew what they were doing. I knew they wanted you, but I couldn't even warn you. It was so easy for me to say all those horrible things to you because I didn't fight back. It's not just that I couldn't, but I wouldn't. I didn't even make an effort. I brought this into our family. The fault all lies on me."

"You need to take care of Myra now," Ricky said.

"And what happens if I go back to it? I'm lucky that when it left, it took all of my cravings with it, but I am still an addict. I always will be. I can't guarantee I won't go right back to it. I've tried rehab but never lasted. I'm not sure if you're aware of how many times I was in rehab or jail, but I guarantee it's more than you think you know. This is the only life I've known for the last twenty-plus years. You can't trust me because I can't trust me. I'm still vulnerable if these demons ever wanted to come back. What if another demon senses my weakness without you around? What if the next one is even worse?"

Ricky made eye contact with her. She had never once admitted to being a burden or to what she had done. Every time Grandma Bea had tried to tell her something, she blew up and blamed everything and everyone around her, but never herself.

"I didn't consider that."

"No, you didn't! And you shouldn't have to, but it doesn't change the truth. Don't do anything for me. I don't deserve it, but I want to earn it. Do this for Myra. The only way I can guarantee her safety is if you're part of her life. You can't do that if you're in jail or the state decides to kill you!"

Ricky felt Myra tighten her hug around him.

"Please, Ricky. Try to fight," Myra said. "Like Freddy said how you fought the demons downtown."

"What about what happened, Myra? All those people. Ellie."

Myra looked up at her brother. "Ellie knows it wasn't you. She didn't have to forgive you because she said there was nothing to forgive. She knows."

"How could you possibly know that?"

"She told me. I've been dreaming about her. She told me she's sad that she's left us, but she's happy that she died knowing you loved her and that you knew she loved you, too. She just regrets she won't be around to grow old with you and said to say she was sorry about Homecoming, too, although I don't know what she meant by that."

Ricky said nothing for a moment. No one else knew about Homecoming. No one.

"You've been dreaming about her? Are you seeing anything else?"

Lori grabbed his hand. "Myra's been seeing Grandma and Ellie since everything happened. They were talking to her almost every day. She was hysterical at first, thinking she'd never see you again. Being able to talk to the two of them helped her get through it, but I think they're gone now. She hasn't seen them in almost a week."

Ricky kissed the top of her head. "I love you, Myra."

"Even when you make fun of me and mess up my hair?"

"Especially when I make fun of you and mess up your hair. Don't you know that's the ultimate way a brother can show how much he loves his little sister?"

And for the first time since everything had happened, Ricky smiled.

"I'll talk to the lawyers. I'll fight, but I don't see how it's going to matter. There are videos and pictures everywhere. There's no hope."

"Don't forget what Grandma Bea used to tell us when we were sad," Myra said. "There's always hope."

CHAPTER THIRTY-SIX

ON THE FIRST DAY OF THE TRIAL, RICKY WAS SURROUNDED BY A vast crowd of onlookers as officers escorted him to the court building.

A cacophony of overlapping voices filled his ears. "Killer! Freak! Satanist!"

He didn't blame them. He couldn't blame them.

The federal judge had ordered a full media, recording device and cell phone ban in the courtroom. He brought in additional bailiffs to enforce the rules.

The District Attorney's office represented the prosecution, and the opening statement took almost twenty minutes. They stated how a mass murder was committed and that it was all attributed to Richard Luna and how they would provide evidence and multiple witnesses to prove their case and ask for the death penalty.

Ricky's defense team responded with a brief opening, stating how although the events that occurred in downtown Stone Creek were a tragedy, there was no direct evidence that could prove that Ricky was guilty of killing anyone.

The trial lasted almost two weeks. There was a looming

feeling of fear as each witness appeared for the prosecution. A mother of one boy who had been killed talked about how her son had been friends with Ricky since they were little, but now her son was dead and Ricky was responsible. Another witness talked about how Ricky was evil and that he must have worshiped the devil with all the unnatural things he was able to do, such as throwing cars and light poles and people into the air without touching them.

Similar testimonies followed. Most were distraught parents, just trying to make sense of it all.

On the fourth day, the prosecution brought out the videos.

The lead prosecution attorney stopped and started one video so many times it took almost two hours to get through the first witness. This was the day the police officers testified.

The police testimonies changed the tone of the trial and brought a completely different mood to the courtroom compared to what they had heard from family and friends in the opening few days. The first officer fumbled and hesitated to state the details of what he saw other than how some of his fellow officers had died. Other officers were the same. They spoke of their fallen brothers and how the station was dealing with their deaths and trying to assist their families, but none offered any specific details until the end.

The second to last officer was a sniper who had positioned himself on the roof of one of the downtown buildings.

"I saw the other officers down, and something was flying around. I fired seven shots, but hit nothing."

"Are you considered a poor marksman?" the attorney asked.

"Ma'am, I'm considered a sharpshooter. I'm the only sniper on our small force. If I'm aiming at a suspect, I'm going to hit him within half an inch of where I'm aiming. I'm not saying that to be cocky, I'm stating it as fact. It's the one thing in my life that's special. My shot didn't miss. Something stopped my bullet from striking its target. I can't tell you what that was and I can't with a right mind tell you what I think I saw, but as that video shows, there was something there. Something that I can't explain."

The last officer to testify was Jimmy Brown, a rookie who had only been on the job eight months and was also the only officer who hadn't grown up in the area.

"This is the first time I've ever seen other police officers die," he said as he choked up.

"And how did it happen?" the attorney asked.

Up to this point, with the exception of the sniper, all the other officers had simply answered they were struck by bullets without elaborating, but Officer Brown was struggling with his reply.

"I can't really tell you what happened," Officer Brown stated. "By the time I arrived, two officers were already dead, so when the rest of us reached the scene, we immediately pulled out our guns. That's the first time I've ever had to draw my weapon. What I saw just isn't something that I can believe."

"What did you see?" the attorney asked.

"I, I truly don't know what it was I saw. But it was chaos and evil. Pure evil. I know as a police officer it may cost me my reputation, but I haven't been doing this long and I don't have a reputation to protect yet. Either that boy there is evil, or something evil was inside him. Either way, I can't prove that he's responsible, but it sure appears that he killed a bunch of innocent people. He killed my fellow police officers. My friends. Do I think this entire thing happened under circumstances we can't understand or explain? Yes, I do."

"Please," the district attorney asked. "Explain what happened in the video where it seems like multiple officers dropped their guns at the same time when they had a clear line of sight to Mr. Luna."

"I raised my gun as soon as I got out of my vehicle. Then I saw... I saw something. Something in front of that young man. It was a blur in the shape of a body, like someone was there, but they weren't there. Then my gun. All of our guns started glowing like fire burning from inside the metal. My gun was bright and so hot. Maybe one misfire could cause something like that, but it happened to all of our guns at the exact same time. It just doesn't make sense."

Under cross examination, Ricky's attorney summarized what Officer Brown had just testified to, then asked his only question.

"So, at no time did Ricky Luna, this young man, touch you or your guns in any way, shape or form that would have made your guns burn up? I believe the words you used were, 'like fire?' Was there any plausible way this young, unarmed boy could have done that?"

The officer stared at the prosecution, then at his fellow officers, and slowly shook his head.

The prosecution refused to ask him any additional questions and rushed to move on.

Throughout the first days of testimony, the defense's cross examinations were all similar for the non-police officers. They asked varied questions, but there were two questions they asked every single person.

The first question was, "After everything you witnessed that day and what we have seen on the videos, can you say with absolute certainty what caused all the officers to drop their guns or what caused all these windows to break and debris to fly throughout downtown?"

Most gave similar responses, some describing what they saw in the chaos and how Ricky seemed to conduct the carnage, but none of them could answer yes. If they tried to say what they thought, they were met with an objection to answer the question. A few stated they saw or thought they saw something moving in the windows or near Ricky, but couldn't say what it was. No one even described the shadow demon.

The last question in each instance was, "Aside from the physical fight with Corbin Brock, you never saw Ricky Luna physically touch any of the victims, did you?"

In every case, the answer was no. No one saw him do it, but they knew he was responsible.

There were still enough prosecution witnesses to the incident to take up three more days of testimony, but on the next day, the lawyers for the defense stated that if the long list of witnesses were going to offer similar testimonies, they were willing to concede the overall point that the prosecution was trying to make. They all saw something, believed it was evil and that Ricky was somehow responsible.

When it was the defense's turn to plead their side, they started with the experts. A Physicist was brought in to prove what was on most of the videos defied the basic laws of physics, such as how the motorcycle and the streetlights shot into the air and the odd angles that they followed.

The fire chief testified on the smoke patterns and another expert tried to explain how all the windows that had shattered at the same time could have only occurred internally, like a gas explosion, although there was no evidence of a gas leak.

The next expert the defense called was Doctor Jacqueline Baker, testifying as the Dean of Anthropology and her status as a leading authority on the subject. Her testimony took almost an entire day.

Risking her reputation, Professor Jackie left nothing out. She discussed the sugar skull, her research and books, even the unpublished papers, and the type of work that she had done over the last few decades with Ricky's grandmother.

"This is something that Ricky's grandmother Bea and I

have studied for years. In almost every region we visited, we witnessed things we couldn't explain. You can call them supernatural or almost magic-like, but it doesn't change how entire villages and tribes believed them or that we witnessed these seemingly impossible events. This isn't something we could publish or discuss openly without risking our jobs. People tend to ridicule what they don't understand, but just because it isn't something that's generally accepted doesn't mean it's not true. We were tenured professors and we kept a large part of our findings to ourselves or published under different names. We witnessed many strange and inexplicable events in our years of research. But these notes I'm presenting today, many of them handwritten, discuss items that we never intended for public release."

"Why risk your reputation now?" the attorney asked.

"Because I believe in doing what's right. I've known this young man and his family most of their lives. This boy no more killed these poor folks than anyone else sitting in this courtroom."

She presented her notes and showed slides of what they had. They were compelling, but still only words.

"So, can you summarize what you've shown us here today?" the defense asked.

"This boy was possessed. I am one hundred percent sure and I would stake my reputation on it."

The cross examination by the prosecution showed no mercy.

"So you expect us to believe that a demon possessed this young man's mother, an addict no less whose deposition we're supposed to trust, and then got inside of him and forced him to kill everybody that day just to 'feed' off him?"

The courtroom buzzed and the judge had to slap his gavel down twice to settle everybody down.

"It doesn't matter whether you believe it or not. Just because your mind can't handle it doesn't make it false."

She finished her testimony, knowing the prosecution had gotten the best of her, but she had no regrets.

On the next-to-last day, the prosecution called in a rebuttal witness and entered their final piece of evidence that caused the courtroom to let out a collective gasp. It was a ceramic sugar skull.

Ricky couldn't believe it. He was sure he had destroyed it when he threw it through the downtown windows, but he knew it was the same skull he had bought during Fiesta only a few short months before.

The expert testified that it was a normal ceramic skull and had nothing unusual in its structure. He showed thermal images of its insides and compared it to another ceramic skull, just like it with different designs. There was no difference.

"So should we believe this normal, unspectacular trinket held his grandmother's essence or spirit, as Doctor Baker testified?"

The expert laughed. "I don't believe in fairy tales or ghosts. That's scientifically ridiculous."

The closing arguments were the next day. The prosecution only took ten minutes and the defense took thirty. It was a long, hard-fought trial, but it was time for the jury to decide Ricky's fate.

The word was out that they were ready fifteen minutes after entering deliberations.

The jury foreman stood up, and she read "Guilty" for every charge.

The judge took a moment and looked at the jurors. "And all of you are in agreement with this verdict?"

Each juror nodded.

The judge looked over the verdict as the prosecution congratulated each other and those in the courtroom cheered.

The judge cracked his gavel.

"I need everyone to sit down."

The lawyers for both sides looked over in confusion and the courtroom quickly quieted down.

"First, I'd like to address the court reporter. Joanna, none of what I am about to say is to be transcribed. Understood?"

Joanna had just typed "Understood" and lifted her fingers to stop.

She looked up.

"Yes, Judge."

"Now we have been here for close to two long weeks. In this time, we've heard tales of the supernatural and possession and good and evil. We have video. We have pictures. We know many good people died. However, not one piece of evidence shows Ricky Luna touching anyone. What do you think will happen to our proud little town if it gets out that this court convicted a teenager based on demonic possession? We will not be known as some backward community that became a second Salem where witches were falsely accused and burned. History has shown how power-mad leaders and educated adults randomly decided, based on little evidence or behavior they simply didn't understand, to burn and kill innocent women. I cannot in good conscience, as a representative of the law and protector of the sanctity and integrity of this court, allow this verdict to stand."

The spectators and prosecution erupted.

The judge slammed his gavel and yelled, "I will hold every single one of you in contempt and pack you in that jail like sardines if I have to. I will have order!"

The crowd calmed down.

The judge called over his bailiffs and whispered to them. They dispersed around the seated spectators.

"I have just instructed my bailiffs to clear the courtroom of all spectators."

The screams of protest returned. The judge banged his gavel down once. "Clear this courtroom now! The bailiffs can escort you outside the building or into a cell! Your choice."

The screaming subsided, but many continued to mumble in protest. Lori and Myra were the only spectators allowed to stay. After a few minutes, two bailiffs returned.

"Are they clear?" the judge asked.

"Yes, your honor," the lead bailiff replied. "The remaining bailiffs are making sure no one tries to return or approach the doors."

"Thank you," the judge said.

"I am reversing this decision and invoking a judgment of acquittal based on the evidence and the danger it presents if this guilty verdict stands. Innocent people died, and there must be justice, but even for those who may not believe, the witnesses to these events all agree they saw something that can't be explained. These are teachers, doctors, and police officers. Witnesses young and old. The videos also show this was not a mass hallucination. Something happened, and that is not in dispute. However, and I will deny any of this if anyone here repeats what I'm about to say, I believe something evil was in this town and manifested itself as an entity or entities, which some could see and some could not, and they are to blame for this. They manipulated this young man. The videos clearly show he did not want to do this and I saw the struggle on his face. So did all of you. When you see these videos again, as I know they are on social media, look at Mr. Luna's face and you will understand what I mean. I will not sentence this young man to a life in prison or death on something I am certain he did not do by choice. We will not make a mockery of this town and court, and I believe this is the best decision for all of us who call Stone Creek home."

The prosecuting attorney stood up, but the judge pointed his gavel at him. "You will let me finish. Sit down!"

He did as instructed.

"In order for this verdict to stand, we would all have to accept the existence of a demon or some type of otherworldly entity. I can tell you right now, before this case, I never believed in anything like that. I believe in God and my country, and I believe in evil and that the Devil exists, but demons skulking around and possessing people? Not a chance. Now Mr. District Attorney, I want you to bring up one of the videos again. The one from the city camera that shows the moment where all the windows shatter."

He walked up with the remote and got it to that point.

"There," the judge said. "Slow that part down and stop when I say stop."

The monitor showed the skull flying toward the window.

"Pause it. Go frame by frame."

He did as instructed. Just before the skull landed, the judge stood up and yelled, "Stop!"

Ricky saw the mirror demon's face. It wasn't crystal clear like what he saw with his own eyes, but it was there. He looked at the jury and back at his family. Most faces were blank, but Myra's eyes were wide and two jurors wore shocked faces.

"This camera was one of the high quality city cameras and its footage was one of the few not leaked to the media," the judge said. "This courtroom is the only place where it's been viewed and it had the best view of those windows that shattered, considering most people with their cell phones weren't paying attention to them. When this was presented a few days ago, it was mostly viewed in full speed or paused on different sections. I have gone over this video many times since it was first presented as evidence and I don't think everyone can see what I, and I think a few others, can see in the reflection of those windows. Once again, off the record, I will tell you I see the face of something evil, something terrifying, something that I suspect will haunt me for the next few years and that I hope to never see again. I do not believe this boy could control that thing. Pardon my language, but I tell you that scares me shitless and I wouldn't be able to fight something like that. Yet this boy was able to resist it at one point. He stopped it before it could hurt even more people."

The judge looked at the lawyers and then back at the jury.

"We have two choices here. First, I can and will overturn this verdict because there is no court of law that can prove that what I'm seeing is what I know it is. You attribute the deaths to this boy but consider this: If he still had the ability to cause this kind of carnage, why isn't this courtroom on fire or in shambles right now? Why aren't any of you being tossed around this room like rag dolls? It's because whatever did do this is no longer present."

The courtroom fell silent. Everyone was speechless and just looked at each other.

"Also, if I do overturn this verdict, there will be a record that the jury found Mr. Luna guilty. That alone will stain this town. So, members of the jury, this brings me to our second option. Right now, I want you to discuss among yourselves if after hearing what I just said, you want to change your verdict. I will not argue if you still find him guilty, but I will reverse this decision either way. I am simply giving you an opportunity to reconsider and think about how it might feel when your neighbors, the outside world and media are ridiculing you and your family and how your decision must have been so bad that a judge reversed it. I am a federal judge. I'll retire in a few years. I'll survive this. Will you? I am giving you five minutes to decide if you want to be on record with your guilty verdict or if you are willing to change your mind. Madame Foreman, please huddle with your fellow jurors."

The jurors turned toward one another and started rapid, muted discussions. It took 90 seconds for the foreman to turn back toward the judge.

"Your honor, we, the jury, find the defendant not guilty on all counts."

The prosecution stood and screamed their objections.

The judge's gavel struck several times.

"Order! Sit down!"

The attorneys obeyed.

"The decision has been made and the previous verdict will not be recorded. This is the best for every citizen in this town. Once more, I will state all that transpired between the original verdict and the final one is off the record and in the eyes of the law, never happened. And if anyone present in this courtroom repeats what happened or what I said, not only will I deny it but I will sue you all for slander, and I will win. Consider that before you leave this courtroom. You just tell anyone who asks that the prosecution couldn't prove its case. Tell the spectators that were here that classified evidence was presented that required their removal and it was enough to convince the jury to change their minds. There will be conspiracy theories on social media with all the videos already out there, but they will still be as confused as we are. I know this isn't a popular decision, but when everything calms down, I hope you will all understand why it's the right one. Go home and hold your families and pray like you've never prayed before that this town never sees anything like this again."

The judge cracked his gavel one last time. He looked at Ricky with a sympathetic face. "May you be free to heal, son, and I hope someday you'll be able to live a normal life again. God be with you."

When it was over, one news outlet showed multiple clips

of the camera videos and stopped it as items flew into the air with the caption: "What do you believe?"

That night, the house where Ricky and Myra had grown up was set on fire.

Ricky was kept in a holding area for his safety and officers took him, his mom and Myra to a hotel in an unmarked vehicle. They didn't want to risk someone following them to Professor Jackie's house, and Freddy's was too close for someone not to notice. The entire neighborhood was on the lookout.

A few days passed before things settled. Ricky and his mom were deciding where they would go. With the money Grandma Bea had left them and the upcoming insurance settlement on the house fire, they had enough money to go anywhere they needed to. They had even received donations from a fundraising site where most people interested in the supernatural donated, wanting a piece of this unexplained event.

Ricky, Lori and Myra didn't want to leave their hometown, but they all knew they had to get as far away as possible. They needed to be anonymous so Myra could have a chance to grow up in a normal environment. They told no one when they were leaving or where they were going.

Sometimes hope was a lonely place.

CHAPTER THIRTY-SEVEN

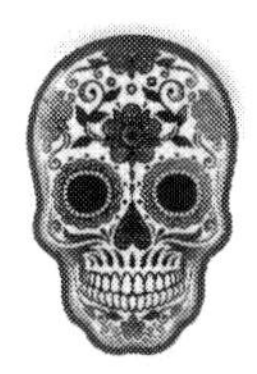

THE LUNA HOUSE WAS ALMOST UNRECOGNIZABLE. IT HAD BEEN over two weeks since a group of angry parents and siblings of the victims had set it on fire.

People were scared after the verdict and let their raw emotions drive them to burn the house like a lynch mob. A group of almost twenty showed up that night and approached the house to torch it, convinced it was the only way to get rid of the evil in their town. Some expected the house wouldn't burn and whatever demon or creature that had caused this would linger, taking them as their next victims.

The crowd had lingered for a few minutes, cheering and finding justice in the flames as they watched it burn.

Today, however, there were no more protesters near the now abandoned house. People were coping, the last of the funerals long over. Most of the town was getting ready for bed or already asleep, deep into their dreams or nightmares, a persistent side effect in the coming years for those who witnessed the Downtown Demon Massacre, as it came to be known. The nightmares were of death and shadows and mirror demons, and some featured Ricky, the mass murderer who could kill you with his thoughts and a motion of his hands. Many of the bad dreams were of sinister sugar skulls, laughing and flying towards their dreaming victims.

On this overcast night, a different kind of shadow moved inside the burned house. Charred wood cracked beneath a pair of sneakers that were desperately trying to stay silent.

Ricky had returned to his Grandmother Bea's house. To his house.

Lori and Myra had removed some of the critical items when they had initially left before the trial, but most of Ricky's things had remained.

He eased through the darkness and risked flipping on his phone light.

He moved through what was left of the living room. The kitchen was completely destroyed and there was no more front door. The front of the house where the fire had started, was mostly left in ashes.

Ricky moved across, staying low with a hoodie covering his head and face.

He heard a snap behind him.

He held his breath, hoping it was an angry neighbor or a cop and not the demon returning to take him over again.

It was Freddy.

"Hey," he whispered.

"How did you know I was here?"

"I've been keeping an eye on your house and I figured you'd come back. I know I would."

Freddy knew him better than he even realized.

"I know we already said our goodbyes yesterday, but I was still hoping to see you."

Ricky nodded. "It's okay. I wanted to see you, too. Just didn't want to risk your family getting hurt."

"My mom was here with Lori and Myra when Ellie and I

left to go downtown that night. Myra is the one that told her what had happened and convinced her to take them downtown, too. My mom understands what happened and doesn't blame you."

"I'm just glad you're all okay."

"Why did you come back?"

"Just needed to look around. I don't think I'll ever be back to this town again, so wanted to see if there was anything I needed or wanted that might have survived."

They stood in front of each other, neither one wanting to say another word, but Ricky sighed.

"I know it's not our style, but I'm glad you're my friend. My best friend. Even with all the friends we had, it was always you and Ellie. I love you both."

Freddy smiled, and even in the darkness, Ricky could see his eyes were watering.

"Pussy," Freddy said as his voice cracked.

They hugged each other. Something they hadn't done since they were much younger on a day when Ricky had broken down after seeing his mom leave them again.

"I'm gonna miss you, brother," Ricky said.

"I'll miss you, too," Freddy squeaked out. "You want some help looking around?"

"No, I think I need to do this myself."

"Okay. I'll let you go. If there's any way..."

"I will, Freddy. I'll find you or let you know where I am and someday I'll see you again. Once we figure things out and get back to some kind of normal. I have to change my identity and my online information, but I'll contact you with new usernames and numbers when the time is right and I think it's safe."

Freddy nodded. "Like witness protection."

"Something like that."

They took a moment to look at each other, each remembering various points of their past, neither one wanting to break.

"I'll see you, brother."

"We'll always be brothers. Time won't change that. Thank you for everything, Freddy. You turned out to be one of the bravest people I know."

"Who would have thought, huh? Took being the most scared in my life and a couple of demons to make me brave."

Freddy looked up for a moment and then turned around and walked out. Neither of them said any more.

Once he was sure Freddy was gone, he moved to his room. He told Freddy he was just checking for what may have survived, but he knew what he was looking for. He just hoped it wasn't burned to a crisp.

He went through the mess of his room. His computer was there, but charred to pieces. His corkboard was on the ground, too, with burned pictures melted onto it. He walked to where his closet should have been and kicked the debris around.

Then he saw it. A tin his mom had given him after coming back from Paris. It had a picture of the Eiffel Tower on it, which was scarred black. He lifted it. It was dented and beaten, but still mostly intact. He opened the lid and saw the contents inside were still there. Papers, his old temporary driver's license and pictures.

He held up the handful of photos.

The top photo was of him and Myra with Grandma Bea during a beach vacation the three of them had taken one summer. He thumbed through a few more and then pulled one out. Its edges were burnt, but the picture was still intact.

He stood in the middle of Freddy and Ellie. Their arms were wrapped around each other and they were smiling. It was the time where Grandma Bea had taken them all to the State Fair in Dallas. It was the first time he had ever been there and got to take friends. Mom had been gone for over a year at the time, and Grandma Bea decided to cheer him up when his birthday had passed and he hadn't heard from her.

They were happy. It was one of the happiest days of their young lives.

Ellie and Freddy were the two people besides his mother, grandmother and sister that he loved most. It was a wonderful time he would never get back, but that would live in his happy memories until the day he died.

He put the items back into the tin and stuck it inside his hoodie.

He was at peace for just a brief time as he looked at the picture. He didn't think of the pain or guilt that had consumed him constantly over the last few weeks but thought only of what was to come--a new life, starting over with Lori and Myra. Whether or not it worked out, it was still moving forward. Doing his best to continue to hope.

He made his way out of the house, retreating through the back doorway where he had come in. Part of the frame was still standing, although the door was permanently open. He stepped on a cracked mirror and looked down. He felt himself cringe, but sighed in relief as he saw it was just his own reflection staring back at him.

He took one long, last look at the darkened remains of the house where he grew up. In his head, his memories completed the picture. He saw everything as it used to be and pictured the couches as they were and Myra running through the halls laughing while he chased her, and Grandma and Lori laughed at them from the kitchen.

It was time to say goodbye.

Ricky started to walk out through the back door when something crunched beneath his feet. He turned and jumped as he saw a decayed, clawed hand reach towards him, then realized it was just a charred piece of board he had stepped on in the dark.

Ricky took in a breath and shook his head, hoping to never see another shadow again. He walked out without looking back, thinking of Ellie.

A small figure appeared behind one of the shattered windows, looking out as Ricky headed into his new life.

The little girl in a bathing suit waved.

"Bye, Kitty. See you soon."

GET A NOVEL, TWO NOVELLAS, AND A BOOK OF SHORT STORIES

I enjoy engaging with readers. The first few years of my career, most of that time was spent at book events and classrooms when I primarily wrote MG supernatural books.

With YA/Adult books and short stories now in my catalog, I will occasionally send newsletters about new releases, special offers and general news relating to my work.

If you sign up to my mailing list, I'll send you several freebies:

1. A copy of my YA novella Our Possessions, a prequel to my "Sugar Skull" series.
2. A copy of my YA novella The Conductor.
3. A copy of my MG novel Lobo Coronado and the Legacy of the Wolf.
4. A copy of The Dead Club: Short Tales, a prequel to my MG Dead Club series.

Get your free Starter Library here:
manuelruiz3.com

ACKNOWLEDGMENTS

My Alpha and Betas are invaluable, and I can't thank them enough for their time, generosity and feedback.

Alpha Readers

David, Mari and Daisy

Beta Readers

David Riskind
Michael Sawyer
Mari Molina
Belynda Chapa
Pam "PMoney" Marino
Daisy Ruiz

AUTHOR'S NOTE

Although this book is not "Based on a True Story," several of the scenes are based on True Events. A modified version of the opening chapter happened to me when I was about eleven or twelve years old, visiting my Grandmother's house in South Texas.

I am the oldest of three brothers. Marc by four years and Matthew by ten. We grew up in Robstown, a small town just outside of Corpus Christi, Texas. The bulk of our extended family lived about thirty miles to the West in Alice, Texas, and we spent most of our summers and weekends there, trading time between our paternal and maternal grandparents and cousins.

The paternal Ruiz side is the larger family, and we were considered the cousins who stayed up way too late when we visited. Most of my aunts and uncles lived within blocks of my grandparents' house, and their families were all usually tucked in bed by 10 pm. When we came to visit, however, we'd stay up playing games, laughing and going to bed at the latest possible time allowed. On this particular night, my Aunt Norma cursed us in Spanish for keeping everyone up late, saying *"Te va salir El Diablo!,"* which is a common warning to misbehaving children that can have multiple meanings, but in this case roughly translates to, "The Devil's going to get you!"

She might have been right.

Later that night, Marc, my first cousin Rick and I were in one bed next to two open windows with our youngest Aunt, Melba, asleep in the same room. It was late, well after midnight, and we didn't want to fall asleep and kept laughing and cutting up until a young girl in a bathing suit decided to walk by the windows, looking for her Kitty.

Thanks, Aunt Norma.

This isn't the only strange event that's happened to me, and several of those darker and scarier experiences appear in this series.

This is my first Young Adult book after having published four in Middle Grade. I truly hope you enjoyed Ricky, his family and friends, and more importantly, their story. There are still two more books left to finish this tale, and I hope you'll come along for the ride.

Please feel free to contact me for any feedback or just to say hello!

-Manuel

ABOUT THE AUTHOR

Manuel Ruiz is a life-long Texan with a passion for reading, video games, and music. He works in IT, plays in an 80's band, and owns way too many toys. He writes teen and adult fiction, usually with a supernatural twist, and loves to keep his readers on their toes.

Manuel lives in Central Texas with his family where he spends time giving the characters in his head something fun, dark, and interesting to do.

To find out more, please visit :
www.manuelruiz3.com

ALSO BY MANUEL RUIZ

MIDDLE GRADE

The Dead Club Series

The Dead Club

Grey is an eleven-year-old boy who is curious, a loyal friend and just realized that he's dead. He is joined in the afterlife by a tomboy, a baseball player, a beauty queen, and a science geek and together they learn that Purgatory is broken and are soon thrust into a frantic search to discover what has unleashed chaos in the Underworld.

Councils and Keepers

The Dead Club survived their first afterlife adventure, but the fallout left cracks in the Underworld that have awakened something much, much worse.

The heroes will need more than their growing powers to face an enemy linked to the Oracle's past with the ability to return the Underworld back to its darkest time.

Underworld Rising

The Dead Club is fractured. Ancient enemies have returned to demand vengeance on the Oracle and Underworld Council. The heroes are desperate, planning for war without the Oracle or Grim Reaper while facing the possibility that one of their own has turned against them.

All hope rests on a shattered Dead Club as they prepare to fight the final battle that will determine the fate of the Underworld.

Lobo Coronado

Lobo Coronado and the Legacy of the Wolf

Lobo Coronado is about to have the most exciting day of his mundane life. Kidnapped by night shadows and introduced to his long-lost grandfather, he is transported to another realm where he meets a queen, a vampire scribe and a little angel with a big attitude problem. Lobo learns that an unknown enemy with a demon army and ties to his late father is endangering multiple worlds. Teamed with his new companions, this Freaksome Threesome must work together to unleash the full potential of Lobo's famous bloodline and prevent the annihilation of Earth and the Celestial Realms.

YOUNG ADULT

The Sugar Skull Series

The Sugar Skull

17-year-old Ricky wants nothing more than to finish school, win the hand of his best girl, and get away from his troubling home life. But when two seemingly unrelated things pop up -- a curious midnight visit and the arrival of an enchanting sugar skull -- his world turns upside down. It's soon clear that the skull holds secrets far more dangerous than any high school adversary ... and its sights are set on Ricky's soul.

The Sugar Skull is the first in a 3-book series, inspired by Real Events.

Made in the USA
Las Vegas, NV
23 November 2021